THE DUBLIN HIT

BOOK 1 OF THE SAUWA CATCHER SERIES

J.E. HIGGINS

MERCENARY PUBLISHING

ALSO BY J.E. HIGGINS

The Bosnian Experience: Book 2 of the Sauwa Catcher Series

Cyprus Rage: Book 3 of the Sauwa Catcher Series

The Montevideo Game

1

The first litany of explosions pounded the earth like a stampede of enraged bulls were tearing through the camp. The blasts ruptured the ground, shooting waves of dirt and uprooted plants.

Sauwa grabbed her sister, Rena, and held her tight while mortar shells pummeled the landscape around them. Thick clouds of smoke rose from the bombed areas, creating a haze that encompassed the sky in an impenetrable fog.

Rhodesian soldiers—men and teen boys clad in well-worn, dark olive camouflage fatigues—ran to take up fighting positions. The women collected the scurrying children and herded them to cover as the attack worsened.

After the first blasts came the gunfire.

Sauwa held her sister's face to her chest while bodies fell to the ground in blood-soaked masses from piercing rounds shot from the bushes. A few feet away, James, the young Selous Scout, who only a short time ago had been enjoying a friendly conversation, dropped dead, nearly cut in half by machine gun fire.

Still clutching her sister, Sauwa ran through the chaos and took cover in a sandbag-lined hole. Next to her, men shouted. Dark olive fatigues moved through the smoke around her. Soldiers manned their mortar tubes and attempted to fire back. Enemy shells exploded so close, the deep, penetrating vibrations rattled her bones. Her frightened sister's tears soaked Sauwa's shirt as Rena's baby arms wrapped tightly around her neck.

Her sister screamed. Bullets tore into the burlap of the sandbags just inches above their heads.

Then…nothing.

The shouting stopped. Rhodesian soldiers were sprawled lifelessly above her, their uniforms saturated in blood. The youngest one, a boy no more than sixteen, looked back at her, his lifeless eyes displaying a look of terror from the last thought that had run through his mind.

"SHIT!" Sauwa cried as she woke.

Rising from where she lay, it took her some time to accept that it had been a dream. Her heart beat wildly and her undershirt was drenched in her own sweat. Slowly, her mind began to grasp where she was, and her breathing gradually returned to normal.

The rank odor emanating from the ship's hull was nauseating, to say the least. The combined force of sea water, rotting wood and residue left from decaying fish overwhelmed her. However, in her current situation, Sauwa couldn't afford to be picky about her accommodations. The captain and his crew were taking a serious risk hiding her. Under the circumstances and time constraints, she was thankful to have been able to arrange this much.

Making the best of the situation, Sauwa managed to find a few soft bags of beans that she'd made into a semblance of a bed. A half-full bag of flour served as a pillow.

She stretched out on her makeshift bed as much as she could and tried to get comfortable within the cramped space. Her lodging was located in the galley storeroom, a small room, only a few feet around the perimeter. Even without the additional supplies crammed inside, it was a tight fit.

Still, it was the best her smugglers could offer her and the first moment of peace she had enjoyed in three days.

The acrid aroma, animalistic living conditions and winter cold temperatures diminished next to the pleasure of several hours of sleep. Despite the additional risk, she had offered to help with chores on the ship, an offer that was sternly rejected by a nervous captain who warned her not to leave the storeroom until they hit port.

Pulling a wool cap tightly over her head and scrunching up the grey flannel coat that hung over her body, she felt her eyelids grow heavy and slip over her eyes.

Taking a few minutes to reflect, she came to the same conclusion she had reached so many times since this all began. Her past, consisting of the last week, had been a series of dramatic events and narrow escapes. Her future, as she looked into the dark room, contained no certainty after the ship ride.

It wasn't much to think of—how her world had

changed so dramatically in the proverbial blink of an eye. She wanted to shed tears at the thought of what her life had suddenly become. But it did no good to dwell on things she couldn't change. She turned her mind to the future, to forming a workable plan, until the hum of the ship's engine lulled her into a deep slumber.

Her rest came to an end with a loud pounding at the door and the familiar growling brogue of the Scottish captain.

"Time ti gu, Lassie. We hit purt, and I want yer arse off me fuckin' boat niew!" He was gruff and demanding, as he had been since the beginning of the voyage.

"Just a minute!" she called back. She grabbed her sandy brown military kit bag and climbed awkwardly through the labyrinth of flour bags and steel shelving that held rows of neatly organized cans.

The captain's pounded with unrelenting fervor. Coming within arms-length of the door, she extended her arm and turned the knob. The door creaked open a crack before the captain grabbed it and flung it violently the rest of the way.

Sauwa faced the brawny giant.

"The door wasn't locked," she said, assuming the reason for the captain's reluctance to open it himself.

The captain's squint through the rough, thickly lined face told a story of many fierce sea adventures. "E'm noot ta berberan yi think mi," he growled back, offended. "Ee dunna berge in un a lady wer she meghta noot be a'decent." The captain apparently took his gentlemanly conduct seriously.

He stepped aside for Sauwa to pass him. She turned to thank him but was cut off by his arm waving for her to continue walking. Not wanting to exacerbate the situation, Sauwa threw her bergen over her shoulder and went through the small galley into the mess and out into a dreary looking, narrow gangway.

The captain followed closely behind, ready to prod her the moment she faltered in her journey to leave. Ascending a few creaky, wooden steps she exited through the old weathered door.

The night was pitch black, save for the dull lights barely visible from the pier in the distance and the equally dismal ones lining the ship. The air was even colder than her galley storeroom. Almost immediately, she felt her bare hands going numb. Outside, from the bridge, the fishing boat seemed much smaller than it actually was. It sat low in the water, probably because of a large catch of fish the crew netted before continuing on to their destination.

In the faint light, she could see the outline of a small craft, a motorboat with a single figure aboard. It drew closer, then roped off next to the ship.

The captain pressed gently against Sauwa's back urging her to continue walking. He moved past her toward the motorboat that was now tied alongside. Not knowing what to expect, she followed slowly. Her eyes darted from side to side as she kept abreast of everything going on around her. Though dark, she could still see the outlines of the crew, and she watched for any strange or unusual movements that might alert her to a pending ambush or other danger. That these men had taken a great risk to help her, did not mean they couldn't suddenly decide to the contrary.

Once standing over the motorboat, Sauwa peered

down at a thin, frail-looking man, mid-sixties, and wearing a dark overcoat, which made it even more difficult to see him.

"I was told I'm picking someone up from you all," the old man said in a general statement to whoever was listening.

"We do have someone who's getting off here," replied a man from the fishing crew, who was clearly better spoken than the inarticulate Scottish captain.

Sauwa moved toward the craft. The old man stopped her. "This person would be a foreigner."

"I am sir," Sauwa replied nervously.

"You sound English," the old man responded with a hint of suspicion in his voice.

"She is," interjected the crewman again.

The old man stood poised for a moment, as if debating something with himself. Finally, he shrugged. "Well, let's be about it then. Come aboard, girl."

Sauwa approached the edge of the ship and started to climb over. She was immediately hit with a freezing cold splash of water. It sent shivers up her spine. She wanted to shriek but remained silent. She felt the hands of the old man grab onto her to help stabilize her. His grip surprisingly strong given his frail appearance.

"I've got this," he said as he went to lift her bergen off her shoulder, relieving her of the awkward weight. The wind was little more than a light breeze. Still, it was enough to disrupt the transfer.

With her jeans now soaked from the persistent splashes of water, Sauwa was relieved to feel her feet finally touch the floor of the boat. Despite sliding carefully, she nearly slipped over the bow when a larger wave rose up and caught her off balance. The old man steadied her. With one powerful heave, he pulled her back and threw her head first into the boat. Crashing into a pile of ropes, she felt the rough, scratchy nylon strands as she struggled to her feet.

The old man detached his vessel from the fishing boat and was working to activate the motor. The small craft began to drift on the waves. It wasn't long before the fishing boat was a dim outline.

The small boat rocked violently in the water, making it hard to balance. Sauwa sank back onto the pile of ropes while the old man began pulling the cord to start the engine. After a few tugs and no results, she stood up to offer help. Before she could say anything, the engine suddenly roared to life.

"You stay where you're at, girl," the old man said gruffly. "I've got this engine. You just sit down and stay quiet."

Not wanting to argue and feeling the numbness kick in from the cold air and soaked clothing, Sauwa moved to the other side and sat down. The boat sped steadily over the water against the encroaching ocean waves. Water sprayed into the craft with each splash. It was all she could do not to squeal as the ice-cold water ran down the length of her back, but she was determined not to be a burden or an annoyance. She would tolerate her situation and hope something better awaited her at the end of the journey.

"We're only a few minutes out from our destination," the old man said, perhaps sensing her mood.

Sauwa was startled by the thump of an object suddenly landing on her lap.

"It's a rain cover," he explained. "It should protect you from the water and the air."

Wasting no time, she unwrapped the bundle and threw it over her body. Huddling with her knees tight to her chest, she breathed hard hoping to warm the environment. It worked, a little.

Gradually the waters calmed, and the spray eased as they neared the shore. The boat slowed to a mere idle. Sauwa came out from the meager warmth of her cover, her body clammy.

The motor went silent. For a moment, she tensed, fearing something had happened. Easing back her flannel and reaching under her sweatshirt, her fingers touched the grip of the Makarov pistol she kept in her waistband. She held off lifting the cover to avoid creating additional noise. Sauwa waited, motionless, until the old man announced their arrival.

Her body relaxed. All was well. Her journey was at an end.

Emerging from the cover, she felt the sharp shock as the cold hit her body again. She began to shiver and tried not to let her teeth chatter.

"A warm meal and bed await you, Lassie," the old man said, his voice warmer.

He threw a rope around one of the posts and began to secure the craft then reached for an object that crinkled as he took hold of it. He handed it to her after she stepped onto the pier.

"I took the liberty of putting your kit sack in a plastic bag to protect it from the water."

"Thank you. I appreciate it very much," Sauwa replied and took the plastic in hand.

The old man followed her up the small ladder along

the pier. He gently took her by the arm and proceeded to escort her down the darkened path toward land.

From the fishing boat, the pier was visible due to a few old, dim lights. If an ambush lay at the end of the walkway, she would never know until it was upon her. She couldn't make out how many other boats were at the pier, or if there were any buildings at the end.

Staying close to the old man, she walked briskly. His hand remained around her arm, which gave her a feeling of safety. If he was setting her up, he would have tried to lengthen the distance between them to avoid any crossfire from an ambush or prevent him from becoming a hostage.

Their feet finally hit the pavement and soon they were standing in front of some sort of truck. Buried in the shadows, it was difficult to make out what type of truck it was. Sauwa could only see the general outline of either a truck or some other frontier conducive mode of travel. The old man took the liberty of getting the door for her. Looking in the passenger side, she saw a cab fitted with extremely worn, weathered seats and the floor caked in a layer of dried mud. There was a variety of personal knickknacks lined up along the dashboard, on the floor, and behind the seats.

This was the man's personal vehicle, as opposed to a throwaway used only for this particular mission. Slipping into the truck, Sauwa settled into the seat. The worn leather was a welcome upgrade from the cold, hard wood of his boat or the hard, lumpy bags that had been her previous accommodation on the fishing boat.

The door shut after her. Left in the darkness, she waited quietly but alert, not allowing herself to relax, her bergen tucked tightly against her body. Outside, she heard the crunching of the loose dirt with every step the old man took as he walked around to the other side. Gripping the door handle, she tracked his movements. If he veered off, she was ready to jump out and run, even not knowing what the area looked like or where she was at now.

To her relief, the old man opened the driver's side door and slipped in next to her. In the light, she was finally able to get a good look at him. He looked far different than she had assumed. His hair was charcoal and grey, gathered in a loose ponytail and partially covered by a wool knit cap. His skin was worn, the sign of someone who was used to hard work. Yet, unlike the fishing boat captain, he had a more distinguished appearance; he did not have heavy jowls or the thick crevasses. He had a neat, well-kept goatee, like a professional type or an artist. (Not a hint of a strongman, a kidnapper or a killer, but then again, people were not always what they seemed.)

He shut the door, leaving them in darkness.

2

"Are you comfortable, love?" the old man asked.

"Yes," Sauwa replied quietly.

They drove along a dirt pathway, then onto a paved main road.

"Get some sleep," he commanded. "We have a distance to go." Sensing the girl was still quite cold, he turned the heat to full blast.

Within seconds, a freezing Sauwa was relishing the powerful gusts of heat rolling over her body, a welcome comfort. It had been days since she had felt anything but cold. Between her fatigue and the soothing warmth, she fell into a peaceful lull and—though she fought hard to combat it, to remain awake and alert—her body and mind eventually succumbed. Her muscles relaxed. Her eyelids once again grew heavy.

Sauwa awoke to a strong hand on her shoulder. The truck had stopped, and a darkened figure was standing at the opened passenger door. Before her mind had caught up, her hand had instinctively found the hilt of the double-bladed gripping knife she used for close range attacks.

But it was only the old man.

Her hand relaxed. She slowly unwrapped herself and shifted out of her seat. In the background, lights appeared from what looked to be a farmhouse.

"I've got this." The old man grabbed her bergen and started walking before Sauwa had a chance to protest. He marched up a small hill over a loose configuration of rocks meant to be a pathway.

"I can get my own bag, thank you," Sauwa attempted to argue, traipsing closely behind.

The old man said nothing on his way to the house. With a push, he flung the front door open. The light from inside blazed, burning their eyes. They had spent the last few hours immersed in pitch darkness, and it took a few seconds for Sauwa's eyes to adjust. When they did, she was looking into a kitchen that easily dated back to the turn of the century with a strange intermixing of modern appliances throughout.

A woman stood in the center dressed in a pair of jeans and knit sweater covered by a white cloth apron. She was about the age of the old man, mid-fifties to early sixties. Like the old man, she had the appearance of someone who was no stranger to hard living but also had clean distinguished features. Her hair, also a charcoal grey, was gathered atop her head.

"So, did everything go well?" The old woman took the man in a warm embrace.

"Aye, it did," he replied. "No patrols on the road tonight, so I didn't have to navigate the back trails like I thought I was gonna."

The old woman stepped away from him toward Sauwa looking at her guest over — garbed in her large grey flannel and wool knit cap — and carefully assessing her. "So, this is the one the folks in Belfast are so concerned about," the old woman said, surprised. "She's barely more than a child."

"She is that my love," the old man replied. "But, don't let that fool you. If even half of what I was told is true, she's a dangerous one."

She looked back at Sauwa. The old woman's eyes betrayed the mind of a woman who wanted to be motherly, but her posture remained cautious.

"Well, you must be freezing in those wet clothes. I'll draw you a bath and get you into something dry. Then a hot meal for the both of you before you're off to bed."

Sauwa was not allowed even a word before the old woman marched her out of the kitchen and up a narrow passage of creaky, wooden steps leaving the old man to his own devices in the kitchen.

The woman stayed a distance behind Sauwa, just out of reach in case Sauwa had a mind to turn and attack her. The narrow stairway, combined with her bergen still strapped over her back, made any such notion impractical. The old woman, though behaving like a homemaker, had all the mannerisms and instincts of someone quite accustomed to dealing with nefarious types.

Reaching the top of the stairs, Sauwa was directed toward a room just off to the right from the stairwell. It was a small storage closet deep enough to walk into, though too narrow to turn in. The old woman instructed her to walk into the closet and wait. Reluctantly, Sauwa obeyed. She entered the tiny room — made more uncomfortable by the addition of cleaning supplies and towels — and listened as the old woman ascended the steps.

It was an easy assumption that the closet was just a precaution. Pushing Sauwa into a tight place ensured she couldn't ambush her hostess as she came up the stairs. Another possibility was the thought that this was a setup, and she was now defenseless.

A minute later, the door opened. "Come, my love," the old woman said in a soft, warming tone.

Backing awkwardly out of the closet, Sauwa turned to see the old woman, who smiled and waved her hand in the direction of what appeared to be a spare bedroom.

"This will be where you'll stay during your time with us." She took Sauwa gently in hand and led her the rest of the way.

The bedroom was like the rest of the house, nineteenth century, adorned with collections of furniture from the many different eras the house had seen in its time. Looking about the room, Sauwa felt a sudden pang of homesickness. There was a strange familiarity about it all. It reminded her of the old farmhouse she had grown up in on the Transvaal.

"I hope this is to your liking." The old woman interrupted her nostalgic thoughts. "We weren't told how long you'll be with us. This room will be yours until you move on."

"This is fine," Sauwa replied faintly. "It's actually better than what I've had for a long time."

"Well, love, we need to get you out of those wet clothes before you catch your death. You need to take a warm bath and then have a bit of supper." She worked the bergen off

Sauwa's shoulders. "Do you have dry clothes of your own?"

"Yes ma'am, I do."

"I'll get them. I have to search your things anyway." The old woman was apologetic

"I know." Sauwa stepped a few feet back and allowed the older woman to work. "If the situation was reversed, I would demand the exact same thing."

Flipping open the bergen, the old woman untied the strap around the plastic bag lining the pack for waterproofing. "You're clearly a frontiersman," she joked as she began rummaging through Sauwa's things. Both women kept a steady eye on the other. The search ended with the old woman producing a grey, long-sleeved shirt and black and white plaid flannel bottoms, which she laid on the bed.

The old woman straightened, waited and observed as Sauwa began to undress. It was slightly uncomfortable for Sauwa to be watched so closely. Still, she had to respect her hostess's concerns. At least she could take solace in the notion that it was another woman doing the observing and searches as opposed to some man. It was a luxury she didn't often enjoy in her world.

Knowing what the old woman was looking for, Sauwa immediately threw the Makarov pistol onto the bed, followed by the double-bladed gripping knife. The old woman's face revealed not the slightest concern for the fearsome weapons displayed. Instead, she merely nodded obligingly, as if to thank the young girl for not trying to hide them.

With the exception of her soggy, cotton underwear, Sauwa

was completely naked. Collecting the dry night clothes laid out on the bed, the old woman led her young charge into the main corridor. Sauwa grabbed her pistol and followed. The two crossed to the other side of the hall and stepped into a bathroom. It was homey. The wood flooring and carpet cover over the toilet seat all added to the grandmotherly persona the old couple was definitely trying to achieve.

"I'll let you keep your weapons," the old woman said. "You have no reason to trust us, and we intend to be careful of you, too. We also realize you wouldn't take to being completely defenseless. I don't know much about you except that those we report to said you were dangerous."

"That means I could also be a dangerous threat to you," Sauwa replied as she perused the bathroom.

The old woman nodded. "Aye, ya could. But, I've been doing this a long time. If you intended harm, you most likely would have done it by now when you had both of us together. You wouldn't have let yourself be put in this position. I also suspect, as scared as you are, if we tried to take the weapons we know about from you, we'd either get killed or you'd just find something to replace them with that would catch us even more off guard. A professional such as yourself relies on instincts and skill to ply your trade, more than an over-reliance on specific weapons. This way, I know what you have, and I and my husband will take our own precautions, so we can stay with this stalemate for now."

Sauwa took a deep breath before saying, "I didn't have a chance to thank you and your husband for taking me in like this."

The old woman chuckled softly. Her guest cut a most

extraordinary figure: toned with the well curved and proportioned body one expected from a professional athlete. Her skin was nearly snow white, which — when added to her coal black eyes and the long silky raven black hair running straight down the length of her back — gave her the haunting appearance of the iconic angel of death. Indeed, it was a most fitting image for such an infamous killer, as the young girl was reputed to be. "It's alright my child. No thanks are needed. Our people have told us to give you sanctuary, and that is what will do until told differently. Oh, and since you may be staying a spell, you can call me Shanna, and my husband is Rowan."

Sauwa lowered her eyes. "I assume those are not your real names."

"No, my child," the old woman smiled pleasantly.

"I guess they told you what to call me?"

Shanna bent to work the faucet of the bathtub. "Aye, Willow is what we're to call you. And that be the only name I want to know," she said with a twinge of nervousness. "I've heard only that you are a dangerous person, who did many violent things for those whom you served. And, since the orders directing us to help you are coming all the way from the Belfast command, it can only mean you're someone of great importance. That is all I and my husband want to know. For us, too much information makes us liabilities. I have seen my share of killers over the years. While I don't see you as the merciless killer type, you do seem the type who wouldn't hesitate, should the need to kill occur."

Sauwa felt cold in the pit of her stomach at hearing this gracious, motherly figure so easily assess her as a professional killer did not sit well. Violence and spying had been her life for the last several years fighting a dirty war. But the war was over. She, like any other soldier, wanted to go home and live peacefully, but that was not an option yet, not for her. She had to live with the reality that she would never again set foot on her homeland soil. She was a fugitive for the foreseeable future, wanted throughout the world as a war criminal. Still, Shanna's words cut deeply in a strange way. She didn't have to keep working as spy and terrorist. Nor did she intend to. She would get a new identity and, until circumstances changed, blend into a whole new life as a whole new person somewhere. She would get a job, find decent work and put her former life behind her.

The bathtub was now filled with steaming water. Shanna placed a towel atop Sauwa's night clothes before giving her another warm smile and leaving the bathroom. Discarding the last of her garments, Sauwa slid slowly into the tub. The warm, heavenly water gradually encompassed her tired and cold body.

When Sauwa came downstairs, she found the couple sitting at an old oak table in the center of the kitchen. Both were enjoying a glass of some pitch-black liquid that Sauwa assumed was beer. She stepped into the kitchen dressed in her grey, long-sleeved shirt and flannel sweats looking every bit like a teenager settling in at her parents' home.

Shanna rose to her feet and walked over to the antique stove where a large pot was bubbling and emitting a tasty aroma. "I've made some beef stew and some greens for dinner," she said happily. She opened the pot and began dishing up some brown, mud-like substance into three porcelain bowls. "I figure, since we're still getting to know each other, I'd wait and have all of us eat at the same time. Ya know, so you wouldn't worry we had tampered with anything."

"That's all right," Sauwa replied. "You didn't have to wait." It wasn't true. She wasn't about to eat anything before these people hadn't eaten it in front of her first. She had seen too many people die of poisoning or get drugged because they were too trusting or careless.

Piling the stew into the porcelain bowls, Shanna collected them and walked them over to set them in the center of the table. She looked up at Sauwa. "Given the situation, you choose first."

Sauwa reached for a bowl and a nearby spoon before sinking into a chair. The old couple followed suit. They enjoyed the meal in silence, neither side was eager to engage in conversation. Despite the unappetizing appearance, the stew tasted delicious. Shanna had added a spinach salad and a few slices of white bread spread with butter. Sauwa hadn't enjoyed a home cooked meal in a long while. She washed it all down with a glass of a sweet tasting fruit juice and was surprised at how full she was.

"So, Willow," Rowan spoke up, after what seemed an eternity of dead silence. "Tomorrow, I'll be workin' about the house and field. My wife will be off at the market for most of the day buyin' groceries and such. She'll also be the liaison to our command and will be makin' contact with them to let them know we have received you and all seems well."

Sauwa looked at the old man with tired eyes saying nothing.

He continued. "In the meantime, I need ya to stay within the confines of the house and properties for the next few days. Since you have no documents or papers and given your, ah, legal status, we can't afford to have you seen by anyone."

"I understand," Sauwa said. "I imagine this is a tight-knit community where everyone knows everyone."

Rowan smiled. "It is that, love. And with the violence that's been seen in these parts for so many years, people tend to take careful notice of strangers who mysteriously show up. It'll be easier if you just stay close to the house and disappear when neighbors come callin'."

"That won't be a problem," she replied.

"You should be getting off to bed," Shanna chimed in, her voice soothing. "Come, I'll lead you upstairs."

Rising from her chair, Sauwa, feeling drained, followed the old woman. Again ascending the narrow stairwell, they returned to the guest room.

"I've laid a bedpan for you," Shanna said, directing her charge to the far side of the bed. Sauwa looked confused at the sight of the stainless-steel bowl.

Shanna sighed. "It wouldn't do to go creeping about in the night, even to the loo. If someone be creeping about outside, we immediately assume they be meaning us harm. You stay in your room at night and wait until we come for you. If you have to, you'll conduct your lady business in your pan."

Not wanting to abuse their hospitality, Sauwa accepted the situation as she prepared for bed. She tucked her pistol under her pillow, and took a few seconds to bar the door with a wooden board. She didn't want anyone sneaking in during the night, including the old couple, who she still distrusted.

Sauwa slipped into bed, under soft blankets. Finally, a safe, decent place to sleep. No need to be on constant alert or move quickly from minute to minute. She believed she would be at this place for a while. And while she didn't completely trust her current hosts, they seemed less threatening than those she had dealt with recently.

Her head had no sooner hit the pillow when the fatigue of so many days living on edge caught up with her, and she was instantly out.

3

It was late in the morning when Sauwa awoke to a knock at her door. Between her grogginess and the sunlight now beaming into her bedroom, it took her a few moments for her eyes to adjust. Slowly she rose to a sitting position and assessed the room. "We're having breakfast downstairs, dear." It was the pleasant sounding voice of Shanna. "I've gone ahead and unlocked the door, so, feel free to join us when you're ready.

Everything was as she had left it, including the bar against the door. Sliding out of bed, she studied the windows. The dust on the panels had not been disturbed. Content no one had gotten into her room during the night, she set about getting dressed. Her only other set of clothes consisted of some beaten blue jeans, a pale blue Mickey Mouse shirt and another white long-sleeved shirt. She pulled on her boots and knit cap, tucked her knife and pistol in her belt under her shirt and went out the door.

Due to the remote location, she figured it was safer to have her weapons. Besides, if the police should come knocking, she had numerous places to quickly ditch her hardware. The immediate concern was some hit team coming around looking for her or her hosts.

Downstairs, she found Rowan at the kitchen table consumed by his newspaper. "Shanna made some breakfast for ya before she left this morning," he said, his face still buried in the sports section.

"Thank you." She spotted the basket of sausage, a pan of fried eggs and some potato based dish. Grabbing a plate, she leisurely collected food from the choices offered before stepping over to the table. Rapping the paper to catch Rowan's attention, she waited with one eyebrow cocked. He lowered his news sheet to find her plate thrust in front of him. The sight of two forks made it clear what she wanted. Taking one of the forks, he took a mouth full of each dish. Only when he swallowed in front of her did she take a seat and commence eating. Without a word, he returned to his paper.

The sight of an article on one of Rowan's discarded pages stopped her. It was an article discussing South Africa and the announcement of the investigations into the Civil Cooperation Bureau.

Reaching for the sheet, she quickly skimmed it. What she read unnerved her.

The article discussed the appointment of a special prosecutor to look into the activities of the Civil Cooperation Bureau — the CCB — abroad. This was not surprising. She had known about this intention when the Apartheid collapsed, and her commander explained that she and the others in the group were now considered criminals by the new government. Still, this was the first time she had seen anything official.

Deep down, she had hoped what she had been told were exaggerations of a paranoid racist. However, as she read more, any hope she had dissolved. The article explained the creation of some sort of Truth and Reconciliation Commission to investigate the activities of the country's security services.

When she finished reading, all she could think about was that she would never again be able to go home.

Her appetite now lost, she struggled through each bite. Somehow she managed to finish her breakfast at the same time Rowan finished his paper. She slumped in her chair, a disappointed look on her face, the article before her.

The old man stood up. "You interested in helping me with the field today?"

As if being freed from a trance, Sauwa looked up at the old man. A smile cracked across her face, and she nodded. She jumped up, placed her dish in the washbasin and followed him out the door.

The yard work was a welcome distraction, one she needed at that moment. It also felt good to have a chance to return the favor of the help the couple had provided. Her skills, acquired from growing up on a farm, had not been lost, and she found she was able to help fix the rusted old tractor and use most of the aged equipment. The farm was a decent size, not large but not small either. It offered the means for the old couple to subsist with enough left over to fetch a tidy little sum on the market.

During their time in the field, Rowan was cordial and pleasant, much more so than the previous night. He joked and engaged his guest with the offer of some of his home-brewed beer, an offer she politely declined. He was taken by the young lady's abilities and familiarity around the place. He was just as impressed with her work ethic, as she diligently toiled in the field. But as friendly as they became, they remained guarded against each other staying cognizant of their situation. They did not give away details or personal information, ever aware of the veteran experience each of them had in the shadowy world in which they resided.

It was around 1300hrs when Shanna returned from the day's outing. She rode up in a beaten Land Rover. Sauwa had ridden in the vehicle night before. Behind her was another car, a white Mitsubishi model of some sort. Both vehicles stopped just in front of the house, leaving Rowan and Sauwa protected from view by several large, thick shrubs. Rowan waved Sauwa off as he stood up and started walking toward the vehicles.

Slipping deeper into the tree line, Sauwa watched the doors to the Mitsubishi burst open. Two men exited from the front seat. One of the men — a tall, lanky, sandy-haired fellow — met the old farmer in a familiar embrace. A relative perhaps.

All three treated the other man — a short, balding fellow with a highly visible, bulging gut — with more professional ceremony. The fat man must be of particular importance. The old couple acted hesitantly toward him. Sauwa presumed he was an unexpected visitor.

The fat man quickly took charge of the conversation. Even from a distance, Sauwa could see he was abrasive and direct in his behavior. He jabbed his finger first at Rowan and then at Shanna. Both responded as penitent servants having just offended the fiefdom lord — a role the fat man was certainly playing. The brief conversation ended with Rowan extending his arm and pointing in the direction where Sauwa was hiding. The fat man waved the old couple away as Sauwa began walking toward him.

Sauwa held her position and reached for her pistol. It didn't seem likely that a double-cross was in play. The two strange men didn't look or act the part of seasoned gunmen. She had dealt with enough of those in her time to know a professional when she saw one. Lanky and fat man both behaved more like management than field operatives. They seemed oblivious to everything except the old couple. These types usually liked to keep their distance from the violence and criminality.

The old couple came to the bush line and stopped.

Rowan cautioned his wife to stay put as he slowly moved forward. "Sauwa, it's alright; nothin's wrong. We've got someone who wants to speak to ya."

Sauwa emerged from the bushes only a few feet away from the old man.

His eyes fell on the pistol in her hands. "There's no need for that. Someone needs a word with ya."

"It looked like you were surprised to see him." She stared coldly at the old man. "Like him being here was not something expected or common."

"Well..." Rowan struggled to find his words. "He's a man of importance who works for people high up in the UVF. It's not protocol for him to be comin' to safe houses like this. He came all the way from Belfast to speak with you."

Sauwa tucked the pistol back into her pants. "I'm assuming he didn't tell you why he wanted to speak with me."

The old man shook his head. "Nor did we ask. He just

said to fetch ya and offer him some privacy to speak with you alone."

Sauwa followed the old man as he started out of the tree line. She emerged from the cover of the shrubbery in view of the two strangers, feeling naked. The three of them crossed the field, the old couple staying just in front of her. As they neared the house, the two men started walking toward them, the tall, lanky man taking the lead.

"Thank you for this," the lanky man said when they finally met. "This is her, uh?" He looked her over as if unsure he had the right person.

"It is," the fat man cut in, clearly impatient to get to the point. "I know the infamous Sauwa Catcher by sight and by methods," he said, bragging. He stared at her, his eyes expressionless. "You don't know me, but I've seen you a few times when I was in London. I know the man you answered to, Devon Williams."

Sauwa's eyes lit up. For the second time in an hour, the Civil Cooperation Bureau — the CCB — reached out from her past.

The CCB was created to distance the South African government from the more sensitive clandestine exploitations within the covert war. Many covert operations by South African intelligence wound up leading back to the South African embassy. As a result, the CCB was set up to operate independently from the government — through a series of front companies — to carry out a more aggressive campaign against the African National Congress and other Black Nationalist groups.

Devon Williams had run the ultra-secret unit within the CCB, a unit designed to infiltrate British left-wing political groups who — from the safety of the United Kingdom —

were working with South African Black Nationalists. Devon's unit was comprised mostly of Rhodesian born, white South Africans who could blend into the British landscape. It operated to infiltrate the British left-wing political groups that were working with black nationalists. It also had the extended mission to carry out more ambitious attacks against these left-wing organizations as well as high-profile targets in the black movement.

To this end, the CCB relied on assistance from local elements, either criminal or sympathetic, to obtain necessary support and equipment. The Protestant Loyalist of Northern Ireland, particularly the Ulster Volunteer Force, was one such group. It had been an essential ally for the campaign carried out in England.

"I…I've never..." Sauwa couldn't find the words.

"Met me," the fat man finished her sentence. "You never have. I worked in the shadows through intermediaries. But, on occasion, I saw you from a distance. My people, who assisted in some of your complicated missions, bore witness to your abilities and ruthlessness as a killer and terrorist. They were quite impressed. My dear, I'm well acquainted with your professional history."

Sauwa didn't answer. She took an immediate dislike to the fat man.

He continued. "Hence, I wish to speak to you privately about a rather serious matter — one of grave importance. Shall we?" He lifted his hand signaling her to move in a direction away from the house. She looked about at the others and saw only blank looks on their faces as they stood like statues.

Leaving the old couple and the lanky man behind, the two strode side by side. Sauwa could see the sweat stains soaking through the armpits and neckline of the man's white collared shirt. Two birds fighting on the branch of a tree just above them captured his attentions.

"Birds have always interested me," he said as they walked.

It was strange that such a man, so impatient to get down to business before, should now want to waste time on topics of leisure. She assumed he was only making small talk until they had enough distance from the rest of the group. Whatever he wanted, it was not for their ears.

When they were far enough away, his conversation became more serious. "My name is Simon."

"That's not your real name, is it?" Sauwa's voice was a cold, abrupt whisper.

The fat man chuckled, and for the first time, he cracked a smile. "No, it's not. But, for the purposes of this meeting, it will suffice."

Simon folded his arms across his chest. "I imagine you must be ruminating over the ending of Apartheid. It's never easy to see the cause you fought and risked so much for come to an end. I hear they're even looking at the possibility of a 'darky' being the next president — even the convicted terrorist, Nelson Mandela."

"On the contrary," Sauwa scoffed. "I'm glad to see it end. It was a horrible system that should never have been implemented."

Simon's face remained stoic. "Yet, you fought for it."

Sauwa drew her lips into a firm, straight line. "I fought for my adopted country against black terrorists. The Apartheid was an invention of racists; a system set up under the fervor of Afrikaner nationalism and their belief that they were superior to everyone else, my dear

Irishman. They called English the language of the conqueror and set about forcing Afrikaner culture on everyone, including those whites of British origin. I'm Rhodesian by birth. My ancestors hailed from these very lands we now walk. My people came to South Africa when the equally racist regime of Ian Smith crumbled. They needed our expertise fighting guerrillas and operating covert wars because the violence had spread to their country."

"The way you speak, I have to wonder if you're not sympathetic to the Black Nationalist," Simon said, a little smugly.

"I can't say the blacks don't have their grievances," Sauwa replied coldly. "In truth, it was the government policies that brought everyone to violence. Bantus couldn't even march or protest for rights. As a result, they flocked to the radicals and extremists who advocated a violent overthrow.

My people fled Rhodesia after a black-dominated government emerged under such circumstances. Mugabe's regime was just as racist, more corrupt and has run my country into the ground.

I wasn't going to let such a thing happen in South Africa if I could help prevent it. I chose the lesser of two evils. My hope was that more enlightened minds on both sides would have eventually seen fit to create a more amenable system that benefitted all sides — not just Afrikaners and not just whites." That she was speaking so freely about herself and so intimately on such delicate matters was not lost on her. She had been guarded with everyone, including the old couple who gave her sanctuary. But Simon knew so much about her and her activities with Devon Williams's special unit, it seemed pointless to be secretive.

Simon nodded, but his face remained expressionless. "Given what I know about the infamous Sauwa Catcher, I hardly expected such thinking. In truth, I expected a cold, single-minded killer with a firm racist streak."

Sauwa sighed. "So, what is it you need to discuss with me? A man of your importance doesn't come out to the middle of nowhere for nothing. He certainly wouldn't risk himself to meet with a fugitive unless it was something important."

"Business, my child." Simon stopped in his tracks. He turned to face her. "Regarding your particular expertise."

She didn't turn. She didn't look at the balding, fat man, even though she could feel him eyeing her intently.

Simon pressed on, "My organization has a problem. One that requires an outsider to take care of it. We figured with your current disposition, you would be in the market for such a job. It's important. So much so, I've been authorized by my superiors to offer you a hundred thousand pounds sterling for your services."

Sauwa took a breath. She didn't like where this was going. "I don't do that anymore. In a few days' time, I intend to get a new identity, and from there I plan to turn away from all this and disappear to enjoy a legitimate life. I'm not the one you need for whatever you intend to do."

Simon pursed his lips, then they gradually morphed into an unnerving smile. "Don't play naive with me, girl. Naiveté doesn't suit you. I know you lost your South African connections, and your own country wants nothing to do with you." The fat man stared coldly at her. "You're Sauwa Catcher, the Apartheid's most lethal operator.

You've killed dozens of key people, important people, people who were in organizations that are now becoming part of the political leadership of South Africa. You've also killed British citizens as part of your little war. It's common knowledge that the old security organizations you answered to are now being integrated with counterparts of your former enemies. Your government intends to play nice with the world by opening secret archives and holding investigations into the security services, and what they did in all those years of your dirty war."

Though she didn't show it, a creeping fear was overtaking her. The fat man's words had sent a cold chill down her spine.

Simon paused for only a few moments. As a longtime operator in the shadowy conflict of the Irish Troubles, he had learned to assess the fortitude of young men. He had acquired, over the years, a good instinct for sizing up an operator he was about to send on a dangerous mission. The young woman was certainly hard to read — the sign of a professional.

However, he knew his words were having an effect. He let her soak up their meaning before he spoke again. "It's only a matter of time before the British government has a full record of your organization and its activities carried out in Europe. When that happens, the police here will have a list of all your victims and all the evidence to prosecute. You're already high up on the roles as a criminal in both countries. When those records are made public, you'll be too hot to just disappear. They'll likely set up a whole task force just to hunt you and the rest of your kind down to bring you all to justice."

Simon's words resonated. Sauwa began rubbing her

head as she began to realize the enormity of her situation. The fat man was right. She was wanted now for what had been released from South Africa to the various authorities in Europe. As the government in South Africa transitioned from Apartheid, it was inevitable they would do exactly as Simon was predicting. In a short conversation, a man she didn't even know had completely obliterated her dream of possibly disappearing and eventually being forgotten.

After what seemed like ages, she looked up at the fat man. His face was casting a sinister portrait. "I guess I don't have much choice. What is it you need me to do?"

Simon glanced at the trio they had left behind. They were all standing about awkwardly. "Not here. I'll make arrangements for us to meet at a more secure location in a few days to discuss the mission further. Until then, no one need know of this, so don't discuss it with the farmer and his wife. I suggest you keep yourself in shape and sharpen up on your skills."

With that, Simon started back toward the trio, leaving Sauwa alone in the middle of the field to ponder what had just happened.

4

David O'knomo walked about the Concilium building like a small child venturing into the forbidden lair of his father's private office. It was a strange sensation for the young former MK (Umkhonto we Sizwe - Spear of the Nation) fighter.

For so long, he had known of the Concilium only as a sinister place. It was the headquarters of the infamous National Intelligence Service (NIS) — one of South Africa's prime intelligence organs — and a predecessor to the once dreaded Department of National Security, the old-time foreign counter-revolutionary arm of the Apartheid. So many of O'knomo's friends, compatriots and even family had been killed, disappeared or tortured by the NIS, many perhaps in this very building.

Since the early eighties, the NIS had taken on a different, more professional image under the directorship of Dr. Niel Barnard. It had gone from a thuggish secret police group to becoming strictly an intelligence gathering and processing organization.

Strangely, the Concilium was not what he expected. The building was a structure of dreary, grey walls and severely worn carpeting that had needed to be replaced a long time ago. It was hardly the image he had conjured up of dungeon-like basements, torture rooms and offices littered with maps and photographs glossed over by operatives preparing for some assassination or other nefarious covert mission. Still, it did not make O'knomo feel any less unnerved. He progressed through the corridors thinking about the ominous history housed within these walls.

He felt out of place in his light grey suit. After so many years wearing nothing but green and camouflage jungle fatigues, a business suit seemed to hang about him like a circus clown costume. It had been only a few weeks since he'd been squatting in a jungle base camp in Namibia, washing himself in a river, eating hunted meat and defecating into a hole in the ground.

Moving through the Concilium, about to start his new job with the African National Congress — the ANC — everything seemed surreal to him like it was all a dream or an incredibly obscene joke. He looked at his colleagues wandering about with pensive demeanors. It was clear none of the former guerrillas felt comfortable here.

It took them several minutes of navigating the drab labyrinth of hallways, but O'knomo and his people finally approached a set of brown double doors. The doors were guarded by a tall, lanky man with a neat crop of sandy blond hair. The lanky figure towered over them. He looked like an office clerk —with an awkward manner and a bulge in his gut exposing his unhealthy diet and lack of exercise — who had probably never even seen the jungles, much less fought in one.

"Good day gentlemen," the lanky man said. "Are you the ANC representatives for this afternoon's meeting?"

The leader of O'knomo's group, a small, frail man with a receding hairline and graying black hair looked up from under his horn-rimmed glasses. "We are here to meet Johan Van Wessan and his staff." He produced a slip of paper from his leather briefcase and handed it to the sentry.

Taking only a quick glance, the lanky fellow nodded his head obligingly and opened the doors. Beckoning the ANC party in, the sentry stood to the side to allow entry. The party passed into the room. O'knomo gave no further consideration to the office clerk.

"This will be fun," smirked a young man, who walked next to O'knomo. "I hope the boss shows these assholes who are now in charge."

"Keep focused on the business at hand," O'knomo said in a low commanding voice.

The meeting room was as drab as the hallways — worn brown carpet and no pictures hanging on the grey walls. Inside was a long, wood table surrounded by a loose collection of plastic chairs. An assorted group of men ranging from gruff and weathered old spy veterans to younger, energetic and more academic looking individuals sat across the table taking up half of the space.

A man in his mid-forties and sporting a dark, black suit came around the table toward the ANC delegation with a forced smile.

"Mr. Gahima, I presume," the man asked as he extended his arm to offer a handshake. Mr. Gahima, the small man who had offered the papers to the clerk outside, stepped forward to receive it, his own face showing a painfully forced look of friendliness.

"I am Johan Van Wessan of the National Intelligence Service."

The two former enemies shook hands a little tentatively followed by Van Wesson waving his hands toward the empty chairs around the table, inviting the ANC delegates to sit down. Obligingly, Gahima motioned his people to take their seats.

O'knomo sank into a hard, plastic office chair finding himself directly across from a grizzled, white man who was grimacing at him. It was clear the old spy was not the least bit used to the idea of sharing a table with a Bantu, and a nationalist radical at that. To the young MK fighter's dismay, the arrogant smartass who had made all the comments coming in sat beside him. O'knomo's first thought was to hurry up and sit somewhere else, but it was too late. All the other chairs had been taken, and he was left facing an old racist and next to a cocky upstart.

When all were seated, Mr. Gahima wasted no time. He immediately jumped into the discussion.

"Mr. Van Wesson." He began in a polished English that denoted his extensive education and years abroad. That he addressed the meeting in English as opposed to using a Swahili dialect or the demanded Afrikaans' language was clearly a calculated move. A move designed to set the tone for the meeting.

O'knomo looked across the table to see the disgruntled looks of the Afrikaners — their nationalistic pride ruffled by this action. He wasn't sure where this was going, but he was sure that the ANC delegates needed to assert themselves early in the meeting. Something he was glad to see his superior acknowledged with his action.

Mr. Gahima continued. "I thank you for taking this meeting with us. We are here as part of a special unit sanctioned by the Umkhonto we Sizwe's — known as the MK —intelligence organ. As the new government moves to integrate our military and intelligence branches into state agencies, we have certain agendas we want to make sure are not forgotten and get the necessary attention they deserve."

The white men at the table were silent. No one seemed to know quite what to say next. Van Wesson finally uttered, "Well… umm… of course, we understand completely. The conflict is over, and now we have to begin the transition. My understanding is that your team is here primarily for the purpose of investigating war crimes, and we want to help. However, I feel this is a police matter, not an Intelligence one. The National Intelligence Service (NIS) is strictly intelligence gathering and has not conducted any clandestine missions abroad. But, of course, we are here to assist and offer full disclosure of our information and resources."

"We are not here out of judgment, Mr. Van Wesson," Mr. Gahima replied, raising his hand to calm the room. "We are working across the police and intelligence spectrum of the state's agencies to search for operatives who carried out violent and heinous acts in their service to the Apartheid. Operatives who are now living in hiding. We will find them and bring them to justice."

"What about those who carried out violent and heinous acts on behalf of the Black Nationalists," growled the old racist? "Or are we going to just label them heroes and give them a medal for all the innocents they killed and maimed in the war."

The room was about to explode.

Men from both sides rose and tempers flared. It was only the commanding presence of both Van Wesson and Gahima that cooled the situation. Everyone carefully lowered themselves back into their chairs. Gahima continued, "We are not denying our own culpability in this. That is not the mission of my team. Here, our focus is working with you, your resources and connections to other intelligence agencies around the world to focus on those in service to the Apartheid, particularly those who operated for units belonging to the Civil Cooperation Bureau. We know this was not a function of the National Intelligence Service (NIS). This should make it easier for you to assist us as opposed to the military, whose connection to the organization leaves them compromised."

Gahima had managed to calm the mood in the room. The temperament on the white side was still reserved. The older whites, obvious throwbacks to the old days of the Department of National Security, the successor to the infamous Bureau of State Security, were distressed. They saw this request as a clear betrayal of those who had risked so much and fought to protect their country from the black and communist terrorists. The younger whites, the academics who had followed Niel Barnard only knew of the intelligence gathering missions and considered nothing else. For the Barnard men, the actions of groups like the CCB had often gone too far.

Van Wesson broke the silence. "Your team has been cleared to have full access to our resources in carrying out this assignment," he said to Gahima. "You'll be working within our building, and your teams will, of course, include people from my office. A joint venture as you would say."

Gahima nodded. "This will be more than anything, an experiment. Two once rival organizations will now begin working as a cohesive force. We are here to track down war criminals. In doing so, we are working with the police, who are tainted with their own dubious history, and you, who will help us locate these criminals so they can face justice."

"Justice?" another one of the older whites grunted. "Sounds more like persecution to me. You kaf…blacks won the bloody war and now you just want to get your revenge against us!"

"Why not? We're certainly inclined to do so!" shouted the arrogant loudmouth sitting next to O'knomo. "You should be thanking us that we are not arresting you as criminals for your service to the evil of Apartheid!"

The room, again, nearly erupted into a riot of shouting accusations.

Again, Gahima and Van Wesson rose to calm the hostilities.

When the shouting had died down, Gahima spoke. "I have seen atrocities and other excesses carried out by both sides. But, at the moment, the issue is setting up a task force with NIS that will track down and bring to justice war criminals. Whatever else is discussed here today does not obviate this fact. Our team, in conjunction with people from your organization, has the mandate from both our leaders to carry out this mission."

"And we will give full assistance to you in this endeavor, Mr. Gahima," Van Wesson quickly spoke up, in time to stop another one of his subordinates from making another agitating comment. "I imagine you intend to get started in the next couple of weeks."

"No," Gahima frowned. "My people have a lot of eyes and pressure from the very top of ANC leadership for results. I intend to have my people begin today."

Van Wesson took a deep, uneasy breath. He had not expected these former enemies to move so soon. He nodded his head. "Yes, of course. We can have office spaces prepared for your operation today."

"We will also need to review records and files that have been requested prior to this meeting," Gahima said, his voice quiet but stern.

Van Wesson nodded, again. The meeting ended with a promise that a section of the building would be prepared well enough for work to begin.

As everyone rose to adjourn, Mr. Gahima stopped O'knomo. "May I speak to you please, David?"

"Of course, sir," O'knomo replied, somewhat puzzled.

Gahima pulled O'knomo's arm directing him away from the rest of the crowd. "I know this was not an assignment you wanted; you are a field man, not a desk man. But, I requested you personally for this mission."

"I am aware of this, sir."

"I have a very specific mission I want to assign to you. I'm am asking you to please accept it."

O'knomo could feel the old man's hand tightening around his arm. "Of course, sir. If you ask, I will do it."

The old man sighed. "There was, for the last five or six years a special unit of the CCB that operated predominately in the United Kingdom. It was under the command of one Devon Williams, a former member of the Reconnaissance Special Forces."

"I recognize the name," O'knomo grimaced. He didn't like where this conversation was going.

"While the Vlakplaas police have become the primary target of our investigations regarding crimes carried out domestically, the CCB has become the focus of our interest in activities committed abroad. One of the more secretive operations was a unit that went by the code name: The Dark Chamber. It was a special, deep cover infiltration unit comprised of Rhodesian immigrants who had escaped Robert Mugabe's Zimbabwe. From what little I've ascertained, this unit was responsible for the assassinations of several of our top people and supporters headquartered in London. They also carried out numerous acts of sabotage, terrorism, and other savage acts."

O'knomo said nothing.

"This group operated in deep cover, away from most of the South African intelligence units operating in Europe. Williams is at the top of our list along with someone else. His chief operative: The Angel of Death."

"The Angel of Death herself! You mean Sauwa Catcher?" The name suddenly caught O'knomo like a bolt of lightning. "He rubbed his hand over his mouth. His eyes widened in sheer disbelief. "I had only heard of her. She's spoken about as if she is some terrible legend one shares around campfires."

"Many have." Gahima released his grip on the young man. "And, until recently, many thought she was merely a cover story — a figment, devised by the CCB to encompass the acts done by many operatives to look like the actions of a single person. When we were given access to their operational files, we discovered she actually does exist. Apparently, she is every bit as lethal as we have been led to believe. Which, brings me to you. I want you to head up the unit that focuses on the Dark Chamber. We've obtained volumes of records on the Dark Chamber's activities from the archives of military intelligence. I've arranged for them to be sent to your new offices. We need to bring these people to justice."

O'knomo looked up at the grey walls. He wished that there was something worth looking at to distract him. His first instinct was to say "no" and walk out. His ambition had been to put the whole war behind him and take up something else.

The old man stared up at him waiting for an answer.

O'knomo said slowly, "I don't want this anymore. The Angel of Death is not just some thug who kills. If she does exist and is everything I've come to understand, she's dangerous and not one to be taken lightly." For the first time in several minutes, O'knomo looked down at the old man. "Anyone going after her stands a good chance of being at this job for a long time, maybe even years..."

"I'm well aware this is no small task to be done in a week," Gahima interrupted sympathetically.

... "And should also expect to die in the process."

Gahima turned away. He started walking. O'knomo followed. "I realize I'm asking a lot of you, David. What all you have been through is not lost on me. I know you were hoping to get away from this and start fresh in a new South Africa." The old man faced O'knomo again. "But, as you have said, it's dangerous and not easy. I need someone intuitive and adept at this kind of world. This is why I need you. If South Africa is to heal the wounds of her history, the perpetrators must be brought forth to answer. An investigation is the beginning — a hearing. They're calling it the Truth and Reconciliation Commission. It is intended to bring everything to bear. It will be a means to finally acknowledge what was done, so both sides can come to terms with their past."

"Sounds good, so far." O'knomo shrugged as he dug his hands into his pockets and started tilting forward. "It also sounds like something you can do very well without me or the Angel of Death. If we ever find her, my advice is, take her out or let the British have her."

Gahima shook his head. "No, we can't. The Angel of Death can testify to the true extent of the Apartheid's evil in the world. She can testify to the unspeakable acts she committed for the state. I know so many who have had loved ones, colleagues and comrades die by her hand, and they need to hear her admit it — explain it. When she is finally caught, and we send her to prison, it will be the needed closing of a gruesome chapter of our history."

O'knomo wasn't sure he was hearing dramatic politicking or the ardent conviction of a man seeing a serious necessity. He considered the old man and tried to make a decision. It was, of course, a waste of time. There was no answer but yes.

5

The Land Rover made good time as it thumped across the puddle-ridden dirt road. Sauwa bounced in the passenger seat, her seatbelt the only protection from crashing into the roof of the cab. Rowan was cautious. Military patrols were more likely to frequent the main roads. A honeycomb of farm trails and dirt roads may have added to their time driving, but the backroads also increased their chances of avoiding any security units. A beaten gut and some motion sickness were a small price to pay.

She marveled at the picturesque countryside — lush, rolling green hills and jagged rock lines shielded against a roaring ocean. She was in the Northern Irish County of Down. Rowan and Shanna's farm resided only a few miles outside the town of Strangford. From what she was able to gather, they were heading due south toward the town of Ardglass, traveling in a zigzag pattern that alternated between skirting the coastline and traveling through forgotten farm country. Rowan was clearly no stranger to transporting wanted fugitives. He navigated the windy roads and seemed to have good instincts for anticipating the security forces and even the IRA.

Between fits of nausea, Sauwa scrupulously reviewed a map of the area. The previous evening the lanky man had come to the house and given directions to a farmhouse somewhere north of Ardglass for her meeting. Security forces were in a high state of alert due to the recent peace talks. The UVF men had determined it would be better if the meeting was held somewhere far from any prying eyes. She didn't like it but saw no way around the situation. The lanky fellow had given them his instructions, handed her a map and left, giving her no chance to ask questions.

Rowan provided nothing in the way of conversation. He was focused entirely on his driving. He had only looked at the map briefly before they set out. It was obviously someplace he had been to before.

Sauwa wasn't sure how concerned she needed to be. The chosen location was logical, but everyone seemed familiar with the place except her; this did not calm her nerves. She studied Rowan's facial expressions. He exuded all the mannerisms of a man intent on his mission, not a man anticipating anything dangerous.

Crossing briefly over the main road, Sauwa caught sight of a sign showing the distance and direction to Ardglass. Quickly looking down at the map, she estimated they were only a mile from the meeting site.

The Land Rover turned onto a dirt road and picked up speed.

"Stop," she ordered.

Confused, he looked over at her. She shot back a commanding glare. He brought the vehicle to a halt.

"I'll walk the rest of the way," she said. She grabbed her bergen and slipped out of the passenger door onto the road. "It's about a mile or so to the meeting spot, as near as I can tell."

"Why are you doing this?" Rowan objected. His face was white; he looked bewildered. "I'm supposed to drive ya, ya daft female. Why ya gettin' out?"

Sauwa slammed the door and threw her bergen over her back. Turning to the old man, she said. "Because I don't trust the situation. I like to have some semblance of control over my destiny in these matters." Fixing the straps over her shoulders, she adjusted her bergen. "Tell Simon, I'll be along. Just not with you."

Rowan's mouth fell open. He attempted to speak amongst a litany of gasps. He couldn't find the words. Sauwa moved off the road and up the hill. Behind her, she heard the old man say, "They'll bloody well put a bullet in me fuckin head if I don't bring ya."

"Tell them, I would have put one in you if had," she said over her shoulder.

She listened carefully for any noise that might resemble the sound of a gun about to be used. She fingered the pistol at her waistline in preparation. The only sound was the engine revving up, followed by the crunch of the ground as the Land Rover sped away. She continued up the hill.

It didn't sit well with her; the thought that she was possibly putting someone who had shown such hospitality in a bad position with dangerous people. But, she didn't trust Simon, and she was not inclined to walk into an ambush.

Mounting the top of the hill, Sauwa took a few minutes to get her bearings and allow her stomach to settle. In the green hills she felt, for a moment, like she was back home on the Transvaal. But homesickness did nothing to help her current nausea. She ate the candy bar she had tucked in her flannel — a slight relief — then trekked toward the meeting site.

FIFTEEN MINUTES later she reached the outskirts of the farm designated as the meeting spot. Using field skills she had acquired in her youth and the training at Fort Doppies, she crept closer, careful not to be seen. The farm sat at the base of a hill and contained a large, two-story house plus an assortment of farmstead structures. Livestock and fields of organized crops indicated the farm was active.

Starting her recce from the top of the hill, she looked down on the area through a pair of binoculars. Within seconds she made out the dumpy figure of Simon, agitated and pacing back and forth waving his arms and shouting in the direction of the barn.

She could only assume his ravings were at Rowan. She caught sight of the old man's Land Rover parked in a cluster of bushes next to another small, green truck. Simon turned and, with his hand held over his brow to block the sun, he looked up at the hill.

She had taken time to walk about the area, suspecting the dumpy man would have people lurking, but she saw none. She scanned the road in both directions for any additional vehicles parked in the distance. With the bare open fields, there was no place to hide a vehicle of any kind, and there was no hint of anyone else.

She watched for a few more minutes before deciding all looked good, and she could move in closer. She was thankful the terrain offered little for concealment. While it didn't work exactly in her favor, it also limited the places Simon could have set up an ambush.

On her hands and knees, she crawled down the hill just far enough to be satisfied she wouldn't skyline herself. Then throwing her bergen over her shoulders, Sauwa rounded the hill toward the farm. She still had another twenty minutes before the meeting time, but with her circumstances somewhat desperate, she had no wish to test her current benefactor any more than necessary. Yet, she wasn't about to simply risk herself.

She kept a good pace, moving between a fast run and light jog on soft, moist ground with the high grass continually grabbing at her ankles. Thankfully, the hill was small, and she was able to get around it relatively quickly. Close to the farm, she slowed until she reached a small shed with a tin roof and peeling wood. Chickens clucked inside. She peeked around the corner to see Simon still parading back and forth glowering at his watch, exasperated. She withdrew back behind the coop, ever aware of a possible ambush, and scanning the area for logical hiding places. The house and the main barn were the only possibilities.

The house was big. It towered over the other structures providing a clear view of the entire facility. The coop was just enough behind the house to keep her from being seen. As an added benefit, the windows at the back of the house were small and would offer limited viewing capability.

Peering out from the other corner of the coop, she checked the open windows of the house, for any signs of human activity.

She saw nothing.

The meeting seemed safe enough. Sauwa removed her pack and strode out into the open. Her hand remained firmly on the grip of her gun. If anything happened, Simon would be the first one dead.

It took the fat man a few minutes to notice her. He was in the middle of a rant. When he finally did notice her, his face went red. Pointing an index finger in an accusatory gesture, he growled. "What is this all about? This isn't a bloody game!"

Sauwa looked past him at the barn. She waited to see if anyone was coming out. No one did. She moved to the side as Simon closed the distance between them. He didn't seem to notice she's placed him between her and any possible sniper that might be in the house. Her recce of the ground surrounding the farm assured her no sniper was lurking about the outskirts. "If I thought that, I wouldn't have taken the precautions."

The fat man stopped and glared at her. For a moment neither said anything as the staring match continued. Then, clearing his throat, Simon said, "We're hiring you for a job. I don't like this fucking about."

"I have no reason to trust you. In my line of work — that you love to remind me about — betrayal is all too common, especially among those who see me as expendable," Sauwa replied calmly. "So, can we get to business?"

With a sigh of irritation, Simon waved his head toward the barn. That Simon had not been at all concerned about being between her and the house windows made her more confident a sniper was not hiding there. But Sauwa kept a grip on her pistol as they neared the darkened structure. She studied Simon for any expressions and behaviors that might indicate a threat. Now, the concern was what was inside the barn.

Allowing Simon to go first, she followed directly behind him. Her eyes shifted from side to side, watching for any signs of danger. Her mind raced through the various scenarios that could play out, and how she'd respond. The barn was not as dark as expected. Just inside, she quickly caught sight of a man and stopped short, ready to draw her weapon. It was Rowan.

He was standing awkwardly, looking nervous, until he saw her. "Thank God, you're here." He bound toward her as if she were a guardian angel. Her arrival may just have saved his life. Rowan walked past them out of the barn and turned to face the fat man who was still looking quite annoyed.

"She's here, just like I said she'd be," Rowan said pleadingly. "Now, do ya have any further need of me?" He edged toward his car.

Simon shook his head. "Your part is done. The rest ain't for your ears."

Rowan said nothing more. Nor did he acknowledge Sauwa as he made for the Land Rover.

Simon beckoned Sauwa to come further inside the barn. Now confident the meeting wasn't a setup, she released the grip on her weapon and moved toward him. The barn reeked with odors of animal dung and livestock feed — odors she was very familiar with. From Simon's distorted facial expressions, she assumed the rural life was not part of his world. Sunrays from the overhead openings offered the only illumination. The dusty interior looked almost heavenly.

In the middle of the barn was an old work table. It was bare, aside from a leather briefcase that sat on top of it.

Simon moved to pick up the briefcase. "Right, down to business." He set the case flat, twisted a few knobs on the combination lock and opened it. He spread a collection of pictures and documents evenly across the table. "If you're wondering why no one else is here, it's because this operation is highly sensitive. Therefore, we must maintain the strictest secrecy."

Sauwa inched over to the table to view the documents. She wasn't sure what Simon was showing her. Among the papers was a large, black and white photograph of a man. He appeared to be in his mid-forties, portly and wearing a white linen suit, open-collared shirt and sunglasses. He could have been some rich guy out on a walk.

"This is Marston Donovan," Simon explained. "He's your target."

Sauwa picked up the photo and studied it carefully.

"He's a detective with the Republic of Ireland's Garda Siochana. He's in the Crime and Security branch operating as part of the Crime Special Surveillance Unit."

"You want me to take out a cop?" Sauwa was stunned.

"He's a cop whose job is to monitor and collect intelligence on major threats to the country. That's his official job. His other business is passing information regarding Loyalist paramilitary personnel and our contacts over to the IRA.

Over the last two years, several of our people have been assassinated and many of our safe houses in the Republic attacked by IRA Action Service Units. In addition, people we work with to obtain weapons have also been targeted. About a month ago, our contact in the Royal Ulster Constabulary informed us Donovan has been providing all this information. He's proven to be a huge thorn in our side.

Which brings us to you. Because this man is a high-level, intelligence cop, the Ulster Volunteer Force — the UVF — can't carry out this mission ourselves. We are also in the middle of peace negotiations, which complicates things further. But the information he gives to our enemies is crippling us. We need him taken out, and it can't be traced back to us."

Sauwa returned her attention to the photo. "So, you need a freelancer. I agree. But given the UVF's informal alliance with South African intelligence, won't my doing this still lead back to you?"

The fat man didn't respond. He only looked at her.

Nodding her head, Sauwa realized what was going on. "Ah, an intelligence cop who got too close to a South African war criminal and was killed for it. That's how you want it to look if I get discovered."

"You understand perfectly." Simon's lips curled into a sinister smile. "As I said, we can't afford repercussions on this sort of thing, especially not now." He took up a collection of papers and handed them over to her. "This is his biography, what we know of him on a professional level."

Sauwa took the papers and began perusing them.

Simon went on, "He's well respected within his organization."

Sauwa caught sight of the list of the man's awards and commendations. It was extensive. "Not the sort of man I would think would be on the take."

"Oh, he's not. Believe me." Simon rubbed his chin as he shook his head. "He's a committed adherent to the cause of Catholic freedom in Northern Ireland. While our cop is not overtly political, his younger sister has been a longtime activist working for the Catholic civil rights movement here. That's how we found out about him. A conversation between the sister and a known commander in the Provisional Irish Republican Army was being monitored by the RUC — Royal Ulster Constabulary. In it, she asked the commander to set up a meeting between him and her brother to discuss a new system of communication and intelligence priorities. Since then we have been paying attention. He's not a crooked cop. He makes no money on the gold he gives them personally. But, what he gives is gold, and we have to stop it." He handed her another collection of papers. "This is what we have on his activities working with the Provos."

She glossed over the new set of documents. It was a detailed chronology of recorded conversations mentioning his name by known IRA operatives, as well as sightings of him in public establishments along the border known to be frequented by IRA members. The chronology contained a list of attacks carried out against UVF locations and persons where the information, presumably, had been supplied by Marston Donovan. The list was extensive and, even with her limited knowledge of the Loyalist organization, detrimental to their operations in the Republic and along the border.

Sauwa understood why the policeman's assassination was such a priority for the UVF.

Donovan's commendable service record within the Irish Garda and his position as an intelligence officer with their most sensitive unit, the risks would be huge. Assassinating a respected police officer and an officer of the Garda was going to make another powerful enemy for her. But, with the information she had just been made privy to, she was in no position to decline the job.

"If I do this, I have to make it look like an accident." Sauwa switched her attention from between one document packet to another. "Anything else, and I've got an immediate manhunt to contend with."

"That will suffice," Simon said, disinterestedly. "As long as he dies."

Sauwa ignored him. "The next question to hash out is my means of escape. It will be dangerous for me to stay in Ireland after this, I'm a liability to you as long as I'm here."

"Before this meeting ends, you'll be given a name and number of a person we work with to obtain weapons in Dublin. After today, you'll work exclusively through him. All he knows is we have dealings with a criminal firm back in London. This group has reached out for our assistance to do a job, and we're merely acting as a go-between to ensure their hitter — that's you — has resources to carry out the job. He'll know nothing of your target. He'll think you're a contractor working for another syndicate."

"That can work. Will you have any control over the arrangements this man makes for me to escape?"

"When you've made the hit, he has several contacts who deal in arms trafficking and have connections overseas. He'll arrange through them to smuggle you out of the country. We'll have no control or even any knowledge of how he arranges it."

"Good," she placed the documents on the table and

retrieved the picture of Donovan. "The further from you I am, the better."

"Less of a liability," Simon said.

Sauwa took out a small notebook from her pocket and jotted down a strange assortment of symbols. "If Donovan's death is accepted as an accident, then killing me becomes imperative to ensure the truth never comes out. If he dies by an obvious assassination, it's in your best interest for me to escape so that it takes the attention away from you. Then you'd just arrange for me to be killed overseas. The less connection that exists between us after this meeting lessens your exposure, and your control over my escape. In the end, you wouldn't risk yourself by trying to kill me with resources and people that can be traced back to you and inevitably brings to light your involvement. The very thing you need to avoid."

"That's what our thinking was on the matter," Simon replied, as he watched Sauwa review the papers and make notes. "What are you doing?"

"Using a code," she replied. "I'll need to have notes to review since I imagine you aren't going to let me leave with any of this information, and I don't have time to memorize all of this. This way, if my book gets seized, they won't be able to decipher what's written. It protects both of us."

The fat man was incredulous. "That information was hard to get and could be compromising if seized."

"Then be thankful that it is written in code. Most policemen would simply disregard it as an adolescent's doodling." Sauwa didn't bother to raise her head and look the man in the eye as she worked. "If you would like this job to be successful, allow me my notes."

Simon stood silently as she read the papers and made her scratches. When she finished with the documents, he collected them with a meticulous eye to ensure all was accounted for, and she held onto nothing. He next produced a thick white envelope that he dropped onto the table. "This is your expense money — ten thousand pounds, Irish. This should be enough to meet any basic needs moving about. This amount will not be subtracted from the hundred thousand pounds that will be paid upon completion of your mission."

Sauwa took the envelope and looked inside at the thick stack of money. "How will the money be paid? I'm assuming your contact will be the paymaster."

"He will," Simon replied. "He will be given the money by our people and told not to give it to you until the job is done. At your first meeting, he is to show it to you, so you know the money exists."

She raised her eyebrows. "So, when done, I'm going to be stuck carrying around a hundred thousand pounds while trying to escape the country?

"Yes," Simon replied. "We are low key about this, remember. Besides, you're not going to leave the country going through customs anyway. At some level, this is a moot point.

"What stops me from just robbing him?"

"The fact that you'll lose your escape route," the fat man replied nonchalantly. "Without the assassination, you can look forward to being stuck on an island with the UVF combing for you along with the Irish and British security services, to whom we would be inclined to leak your whereabouts."

"I figured as much," Sauwa replied, as she tucked the

envelope into her back pocket. "What stops him from taking the money and leaving me stranded?"

Simon chuckled. "We are very careful about who we entrust with these types of affairs. We tend toward those in the criminal world with a better view of the horizon to see past the immediate temptation. The man we have as your contact has been in business successfully for many years because he thinks ahead and sees the big picture. He knows you're a professional killer and is cognizant of what you'll do to him if he fails to deliver your payment on demand. He was told you were a killer, hand-picked by a big London syndicate, and a dangerous person to cross."

Simon handed over a folded piece of paper. "Here is the contact information for your man. Call him from a pay phone the moment you hit Dublin. He will handle your logistical support for this mission."

Sauwa took the paper from him and read the name, Banker; a location, the Rory Club; and a phone number.

"Understand, Lassie," Simon warned. "The name Banker is his code name only for you. You call and ask to speak to Banker. When the person who answers tells you there's no one by that name, you reply by saying your name is Bridget, but that you go by the nickname Swan. Your contact will be looking for someone calling those names. You leave your name and the number at the phone booth and wait for him to call you back with instructions."

"And if he doesn't call back?" Sauwa asked, a little concerned.

The fat man glanced at her, perplexed.

"It's been my experience that things can go wrong very easily, especially when dealing with underworld figures. They often get nicked at the most unexpected times."

"He'll be there," Simon shrugged and collected his things. He turned to look at the paper clutched in her hands. He didn't have to say anything. She jotted down the information into coded scribbles in her notebook and promptly handed back the paper. With a cheap lighter, he burned the information into a small charred pile.

She didn't like the situation. However, Simon was right. There wasn't much room for convenience in this affair. She was going to have to get used to the idea that this whole operation was being done through questionable, backroom dealings that she would just have to work around.

Simon started out of the barn. As he left, he explained that the farmhouse was empty. The owners had taken a few days to go on an outing. She, therefore, could spend the night and take whatever food was in the house for provisions. He further explained that the nearest town was only five miles away once she hit the main road. She pointed out that she had no viable identification except a driver's license from one of her covers back in London. He told her she was known to be resourceful and could lift someone's identification in town once she got there.

He stepped out of the barn leaving her to reflect on all that had happened.

6

Dark clouds of black smoke grew thick as the fires outside became roaring monsters that danced angrily. Sauwa's family huddled tightly in a corner as wailing and high pitched screams — a horrifying noise — cut into the night. They remained silent, the sound of death surrounding them.

Little Rena buried her head in the folds of Sauwa's thin, white T-shirt. Portia — her other sister, eight years old and terrified — gripped Sauwa's shoulder, the screams growing closer. Their mother's arms encompassed all three of her daughters.

Looking up, Sauwa saw the large, brawny figure of her brother, Colin. He knelt on one knee, his rifle, a long automatic piece of some sort, clutched tightly in his bear-like hands. Next to him, in similar postures, were two other brothers, the twins, Regan and Martin. They held their stances, eyeing the windows and doors waiting for the inevitable moment. The blood-curdling screams outside were gradually giving way to the deep, loud groans and mutterings of men approaching. Among the orchestra of terror, the swish of machetes could be heard being wielded through the air, slicing into human flesh.

Portia's grip tightened, just as Sauwa's arms tightened around her youngest sister, Rena. Her only thoughts were of her father and oldest brother, Lucian. At the start of the violence, they had grabbed their weapons and, along with several other men from the settlement, dashed out to meet the threat.

Earlier, the rest of the family had heard shooting from a distance and assumed it was their father and Lucian fighting off the guerrillas. Then the shooting stopped, only to have it replaced by the sounds of screams of the villagers down at the foot of the hill. They were being slaughtered by the guerrillas. The villagers weren't of Shona origin and had no connections to the Zimbabwe African National Union (ZANU), nor did they give them support. The ZANU was one of the main guerrilla armies fighting the rule of the Rhodesian government.

The sounds of violence grew more intense with each passing moment. Sauwa could feel Rena shivering with fear. The little girl's tears had become heavy enough that they began to soak Sauwa's T-shirt. Sauwa hugged her sister and whispered into her ear, telling her it wasn't as bad as it sounded and that her brothers were just being overly cautious. It did little to help. Rena's sobs only deepened.

The attacking men howled with excitement, heckling and raging louder with each passing minute, loud enough to drown out the shrieks of their victims and the roar of the blazing fires.

The faces of her brothers were white with nervous

anticipation, their breaths heavy. Colin was looking around the room at his family. He was now the man of the house; he was now the one in charge. He readied his rifle, as did the twins.

SAUWA AWOKE IN DARKNESS. It took her seconds for her eyes to adjust and realize she was in a room lying in bed in a cold sweat. Her nightshirt was completely soaked with perspiration. She sat up, gathering her faculties.

Another nightmare. One of the many horrible memories from her childhood in Rhodesia. She only had them now and then. But, when they did occur, they were vivid and powerful. Her work with the Civil Cooperations Bureau —CCB — had added to these evening tales that occasionally plagued her.

Through the cracks in the shades, she could tell that the sun had come up. Slipping out of bed, she fumbled about the floor feeling for her bergen. Clutching it, she stood up and carefully navigated her way to the door.

The farmhouse was a historical model that easily dated back to the eighteenth century. Aside from modern plumbing and electrical wiring upgrades, there was little modernization.

Making her way down the dreary, darkened hallway, she found herself in the kitchen. There was no way to know who was likely to frequent the place, so she had opted to keep all the shades drawn, but that made visibility poor. With the help of a flashlight she had been able to find during her recce (South African word for recon) of the house, she also found a small alarm clock on the counter — it read eight o'clock.

As Simon had explained, the refrigerator and cupboards were well stocked. From the looks of things, the food had all been purchased recently. Apparently, the UVF wanted to make sure she had provisions when being left out in the middle of nowhere.

Finding a pan and some plates, she collected some eggs from the fridge and set about making breakfast. She had eaten some fruit and cold cereal last night. The possibility of a military night patrol had made it too risky to use lights or cook some food. There was a fifty percent chance that any soldiers in the area would know the family who lived in the house. Her accent was not indigenous to the area, so even a chance encounter of a patrol knocking on the door would make any halfway intelligent officer suspicious and start asking questions. Questions she would have a hard time answering.

She had wrestled with the idea of using the house or staying in a darkened spot in the corner of the barn. If a security patrol had dropped by, there were no real means to see out the back or any good means of escape. The house backed up against a hill and offered no cover. However, she could more easily slip out of an opening she spotted in the far corner of the barn. It led to the fields outside and the wild grass, but she would be caught by any flashlights or someone scanning the area using night vision optics. She figured the best answer was to stay in the room offered on the bottom floor, keeping the curtains drawn and not answer, if someone called at the house. Besides, a young girl, alone at the house, sleeping through a night visit or being hysterical at the thought of someone prowling around, would cause less suspicion than a homeless wanderer camped suspiciously in a barn.

Lifting the curtain an inch, she peered through the window to scan outside. The farm was as deserted as it had been the day before. Since ASU's and other paramilitaries tended to operate mostly at night, the threat of a security patrol was greatest then. So early in the morning, it was unlikely a patrol would be so far out.

A few eggs, some oat cereal and a bowl of fruit made for a most delicious meal. A glass of orange juice topped her breakfast off nicely.

After breakfast, she enjoyed a warm shower in the downstairs bathroom. The warm water felt good after waking up in a pool of cold sweat. She wiped down the tub, spent another few minutes cleaning the kitchen and the dishes used, collecting her things, and packed a few days' provisions.

Before she left, she discarded the Makarov in the water trough. She didn't like going without protection but, if caught, a gun was too difficult to explain. She had taken a few hundred pounds from the envelope and stuffed it into her wallet. The rest she tucked into some plastic bags stuffed them into jars of coffee. If she looked innocent enough, soldiers and cops would not be so inclined to conduct a thorough search through her bags.

Confident she was as ready as could be, she strapped on her bergen and started off.

THE MORNING WAS crisp despite a cloudless day. With the house all locked up, she took one last look around before making her way back toward the main road. As a precaution, she rounded the hill and trekked back the way she had come through the open fields. This lessened the chance of running into patrols. With only one fake identity from London, she didn't want to run any more risk than necessary. In a flannel coat, jeans, military boots and her bergen on her shoulder, she could easily be a bohemian enjoying an outing in the countryside.

Sauwa was tired when she finally made it to the outskirts of Ardglass, a quaint little town on the sea, slightly more than a shire, boasting a population of just under two thousand people. Tramping up the road, she acted like a wanderer, drifting and glancing aimlessly around. She gazed at the scenery and a collection of ancient looking houses. This was only partially an act. One thing she loved about the United Kingdom was the wash of history one could take in. Coming from such a young country as South Africa, it was a wonder to see houses that bore witness to so much throughout the ages. The grey stone houses that littered the landscape were truly breathtaking. In the distance, she could see the dull, greyish water of the Irish Sea.

She walked through the village and took careful note of the attitude of the locals. If they seemed mindful of strangers, she wanted to cut her time here short. If not, she intended to stay a moment and get her bearings. Casually looking about, she responded to several quick waves and hellos. They weren't a lynch mob of fear-ridden villagers, yet they definitely noticed a new face in town. Better to keep moving then.

She made her way to the train station, where she acquired a map.

In a discrete corner in the waiting area, after a quick map recce, she determined that her best course of action was to take a trip to the much larger town of Newry. The population there was nearly thirty thousand and would have a bigger transient population where she could avoid notice. It also bordered County Armagh, known for farmland and a vast network of informal farm roads and trails that crossed into the Republic. The IRA conducted all sorts of guerrilla operations there because of the difficulty security forces had in controlling access points that crisscrossed the border.

With all the attention Sauwa had, any documented crossing — where a picture was sure to be taken of her and a record made of any identity she might be using — was out of the question.

Dropping a few pounds at the ticket office, she bought a seat on the next train to Newry. An old man, who looked as if he had been working in that office since the nineteenth century, lazily took her money and punched her out a ticket. She had taken a moment to scan the location for any security systems. Fortunately, the only cameras that seemed to exist were at the ticket office. They were cheap, stationary things of poor quality. Lifting her coat lapels up around her face and pulling her knit cap lower over her ears, she was able to limit what the cameras would be able to capture of her face. A quick comment about the cold weather was more than enough to explain the bundled-up appearance to the old man. An hour later she was on the train.

Newry was an entirely different place. It was a thriving town of thousands with a collection of historic buildings dating back to at least the eighteenth century which ensured heavy tourist traffic from all over. It was easy to blend in as just another face looking to see the sights.

Sauwa grabbed lunch at a crowded local tavern and scoped out a group of college kids gathered around a table. They were well into their libations, and the assorted males and females were ensconced in the pursuit of finding a mate for the evening. One of the young ladies had an appearance similar to Sauwa's. She also had a large handbag that remained wide open.

Sauwa bided her time watching the room carefully, sipping her water and finished the last remnants of her meal. Her look-alike was well into her drink. So was the young man who had captured her look-alike's attention. Sauwa paid her check, casually rose with a beer in her hand and moved to stand at a high table near the door. The young lovers were now nestled in each other's necks, their hands exploring body parts. Soon the couple left their seats and staggered out the door. As they passed, Sauwa caught sight of the girl's wallet.

The couple brushed past her. In one quick movement, she grabbed the wallet. Taking a gulp of her drink, Sauwa casually slipped out the door and walked toward the train station. She assumed it would be at least morning before her twin realized she had been robbed. By then, Sauwa would be in the Republic, if all went well.

David O'knomo's new office wasn't very big. It was a sizeable room portioned off with bland cubical partitions that only added to the dismal setting and an even more dismal mood. To make matters worse, the team assigned to him seemed dysfunctional from the start.

He had been given exactly three people: one was the old racist who had sat across from him in the introductory board meeting. The jowly, grizzled figure, going by the name of Coors Ravenhoof, an MK fighter, who was a throw-back to the days of the Department of National Security (DONS). O'knomo wasn't keen on having such a person working so close to his operation. However, Mr. Gahima had made it clear that this mission was as much about amalgamation as it was about finding war criminals. Besides, Gahima had it on good authority that despite Ravenhoof's obvious racial views, he had not approved the heavy-handed tactics used by his colleagues during the old days. He also had garnered a reputation as a first-rate detective when he was with the South African Police force and had continued proving his abilities as a man who got results working the streets. O'knomo had his concerns, but he also had a big job ahead of him. A job with a lot of powerful people expecting results.

The next member of his team was another MK fighter, Jamie Nawati. Like O'knomo, Nawati had also traipsed across the various countries of the sub-African continent spending much of his youth in combat fatigues. He had been trained in Angola by Cuban Special Forces to be part of a deep infiltration unit. He had later attended advanced assassination training hosted by the North Korean Reconnaissance General Bureau. Though they had not had a chance to discuss histories, it was understood Nawati had carried out numerous acts of terrorism and assassinations. The young man was on the team to provide a more personal understanding of their quarry. A small but well-portioned man with a chiseled frame, Nawati looked the part of a combat soldier and carried himself with a pleasant, quiet demeanor. O'knomo took an instant liking to the man.

The last of the team, another Afrikaner, Dr. Eugene Walderhyn, was a professor of political science. He had obtained his doctorate at the age of twenty-eight. He had been one of the bright, young academics who followed Niel Barnard into the newly formed National Intelligence Service. Not a field man or a covert operative by any stretch, Walderhyn was part of the intelligence-oriented world that focused on collection and analysis. Clean shaven, with a thick crop of perfectly groomed black hair and manicured features, he wore his large glasses and pressed light blue suit as if he were about to attend a university lecture. He hadn't said much but eyed the ANC MK fighters with suspicion.

Having shown up first, several hours ahead of everyone, O'knomo had had a chance to peruse the files that had been brought to the office in a small, secure steel box. He had spent the early hours reading through the files. If he was to lead this band of *merry men*, he would need to start off as the expert. The files that pertained to the activities of the CCB unit that had operated in the United Kingdom — the unit known as the Black Chamber. A note taped to the top of the box and written in Swahili by Gahima let him know that the files marked with red tape referred specifically to the infamous Angel of Death.

O'knomo inhaled.

The first file felt strangely like a sacred archive of some mystic religion. The Angel of Death was a legend —an exaggeration he was sure — rumored to be one of South

Africa's more lethal assassins. When he finally brought himself to open the thick manila folder that sat uneasily on his lap, emotion overwhelmed him. In that moment, he was able to attach an actual life to a long-heard ghost story. The mythical creature actually existed — the Angel of Death was real.

He gazed at a five by five inch black and white photograph of a woman, little more than a girl. Her long, raven black hair was tied neatly behind her head. Slightly almond shaped, dark black eyes — deadpan, hollow eyes — stared back at him. She was the vision of a ghostly being. It was hard for him to put a face to the monster responsible for the deaths of so many. Behind the picture was her dossier. He sat back in his chair and stared at the first page. Stunned he finally had a name to go with the ghost: Sauwa Catcher.

O'knomo had finished most of the document when the first of his team arrived. Walderhyn, one of the two Afrikaner, was immaculately groomed with a conservative grey suit pressed to military standards. He gave a slight bow to his new superior before taking a seat. Within minutes the rest of the team followed; Ravenhoof sauntering in behind Nawati. Nawati maintained a professional military bearing. It was obvious he wanted to be recognized as a professional soldier above anything else.

The team was now assembled. O'knomo took a moment to study their faces. Walderhyn and Ravenhoof wore disgruntled expressions. Clearly, they had been assigned to this new team under duress. The consummate academic, Walderhyn sat with his legs crossed, arms folded and glasses perched on the bridge of his nose. Ravenhoof leaned back and began scratching his chin.

Nawati, by now, had sunk into his chair resting his arms comfortably.

"What have you all been told about this assignment?" O'knomo opened as he rose to his feet and began pacing slightly. The room was dead quiet.

"I was told this was some kind of fugitive unit," Nawati finally spoke up. "I wasn't told much."

"Me neither," chimed Ravenhoof. "Only that I'm to help you persecute the losing side."

O'knomo watched as Nawati's eyes glared angrily at the heavyset Afrikaner. For a moment, the fear of a brawl breaking out seemed real. Ravenhoof remained smug and unapologetic. He had made his views clear. Nawati kept silent, as did Walderhyn, for which O'knomo was thankful. A few more moments of silence confirmed that no one had been told anything. O'knomo would have to start from scratch.

"Yes, it is true we are part of a new joint effort between the African National Congress and South African intelligence," O'knomo said as he looked down at the men. "And, yes, it is also true we have been established with the mandate to track down those who are now fugitives from the law for crimes committed during the silent war." He paused. "I realize this is a tense issue for us all. I understand we have strong feelings on both sides about what that means. But there are those who need to be held accountable."

"As you say," the polished, elegant voice of Dr. Eugene Walderhyn cut in. "You mean those held accountable by the standards of your organization. Isn't that right?"

O'knomo held steady for few seconds. This moment was crucial in defining the path of his team from this point forward. "No, that is not right. We are using the concepts of decency. I'm not here to judge. I have no illusions about my own side. I have a belief that there are those on both sides that need to be held to account for their actions, and we are here to do just that. You can think what you like about this entire program. In the end, it does not change the fact that we are chasing those who committed serious, violent acts, and we need to bring them to justice. I realize for you whites, this may seem like persecution. But, I would say this. There are those on my side who carried out equally heinous acts. Those you yourselves want to see held accountable. If you are to have any right to demand justice of your own, you must be willing to make the first move."

O'knomo took a breath. "You may not believe me, but what we do here is so our country can heal. Healing begins when all sides being held to account, and we acknowledge what we all did. Both sides need to be held accountable. Otherwise, revenge groups and vigilantes seeking their own brand of retribution."

The Afrikaners were still suspicious but seemed to grasp what their new boss was saying. Nawati maintained his composure, studying the man before him, trying to determine if he was working for an idealist or a political hack.

Under the circumstances, O'knomo was happy with the results. He did not expect to have his speech appeal to their sense of patriotism and duty. However, if they were not walking out the door, then at least it was a start. The men sat trying to size each other up.

Walderhyn looked around the bare room and asked, "So, who are we going to be pursuing?"

"This is our fugitive," O'knomo pulled the black and white photo from the file he had been reading along with a small tack and pinned it up on the poster board. The group studied it for a moment. The confused look on their faces said enough.

O'knomo stood next to the photo. "We are a very special unit going after a specific target. Her name is Sauwa Catcher — the Angel of Death herself."

"My God!!" Nawati gasped. "You mean she is real!! She actually exists!"

"You better believe it bru," Ravenhoof growled. "I've never seen the face, and I've only heard the name once. But she's real all right. Real and dangerous. We're playing with fire on this one."

O'knomo was surprised to see the jowly policeman speak so vehemently as if he had a personal hatred of his own for the girl in the photograph.

Walderhyn gazed at the picture with a disapproving eye but said nothing.

Nawati had by now risen from his chair to obtain a closer look. "She is a monster. I have heard so many terrifying tails of her. She was a ghost. An apparition who killed so many and just disappeared." He looked over at O'knomo in bewilderment. "She's our objective?"

O'knomo looked his subordinate dead in the eye and answered only with a nod. Nawati acknowledged the truth of the situation and sat back down.

"Everything you need to know is in here." O'knomo handed the file to Walderhyn first. After a quick review of the pages, Walderhyn handed it to Ravenhoof.

"Great Britain is going to make this investigation difficult," said the old Afrikaner, handing the document to Nawati, who snatched it up immediately.

O'knomo agreed. "In time, we will have to establish relations with Scotland Yard. First, though, we need to begin our investigation with what we have so we approach our British colleagues with help to direct the search. The bigger question will be what to do if she's not in Britain. She's a fugitive not just from our government but the UK as well. I would assume she wouldn't stay there. Which brings up the question of what to do if she's fled the country already?"

At the conclusion of the meeting, Nawati returned the file to O'knomo.

As they were about to leave, O'knomo beckoned Ravenhoof and Walderhyn to stay a moment. "I wanted to speak to you both before we went any further. I know neither of you chose this assignment. I realize this probably isn't what you feel the best doing. If I had to chase down one of my own, who had done things under the assumption it was for their cause, I too would have problems. If you aren't comfortable with this, I'll understand. I won't force you or speak ill of you. But, before we go any further, I have to know your minds on this."

Ravenhoof's jaw quivered, while Walderhyn scratched at his lower lip, as if deep in thought. Both stood silent.

Walderhyn looked up over his wide glasses. "I have never condoned the barbarism of the CCB or any security service that participated in this sort of thing. I understand this was not a clean, honorable war. I certainly had no patience for the cloak and dagger, covert operations. While I can understand the necessity of such methods at times, these agencies took it too far and were completely out of control. I won't judge this Sauwa Catcher for what she did. She was in the field, I wasn't. But, I also agree the country needs to heal; that means bringing people like her to justice. So long as that is our goal, and it's not about playing politics or simply getting even, then I'm willing to see this through."

O'knomo faced Ravenhoof. The old cop cleared his throat. "I know what you may think of me. God knows neither the police nor this agency has the best history in their own right. I never went for this heavy-handed stuff. Real intelligence work doesn't come from midnight killings or beatin' a fella in the back room. I never condoned what either the police or the military did running these covert wars. Nor did I like what we were into when this place was the DONS. The reason I had my job after Barnard took control was that I never got my hands bloody with the rough stuff. Now, I ain't about playing politics either, but the CCB was a nasty little business, and I agree with Walderhyn; it was out of control. So yah, if we're doing this for the right reasons, then I'm in."

Ravenhoof raised his finger warningly, and I repeat, "If, we're doing this for the right reasons. As you said yourself, you boys have blood on your hands, too."

"Hopefully, we will be," O'knomo sighed as he turned to look, once again, at the picture of the infamous Angel of Death.

7

The trip across the border had been daunting. No maps existed that described the complexity of the intricate network that informally crossed the border. A compass and general use of the sun had been the only tools available for someone not personally familiar with the labyrinth of roadways. For, Sauwa, it didn't help that her British accent made her stick out immediately — a problem heightened by the issue of being in an IRA stronghold. She stayed off the roads, keeping close to any bushes and other vegetation that might offer hasty concealment in the event she passed anyone.

Initially, she had wanted to move at night to give herself better protection. However, if she were stopped, a wandering tourist was easier to explain to an army patrol or a passing local in the daytime. Besides, she figured she was also less likely to come across the added problem of IRA gunmen, who would be more active at night. When she finally got to the other side of town, she managed to hitch a ride with a farmer on his way to the coastal city of Dundalk. After a hot meal and getting her bearings, she found a lively pub. Scoping the place out, she found a look-alike deep into her libations. When the young girl wobbled off to the bathroom, Sauwa snatched the girl's wallet from her half-open bag. Within an hour, she was on a bus headed for Dublin.

Unlike the other hamlets she had seen in her travel across the country, Dublin was a modern, thriving metropolis. The city glistened with the massive amount of lights that lit the night causing a glowing aura. After passing over O'Connell Bridge, the bus rumbled along the streets of Dublin's south side by an assortment of old buildings mixed with a variety of new modern structures denoting the greater affluence of the city's wealthier section. Sauwa nestled in her seat; the last few days had been grueling as she worked to make her way to her destination.

After a few transfers and a little confusion, she eventually came within a few blocks of Cope Street, and the neon lights of the Rory Club, her destination. She didn't like the idea of reaching out to a career facilitator on the black market. Not because she had such lofty standards; she worried who might be watching. People who dealt in the importation of illicit material did not go unnoticed by the local authorities, especially if their clients included one of the most violent and notorious terror organizations on the island.

Before making any contact, Sauwa scouted the area. Expensively dressed rich kids cruised the streets enjoying their parent's money while they still could. But, because it was a weekday, the travel lanes were not packed. She didn't really blend with the crowd, so she pulled out her map and played the part of a backpacker finding her way through an alien city.

Heading down the street, she pretended to glance at the map a couple of times and casually looked about getting her bearings. A man too old for the crowd caught the corner of her eye. He was mingling, but his clothes were subpar. He leaned against the wall of a small eatery, trying to look like he was just hanging out, but his focus was on the Rory Club across the street. A small plastic earpiece protruded from his ear connecting to a clear plastic cord that slid down the side of his neck into the collar of his shirt.

Further down the street, another man sat in the front seat of an expensive looking car. Like the man against the wall, his age and manner of dress didn't match the general scene. He had a similar cord leading from his ear down under his grey T-shirt. Neither man paid her the slightest attention as they continued monitoring the Rory club. Police, definitely. She walked until she was sure there weren't any others about to see her. The vehicles she had just passed were not a high-end detail. More likely, they were detectives from the vice unit or narcotics trolling in a known area of criminal business.

As she anticipated, the police knew of her contact — this Banker guy — but the surveillance was minimal. The Garda didn't seem to be fully aware of her contact's entire business dealings. Sauwa kept going, searching for a place to eat, then for a semi-secluded phone to make her call. She wasn't about to station herself anywhere she didn't have a significant advantage.

She grabbed dinner at a deli. There was a phone near Merrion Square Park. The park was a short distance from the club, among a group of four of Dublin's five parks. At the late hour, the surrounding streets were marginally busy, most of the crowd enjoying a little time in the fresh air before retiring for the night or heading to a restaurant to catch a late dinner.

Sauwa scoped out the phone booth outside the front entrance. The location was relatively open, gave her a good visual of anyone coming and provided a multitude of escape points she could use in case of trouble. Opening her notebook, she dialed the phone number.

After two rings, a heavily accented voice of a woman answered. "Hello, what can I do for ya?"

"What place am I calling, if I may ask?" Sauwa replied softly.

"You're callin' the Rory Club here," the woman replied sounding exasperated.

"I'm looking for Banker," Sauwa continued.

"Banker?" the woman sounded confused.

"Yes."

"No one by that name works here."

"Strange," Sauwa continued. "This was the number I was given by a guy who said we should hook up if I came to town. My name's Bridget, but he might know me through my nickname, Swan. We have mutual friends. I'm guessing Banker is a nickname, too."

The woman paused for a moment, loud music was playing in the background. "Well, miss, I'll ask some of the boys workin' and let them know a Swan somebody is callin'."

"Thank you. Can I leave a number?" Sauwa chose her

words deliberately. It seemed obvious the woman had no idea what was actually being said.

The woman agreed, and Sauwa read off the phone number of the pay phone. The conversation ended, leaving Sauwa concerned the woman might forget altogether. In either case, Sauwa slipped away from the phone to take up a seat on the park bench just inside the gate. The shadows kept her concealed from anyone looking from across the street or from the higher floors of the aligning houses.

It was nearly forty minutes later when the pay phone rang. Sauwa walked over and lifted the receiver. "Yes."

"Who am I speaking to?" It was the voice of a man, polished and articulate, unlike the woman earlier.

"Swan, or Bridget, whichever one you prefer," Sauwa replied quietly but with a stern seriousness. "Who is this?"

"I was told you would know me as Banker," the man replied with an equally stern voice. "I understand you were visiting Dublin and some friends thought we should meet and have a few drinks."

"I think that would be delightful," Sauwa replied. "Though, I'm not one for clubs. Is there somewhere quiet where we could get together?"

"Of course," Banker replied, now more cordially. "I know a small place. Pints is the name." The man gave the directions and the meeting was set for the next hour.

It took time for her to find a taxi. Luckily, the drive was short. As it turned out, Pints was only a few blocks from the Rory Club. Unlike the flamboyant party district that thrived on attention, Pints was in a conservative and quieter location, the street and businesses occupied by older, more professional types of patrons. She would certainly blend in much easier here than at the Rory.

Asking the driver to drop her off several doors up, she exited the vehicle and started down the sidewalk toward the bar. She didn't want to enter this unknown establishment blind, but cab drivers, particularly long-serving veterans of the job, tended to have keen eyes for those acting suspiciously or out of context to their usual fares. They either remembered dangerous details for the police later, or they were inclined to bring such suspicions to any policeman passing by. A young girl asking to be brought to a small bar only to walk in an opposite direction from the location would certainly spark such instincts. Sauwa couldn't afford to be remembered by anyone, so she stopped and pretended to be caught up reading the headlines from a newsstand as the cabby drove off. When he was gone, she crossed the street scanning everyone she passed with the appearance of indifference

She had twenty minutes until her meeting with Banker. If he had any intention of double-crossing her, he would have had people set up early, but there were scarce places for such people to position themselves without being noticed. If they were there, they would be across the street. They would try to look like folks having a conversation, situated in a café or restaurant that offered a view.

Pints was a higher end establishment with a large front window. The only café within sight had closed for the evening, leaving no other possible staging point. Pints had clearly been chosen to offer both the perception of an innocent get together and to ensure any surveillance would be easily detected.

Twenty minutes had passed, and a man with black hair and a medium build approached. Sauwa, by now, had taken up a spot under an overhead street lamp, a newspaper in hand, up the street from the pub.

The black-haired fellow stopped just short of the pub's entrance and glanced inside through the large window. He was casually dressed in an open flannel shirt over a grey V-neck T-shirt. He studied the interior of the establishment for several minutes before determining that who he was looking for was not there. Thrusting his hands into his pockets, he looked about the street studying everyone in the near vicinity.

His eyes stopped when he caught sight of a young lady reading a newspaper. Sauwa assumed this was her contact. Rolling up the paper, she snatched up her bergen and joined the man in front of the bar.

"Swan, I assume?" he opened, slightly hesitant.

"Banker," she replied.

Both exchanged cold looks of suspicion as he caught the door and beckoned her inside.

The pub was quiet with a long bar and a large outer room full of polished mahogany tables and matching wood chairs. Aside from the half dozen patrons sporadically distributed throughout the establishment, the pub was empty. Acting as a couple out on a date, Banker led Swan to an isolated table. It was near the window so they could see outside, but against the corner to hinder the view of anyone looking in.

They took their seats and were immediately approached by a happy, heavy-set waitress. Banker took the liberty of ordering two glasses of Guinness for them. The waitress dutifully jotted down the order and retreated. Now alone, the two could speak.

"So, you're Swan from London," Banker opened the discussion. His voice was thick with irritation.

Sauwa shrugged, "At least for now. I understand you're here to assist with resources for my job?"

He made a snarky gesture. "That's what they told me. You're my responsibility while you're here enjoying our fair town."

"You don't seem very happy about this."

Banker leaned down and shot her a serious look. "My work isn't the most honest. I survive in this world by knowing when to be scared. And, everything about you and your business frightens me."

"My business?" Sauwa asked, innocently.

"I don't even know what it is," the man maintained his cold glare. "That's what scares me. This firm you work for has serious clout. Enough that it's got some bloody, powerful and dangerous people jumping about. They tell me nothing other than I'm to help you with whatever you need, ask no questions, and make sure you're paid when the job is done. Then I'm to arrange your immediate exit from our fair country to somewhere outside the UK and Ireland. This is the kinda' stuff I don't like. This has dangerous written all over it."

Sauwa shrugged. "Well, on that we can agree. Neither one of us wishes for this. Neither of us has really any say in it. The powers that be need this done, and it has fallen on us to complete it."

"Do I want to know what it is?"

Sauwa said nothing. She slowly shook her head and gazed at him.

Banker leaned back in his chair, as he rubbed his face. "Well, let's have our drink, and then I'll take you to your lodgings."

The waitress returned with two pints of Guinness. With a toothy grin, she set them gently on the table and made her exit, leaving the couple to continue their conversation.

Banker studied the pale, dark-haired girl before him. In her field coat and cap, she looked more like a London Bohemian than an employee of a major criminal firm. But, the smartest criminals tended not to look or act the part.

"So," Sauwa gave a quick glance about the pub to ensure no one was within hearing distance. "You've been in business a long time. Those who put me in touch with you spoke highly of your abilities."

Banker took a sip of his beer and wiped the drops from his lips. "Like I've said, I survive in this game. I do so by being choosy about those I work with. And, those I work with play it straight."

"Good rules to live by," the young lady leaned back in her chair.

Banker noticed she wasn't touching her drink. "Not thirsty?"

"Not thirsty," she replied, as she looked around the room again.

"I didn't bring anyone if that's what you're concerned about?" Banker leaned forward, exasperated.

"Maybe not intentionally," she leaned in, too. "But I caught sight of police types keeping a watch on your establishment. I'm more concerned about the likes of them following you to see what you're up to."

Banker ran his fingers across his face. "You've been by the club?"

"Walked past it. Like you, I like to know who it is I'm working with, especially when I'm putting my safety in their hands."

Banker raised an eyebrow. "As in any clubbing world, narcotics tend to circulate. Finer clubs like the Rory attract patrons with both money and an appetite for the high-end stuff. So drug dealers frequent our establishment. They don't work for us. But they do attract the occasional narcotics cops to keep watch on us. That's all they are."

Sauwa stood up and slid her bergen over her shoulder, indicating to Banker it was time to leave. Throwing some money on the table, he rose to join her as they both made for the door. Outside, she cuddled up to her date ever aware of her surroundings. A slow and thorough glance around revealed nothing suspicious. No one she saw out on the street looked familiar — no one she had seen at the club or looking to be part of a surveillance unit.

Confident they were safe, she took Banker's arm and motioned him to his waiting car. They drove most of the way in silence, interrupted only by an occasional question from Sauwa regarding geographical concerns about the city, and Banker's quick reply.

The journey ended in a warehouse district just off of Dublin Port. Banker navigated through a maze of hauntingly decrepit, old buildings. Eventually, they came to one building set along the water with a parking that offered some concealment from random traffic. Banker halted the car, and the two exited. Even in the dark, she could see the structure had been around for a long time and showed signs of serious use. The neighborhood seemed like it had been entirely forgotten.

"I figured whatever you're here for, if you're to get out of the country right afterward, the best place to be would be somewhere close to the ports where you wouldn't encounter a lot of people who could recognize or inform on you."

Sauwa took it all in. "You figured right. Normally, I have to fight to get a place as secluded as this. Someone always thinks to put me in a cheap hotel assuming I can disappear into a sea of wino's, drifters and other low-life's. They forget that those places attract police and vice cops looking to make arrests and informants looking to make a pound by reporting suspicious people to their cop handlers."

Banker led her toward the door of the facility. "My thinking exactly. That's why I chose this location. The warehouse belongs to an associate of mine; all legit, of course. But, he isn't going to be using it for the next few months. It seemed ideal for your needs."

Inside was a massive open room. Every step echoed throughout the structure. At the far back, Banker led Sauwa through a doorway into a hall and finally into a room that faced out to the Irish Sea. Flipping on an overhead light, they stood in a makeshift apartment. Though sparsely furnished, the room offered a rolled-up mattress, a pile of old blankets, a desk, a table and chairs. A garage door opened to view an escape route, to the water.

Before saying a word, she performed a quick search of the room for bugs. Banker watched her, begrudgingly impressed by her proficiency.

"You'll find a shower and bathroom area down the

hall. Tomorrow, I'll bring you some toiletries, so you can wash."

"Thank you," Sauwa replied. She finished her sweep and walked over to a window facing into the darkness. "You picked this place well."

Banker let her look at her new quarters.

She turned to face him. "How will transportation work?"

"How would you prefer it?"

"I have a license under an assumed name. If I get pulled over, it should buy me some time. Something small and inconspicuous, so I can move about easily on all kinds of roadways, like a motorcycle of some sort."

"I can manage that."

"Equipment?" she asked. "What can you get me?"

The Irishman shrugged. "Anything really, within reason. I don't do ballistic missiles or things of that sort."

"But otherwise?"

"Otherwise, I have what you'll need."

Sauwa considered him. "Transportation first. No more chauffeuring me about."

Banker nodded.

"I'll let you know what I'll need as my plan develops. However, I'll need a stable means of contacting you."

"Call me at the Rory. I get calls there all the time."

"Too many people involved," she said. "I don't like having others serve as intermediaries taking messages, and I don't like waiting around public phones for you to get around to calling me back. Besides, if you have detectives watching your place, I have to assume your phone could be monitored as well."

"Well..." Banker attempted to defend himself sheepishly.

Sauwa cut him off. "I don't care. I'm taking a lot of risks already. I don't need to worry that I'm speaking into a tapped phone or having to leave messages with perfect strangers." She starred at the Irishman coldly. "Find a pay phone, preferably at a call center, with an assortment of phones so it would be difficult for police to notice even if they did follow you. Give me that number. At an appointed time each night, I'll call you. We'll discuss issues then."

Banker didn't argue. The ice-cold stare from the mysterious figure sent chills down his spine. Despite her girlish appearance, his seasoned criminal instincts told him she would be lethal if crossed. In that minute, he decided he did not want to be seen as either incompetent or a liability by her. He nodded compliantly.

She relaxed, but only a little, pacing about her new quarters. "The final issue — my money."

"I've got it."

"How much?" Sauwa asked, testing him.

"A hundred thousand pounds," he replied. He studied her facial expression. He knew he was being tested. This woman would know exactly what she was to be paid. But, in a world of treachery and no records, double crosses were all too common. If his number had been different, she would have known he intended to steal from her. "I have it locked in my safe at the club."

"Move it somewhere else."

"I don't understand."

Police surveillance aside, I'm not letting you keep my money in a highly conspicuous location, crawling with the types waiting to rip you off. When this job transpires, things will have to move quickly. You could be deterred at the club or seen carrying the money. A man in your profession has a multiple of offices to keep jobs compartmentalized. I'm sure you can find a private site where the money can be stored and transferred quickly."

"I can find a place," Banker replied, feeling even more nervous about the whole project. "It's just...well, I have better protection at the club. If it's in a secluded spot, it...it might be compromised."

Sauwa stepped toward him. "You're really telling me you're worried I might steal that money and leave you holding the bag."

He said nothing, frozen by her barbed scrutiny. She moved away. The tension dissolved, like she had removed a blade from against his throat.

"I will tell you why that can't happen," she said, her voice smooth. I need you to get me out of the country after the job is done. For both our sakes, stealing a mere hundred grand isn't going to get me very far when those who I work for come seeking retribution, and I'm stuck in a country with no way out and nowhere to hide. We have to rely on each other."

Banker's muscles had tensed. He forced them to relax. "I'll move the money. When I have a new location, I'll let you see it, so you know it exists, and I'm not lying about it."

"Thank you."

Banker left the room with the promise he'd be back tomorrow morning to resume business.

Left alone, Sauwa took a half hour to do a full search of her quarters. In that time, she found several additional rooms and offices, all completely bare, and three exits leading to the street. Luckily for her, the doors opened only from the inside, leaving her fewer entry points to worry about.

Grabbing a towel from a neatly folded pile, she set off to the newly discovered toilet to enjoy a shower. Her mind awash with the uncertainties ahead.

8

The blast tore through the mud wall of the hut exploding debris and fire in every direction. David O'knomo felt nothing under his feet. He was flying through the air. His journey ended with a hard, painful crash into the mud wall on the other side of the structure that served as headquarters. His daysack on his tactical web belt back jarred his back. He lifted his eyes to see into a thick, black cloud of smoke and dust.

Voices echoed all around him. He heard screaming in a strangely mixed chorus of English and Swahili.

He managed to get to his feet just in time to feel a powerful set of hands grab him on his forearms and lift him off the ground. The hands thrust him through a side door, which he barely registered before he was falling to the ground outside. The clouds of smoke were all around, forming a dense haze. Throngs of fatigue-clad men raced about, weapons in hand, in a wild disordered stampede.

No sooner had O'knomo made it onto his hands and

knees, the powerful hands grabbed his arms again and lifted him to a full standing position.

He stared into a massive chest covered by a tight-fitting fatigue shirt, then looked up at the large, round head of Oma Muniggi, his childhood friend and now comrade in arms.

Muniggi was yelling, trying to say something. Between the litany of shouts and the hail of gunfire permeating the atmosphere, O'knomo could only make out a few words. The larger man was trying to explain something about attack helicopters. He was pointing wildly toward a collection of hills overlooking the camp from the south, mouthing unintelligible words. But O'knomo understood only one thing clearly: recce units.

O'knomo could deduce the rest. Three or four SADF attack helicopters hovered overhead. In perfect coordination, the massive steel beasts took turns swooping down closely over the camp. They spit fire from heavy .50 caliber machine guns from inside the craft's side doors and blasted small rockets into the larger camp structures.

The attack had come at dawn, following a barrage of mortar fire directed with precision at the defense points manned by high-caliber machine guns, the machine guns that would have been effective against the helicopters raining down on them. A South African recce team had taken position and guided the whole attack. Muniggi pointed in the direction he assumed the recce team was most likely to be. Of course, Muniggi's deductions were all pointless. They did nothing to deter the armored helicopters from tearing up the ground with machine gun fire.

The two men bolted across the camp, dodging corpses of fallen comrades and debris that littered the ground everywhere. O'knomo choked on the thick dust and smoke in the air. Still, he kept running. The command post was demolished and the camp leaderless. The soldiers darted about in chaos, trying to find a way to effect some change.

O'knomo's mind centered on one thing: the machine gun at the east entrance. If it remained operational, he might be able to knock out a few of the helicopters. He took off in the direction of the entrance.

Muniggi stayed close behind him.

They neared two grass huts used for the communications that were now engulfed in flames. From their new position, they sighted the guard post. The smoke grew thicker with the added flames from the burning structures, but they kept eyes on their target, sprinting fast.

As the aerial gunships began a descent on the camp, O'knomo and Muniggi reached the guard post, a gunship moving directly toward them. O'knomo could hear the thunderous sound of gunfire. The dirt before him ripped apart violently. In that moment, paralyzing fear ran down his spine.

"SHIT!" David O'knomo leapt from his bed and pressed himself against the wall of his room, breathing hard.

It took him a minute to realize it had all vanished. The camp in Zambia was gone leaving him alone in a barren room with tan walls and a spartan collection of old furniture. He remained fixed against the wall. His eyes and rational mind told him he was safe; it had just been a dream. Yet, his instincts, honed after so many years in combat remained alert, as if expecting the enemy to come bursting through the door any minute.

Eventually, he was able to work his way from the wall and calm his nerves enough to take a seat on the bed. His breathing slowed to a normal pace. He regained his faculties, felt a cold, dampening sensation all over his body and put a hand on his chest. His shirt was drenched with sweat.

UNABLE TO SLEEP, O'knomo decided to get an early start at work. The sun had barely risen when he reached the doorway of his office.

He had read the personnel file on Sauwa Catcher numerous times. He felt he could recite most of it from memory. Now, he moved to her unit's activities as a whole: how they operated, who worked with them, and who gave them support. His file on the Black Chamber read like a rough draft for an intriguing spy novel. Each page presented a new scope of fascination as he read through the planning and execution of so many missions.

He had finished half of the thick file, when Jamie Nawati stepped in. The young Mk soldier was still waking up. He drifted about the room like he was trying to remember if he had ever been there before. Deciding not to rush him, O'knomo went on reading the file.

It was 0830hrs when Dr. Eugene Walderhyn marched into the office. He was the stoic, conservative image of the professional academic. Twenty minutes later Coors Ravenhoof strutted in armed with a large, steel coffee thermos, which he carried like a weapon he intended to use for violence

The team assembled in a semi-circle around their leader, who stood at the board displaying a picture of their quarry. It was the first day of their mission.

O'knomo gathered himself. "You've all had the last few days to pour over the files, study our target and get a feel for what we're up against. I think the best thing to do is to build a strategy. How do we intend to begin this pursuit?"

"Dark Chamber," Walderhyn opened, "worked outside the general support network of South African intelligence. They did this, as near as I can tell, to protect the government from any connection to their terrorist activities. Based on that, we have to assume they worked through a careful association with both the local criminal network and rightist groups. We should start there."

O'knomo nodded. "You're right, we should look for alternative networks, predominantly criminal."

"I agree," Ravenhoof said, "we should tap the Scotland Yard boys."

"No," Nawati broke in. He eyed the group. "Not criminal. We need to look at political associations." The room remained quiet, the other men waiting for a further explanation. Nawati cleared his throat. "We have to think about this from Dark Chamber's perspective. They weren't just a highly covert organization, they operated on the fringe — a lone wolf unit created to be easily discarded. These people knew this day could come. This sets them apart from other organizations or groups in the Apartheid security forces. We have to assume they thought this out. By now they'll have broken up and gone their separate ways.

We're looking for Sauwa to be working alone at this point."

"Why would you believe that?" Ravenhoof snorted, "I would think they would stay together as long as possible. You know, safety in numbers and all that."

"No," Nawati disagreed. "A group of wanted fugitives is harder to hide. With limited resources, it would be harder to remain mobile, if you have more people to worry about. I'm telling you, they're traveling alone at this point."

"Then surely she's hiding out in the underworld," Walderhyn interjected. "We should be looking for gangsters."

Nawati shook his head. "Sauwa Catcher is a highly sought after international fugitive and a skilled covert operative. She's not going to trust her fate to profit-driven gangsters, who could turn her over to anyone offering a price. No, she'll go to someone who's an ally, someone who would be sympathetic. She wouldn't just go to anyone either. Sauwa would reach out to a group that had an extensive network, one sophisticated and connected enough to get her out of Britain undetected and possibly have connections to keep her apprised of any police progress."

Another pause. All eyes were focused on Nawati. The young MK soldier continued, "I doubt she's still in Britain. She's wanted by their police as well. With more information about to come out, she'll be a high priority. We have to focus on groups fitting this description that worked closely with Dark Chamber fitting this description."

"You're sure of this?" O'knomo asked.

"It's what I would do," Nawati said.

O'knomo looked at the other two men in the room.

"It's a good idea." Ravenhoof shrugged. Walderhyn quietly nodded.

"Very good," O'knomo said. "Ravenhoof, do we know what groups in the United Kingdom fit this image?"

The Afrikaner grumbled. "I can find out. I'll talk up some of my friends in the SAP and see what they know in their country. Then, with your permission, I'll start reaching out to the Scotland Yard boys and see what they might know and if we can put them onto the scent."

O'knomo furled his brow. "Good. Do that and get back to me. In the meantime, Walderhyn is going off this theory. We need to assume that she's out of England by now. As hot as she is, she won't stay in the United Kingdom. Review the intelligence we have and form an idea of how she'll attempt to get out of the UK."

"I can do that," the academic replied quietly. "Are we sure she's even still in that little cluster of islands?"

O'knomo glanced at Nawati, then back to the academic. "Until we see information to the contrary, let's assume she is. She has limited resources, so she can't just move about freely. And moving from England to Wales is one thing. It gets harder when she has to try to cross into a different country without land routes."

The meeting concluded with everyone understanding their task and promising to meet up the next day at the same time for progress updates.

NAWATI WAS the last to reach the door. The young man looked distraught, and O'knomo guessed Nawati had not come to terms with working in the intelligence headquarters of his former enemies.

"Jamie, can we speak."

Nawati didn't wait for O'knomo to open the conversation. "You spoke to the two white guys after I left the other day. Something I should know?"

O'knomo motioned Nawati back in the room and closed the door for privacy. "Forgive me, I was concerned about their feelings chasing down one of their own, and wanted to see where they were emotionally. I felt it was better speaking to them in private first, but wanted to take this moment to speak with you. This is not an easy assignment. We are going after someone our people have feared for a long time. This can't be about retribution. We are here to bring her to justice, not the morgue."

Nawati smiled, "You think I will seize this as a chance for revenge?"

O'knomo smiled back.

"In truth," Nawati adjusted the collar of his crisp, white shirt. "I, more than anyone here, may have the hardest time carrying out this assignment."

O'knomo was perplexed. He had come to know Nawati as a patriot of the anti-Apartheid cause — a professional, someone who could get a hard job done. That the young MK soldier would struggle in their hunt for the Angel of Death had not occurred to him.

Nawati continued, "I'm here to provide insight into her thinking, right? And I can because I carried out the same type of missions she did. I hunted and I killed. In the end, the only difference between us is we were on opposite sides. It's hard for me to look at her and not see someone driven by the same things that drove me."

He turned to the ghostly looking photograph pinned on the board. "I read her file, just like everyone else. She was born in Rhodesia. She came to this country with her uncle, who was a soldier in the Selous Scouts after her family had been killed by the ZANU in a raid.

A few parallels don't make you the same, O'knomo interjected.

In the early eighties, the South African government was hiring as many Rhodesian police, soldiers, and intelligence operators as they could to build their own operational program to combat the growing insurgency."

"You studied her file thoroughly, I see," O'knomo interjected.

Nawati dismissed the comment. "The Civil Cooperation Bureau (CCB) recruited her. It was the early 80s. The South African government was hiring as many Rhodesian police, soldiers and intelligence operators as they could to build their own operation program to combat the growing anti-Apartheid insurgency. The CCB was searching for young whites of British lineage —— mostly young Rhodesian immigrants — who could integrate into English society.

O'knomo was well aware of the history. Many anti-Apartheid nationalist groups were trying to build connections to the European left and help monitor the English-speaking whites in South Africa. Sauwa Catcher would have been in her late teens when she was sucked into the war. O'knomo could fill in Nawati's line of thinking, but let Nawati speak without interruption.

"Her uncle was part of their developing Special Forces units." Nawati was still focused on the photo, running through the file in his mind. It helped him to put things in order, to run through each step of a journey that could easily have been his own. "She was identified early as having a remarkable aptitude in areas coinciding with spy work. She was recruited into a special unit — an extension of the CCB region six office — dealing with domestic security issues. Her role was monitoring whites suspected of working with the South African Communist Party."

"The CCB discovered her talent for more intense covert work when she engineered the assassination of Jeremy Rivers, leader of a leftist political group in Cape Town. She arranged a fire in the basement that burned with wool and plastic emitting a toxic gas that poisoned the radicals and came off looking like an accident."

O'knomo sunk down into his seat, surprised by Nawati's sympathetic understanding and lack of hatred.

He had already studied the biography himself and was well acquainted with the story being recited to him.

Nawati released himself from the hypnotic eyes in the photo and looked at his superior. "I'm sorry, but I can see what drove her to this because I see the same path in my own history. You brought me in so I could help get you into the mind of a professional killer. It also means that I can empathize with her as well."

The older MK soldier's expression was a mix of indecision and mistrust. Nawati squared his shoulders. "I'm in this. I will work to bring her in and give you what you need to the best of my abilities. But I won't deny that I see myself when I look at her. There are not many of us who can perform this work. Had circumstances been different, it could just as easily be my picture on that board, with a team being organized to hunt me down. I can't lose sight of that."

O'knomo took in a deep breath. "We all have demons we will need to overcome. For the whites in our unit, it will be chasing down a former member of their own security service. For you, our target is an agent you share an intimate connection with." He rose to his feet and stretched. "As to your concern, it didn't end differently. She's the fugitive, not you. In the end, our mission amounts to only one thing. We bring her in."

9

Sauwa found it hard to get comfortable in the hard, wood chair in the small deli. Breakfast was mildly palatable, and the owner acted like he was doing her a favor he tending to her, but the deli offered a line of sight to the Sherrfield Café across the street. Her target, Marston Donovan, was known to frequent the Sherrfield, so it was the best place to begin her surveillance and plan her attack.

The notes taken at the farm had provided his home address in some suburb on Dublin's north side. But the neighborhood proved to be a strategic nightmare, a maze of narrow and twisting streets that would have made following him, even with a trained team, difficult. Long-standing neighbors knew everyone around and noticed her presence immediately when she jogged through Donovan's cozy lane. It didn't matter. A trained intelligence detective who lived within the murky world of covert information collection would be on guard for strangers around his home.

Sauwa navigated the picturesque world of Phoenix Park twice as she practiced with the small motorbike Banker had procured for her. Then she rode leisurely past the headquarters of the Irish Garda. Large and well-guarded, it presented too much danger to hang about too long. Monitoring Donovan from his office would not be possible.

The Sherrfield Café presented the best location for her purposes. Settled on a busy street of small shops and eateries, it was a trendy place for tourists and out-of-towners. People of all types mingled here, making it easier for her to blend in and stay inconspicuous.

From the deli, she enjoyed her second cup of raspberry tea and a small breakfast. H.G Wells' Island of Dr. Moreau gave her an excuse to linger. She occasionally glanced out the window and scouted the cars pulling up to the curb, scanning for the makes and license numbers — her employer, the UVF, had given her a list — of the vehicles Donovan used when working. She had to commend the UVF's intelligence network for its thoroughness and accuracy of its information.

For the last twenty minutes cars had accumulated outside the window. The Sherrfield was soon a buzz with an assorted group of people, who congregated briefly and then moved quickly into the coffee shop. Their diversity ranged from casually dressed conservative types to the rougher looking radicals to obvious underworld heavies. They made friendly overtures to one another. Sauwa assumed they were the detectives starting to arrive.

Chewing slowly on a piece of sausage, she observed each car. Finally, a polished blue Nissan arrived and wedged its way into a narrow spot near the café entrance.

The car door flew open and out stepped a man matching the picture of Marston Donovan.

He was heavy-set with a slight bulge protruding from under his buttoned-up, grey sports jacket. His features were groomed and manicured — professional. As he exited the vehicle, he scanned the street, then shut the door before starting toward the coffee shop.

These actions confirmed her suspicion she was dealing with a professional. He was cognizant of his surroundings and anticipated being under surveillance. He would not be an easy target. If she tried to follow him to study his patterns by herself, he would spot her in a few hours or a day at best. He was competent, and would likely be working with a team of equally competent operatives, and he was used to dealing with groups of suspicious of strangers. If they noticed her, she would be in grave danger.

Donovan disappeared inside the Sherrfield. Sauwa switched between the pages of her book and kept a visual of the cafe and Donovan's car. She sipped her tea slowly and swallowed the last of her breakfast. The old couple who managed the deli was busy with the influx of customers. They left Sauwa alone to watch her target and, most likely, forgot her.

A half an hour later, Donovan emerged from the coffee shop. Her target took his time returning to his car, stopping multiple times to converse with others, laughing and backing-slapping. None of these trained policemen — including Donovan — even glanced at the strangers who wandered past their group. The detectives appeared preoccupied with last-minute conversations as they edged their way to their cars.

Sauwa would have to observe this ritual a few more times to establish their routine, but she saw a possible niche she could work with. Donovan not only seemed to let his guard down here, he was also in a perfect strategic location. There was a constant gathering of people crowding the sidewalk, which limited the targets mobility. A row of cars served as a wall that funneled everyone tightly together and provided good camouflage for her to get up close and just as easily disappear.

With a satisfied smile on his face, Donovan swaggered to his car then climbed in. He pulled out onto the street and drove away. The other detectives gradually dispersed. None of them seemed to feel they were in the slightest danger here.

Sauwa gulped down the last drops of her tea. She carefully looked around the deli to see if anyone was paying any attention to her. The patrons were all consumed with their own affairs, gossiping and studying the deli's menu. The deli proprietors were buried in a line of customers five deep. Confident she was a ghost, she quietly slipped out the front door.

THE FOLLOWING DAY, she was pulling into the parking lot of an apartment complex in Dublin's more upscale south side. The lot was nearly deserted with most of the apartment dwellers off to their jobs. Banker had told her to meet him at this place to continue the discussion about the finances. Dressed in a clean pair of stone washed jeans, white T-shirt, and sweat jacket, Sauwa tried to mimic the appearance of one of the young professionals emerging in the growing Irish economy. She would look, to anyone watching, like a new tenant.

The complex was a cubicle fortress made up of four concrete structures surrounding an inner court. Before entering, Sauwa flipped her hood up over her head to mask herself in case of any security cameras.

Following the instructions, she made her way to the third floor of complex B and found room number 317. It was an enclosed hallway with good lighting. She had expected cameras to be posted at each end of the hallway. There were none. Keeping the hood pulled over her head, she knocked on the door. The door was cautiously opened. Banker stood in the doorway, his face expressionless as he beckoned her inside. Ever cautious, she looked past him to check for any signs she was walking into an ambush.

"Don't worry. There's no one here but me. I conduct only my most private business here, so I'm the only one who knows about this place, and I want to keep it that way."

Satisfied it was not a trap, she quickly crossed over the threshold. The door shut behind her as soon as she entered.

Banker reached out gently to guide her by the shoulders — his natural habit with women — but thought better of it. Instead, he directed her into a living room area. The curtains were drawn, leaving a lamp the only real light in the room. The place was sparsely furnished with only enough furniture to convince someone, at first sight, the place was actually lived in.

Banker motioned her to remain where she was, then disappeared into a bedroom. She tensed. After a few seconds later, he returned with a small knapsack.

"Here it is," he said. He walked over to her and placed the bag on the coffee table. "This is the payment you are to receive upon completion of the job. Whatever it is."

Sauwa studied the bag and looked at him. He nodded giving her the okay to check the contents. Reaching for the knapsack, she unzipped it to find it stuffed with British pounds wrapped in tight, neat bundles.

"I guess they figured if the denomination was too large, you'd have trouble spending it unnoticed; too small and you'd be packing around a lot of money while trying to escape," Banker remarked.

"No, it's alright," Sauwa replied. She pulled a few arbitrary bundles out and placed them on the table. In the world of criminality, gangsters often used counterfeit money to pay off people they assumed they would never see after a job was complete. She looked the money over until she was satisfied it was genuine.

Banker leaned up against the wall while observing her.

"How is the money to be paid, since you don't even know what my job is?" she asked.

Banker smiled despite her unnerving gaze. "I asked that myself. I'm to get a call from your go-between telling me to make the payment. Whoever is pulling the strings on this is watching you from a distance."

Sauwa cocked her head. She put the money back.

"Aren't you gonna count it?"

"What would be the point? That was your responsibility. If it's not all there, you're the only one around to hold accountable."

Banker didn't blink. It could only mean he was confident the money was accounted for, or he intended to kill her when the job was done. She assumed he had been thorough. Simon's people had picked their man well. Banker retrieved the bag, took it back into the bedroom, then returned.

"And you trust this place?" she asked.

"It should be safe enough," he said, daring to take a seat. "When I need to conduct business affairs off the grid, I use this place. Actually, only you know about it."

"Why do I get the privilege?"

Banker leaned forward in his chair. "Because you were right. It wasn't just your paranoia. Whatever you're here for is obviously a pretty big deal. The club is no place to be conducting your sort of business. I thought of this place, and since you'll be gone permanently from the country after the job is done, I figured there was no danger in you knowing about it."

Sauwa nodded, "You picked an upscale location. I'm surprised."

"Really," Banker smirked.

Sauwa continued, "Most gangster types tend to fancy the seedy stuff—the backroom pool halls, seedy hotels people bring hookers to or to do junk—as if we're in some fifties crime noir flick."

"Ya," he chuckled. "No one really thinks about a place like this. The tenants all keep to themselves. They see people move in and out. You have fewer busybodies trying to know everyone. Plus, the police frequent these places a lot less."

Sauwa was impressed. Banker was more intelligent than many she had dealt with in the underworld. He was mindful and strategic in the way he approached his business. He was an ally she would need in the coming days. "Well, I've seen enough." She started toward the door. "I'll call you tonight at our appointed time. I'll need some things for the job."

"All right, just let me know," Banker resisted the urge to ask how much longer she intended to be around. He reminded himself the more he knew, the more he made himself a liability. And one thing he had come to understand about the young woman he was dealing with, she was dangerous.

10

Jeffery Talamadge — a member of MI-5's finest — tried to make heads or tails out of the paperwork wedged between his fingers. It was a request from the boys at Scotland Yard for any information regarding the activities of South African intelligence operating within the United Kingdom.

The packet in hand was half an inch thick and inquired about the actions of the Civil Cooperation Bureau (CCB).

A devoted archivist, Talamadge was tucked deep in the bowels of Thames House, the headquarters of the secretive MI-5. He had delivered a thorough report based on the volumes the elite counter-intelligence agency had on the African business within their borders. Reviewing the condensed version of the report, Talamadge searched for details pertaining to a specific unit that had somehow eluded his agency. Scotland Yard's request culminated in one primary issue: a group known as the Dark Chamber and the operatives who had belonged to it.

In the months following the fall of the Apartheid

regime, evidence had steadily trickled in regarding crimes committed on British soil by both the South African government and the nationalist groups combating it. The identities of numerous operatives working within Britain surfaced. MI-5 already maintained a good handle on the activities of the key players. However, some of the deeper cover operatives and their operations were just now coming to light. Many had been detained by the authorities and eventually deported back to their homeland. Yet the police still sought some of the most egregious offenders.

It had rather vexed the British intelligence community that South Africa had chosen to reveal information openly to the police. Irritation flowed within the halls of the building at Millbank SW 1 Westminster. They would have preferred their counterparts to have gone through them and handled the matter more discretely. Instead, the boys at Scotland Yard responded in typical fashion by getting court orders and issuing arrest warrants, making information requests about a political group they had never heard of before. MI-5 found itself in a rather embarrassing position.

Talamadge, a ten-year veteran of the secret service, had guarded the kingdom and had spent most of his career working against African intelligence agencies and the groups they targeted. When this debacle arose, he found himself suddenly holding the title of coordinating officer with the understanding that he was somehow supposed to manage the whole affair.

MI-5 department leaders met to get ahead of the situation and ensure the agency had a grasp of the void of information they were dealing with now. Talamadge's superiors tasked him with reviewing archival documents and the most recent intelligence reports. He checked first to see if perhaps this mysterious unit had been mentioned somewhere before and had just been overlooked by overworked analysts. Next, he reached out to Scotland Yard and the South Africans to piece together the bigger picture.

From what Talamadge could make of the report, the archivist found nothing pertaining to any intelligence unit identified by the name Dark Chamber. Nor did they find any reference to a unit that was working independently from the base CCB intelligence apparatus. The idea that this team was comprised exclusively of African whites, specifically of British lineage, seemed strange in and of itself. This whole unit seemed more like a ghost story.

Even pouring through the files pertaining to the South African intelligence czar, Craig Williams, proved fruitless. Dark Chamber was a mystery organization that came to light only after South Africa intelligence opened its files. British agencies were now scrambling to narrow the intelligence gap.

Talamadge finally caught a break when the South African embassy presented him with a contact — a man by the name of David O'knomo of the South African Intelligence Service (NIS) — whose team was also pursuing individuals belonging to the Dark Chamber. O'knomo's top priority: the fugitive at-large, Sauwa Catcher — a person reported to be responsible for the killing of a London barrister, Lynard Remslyn.

Politically liberal, Remslyn acted as legal advisor to certain Africa National Congress (ANC) officials. A bright star in Britain's far-left circles, Remslyn had also been the

ANC's principal contact for various left-wing groups sympathetic to the Black Nationalist cause.

Perhaps Talamadge had found the source he needed. O'knomo had provided Talamadge with details that implied there was a considerable amount of information the South Africans had yet to reveal about the shadowy forces of the Apartheid's intelligence network.

While O'knomo and his team continued to work out of Pretoria, O'knomo had arranged for one of his people to travel to Britain and help search for this Catcher woman. Apparently, this woman was much more significant than had been originally understood. The MI-5 veteran was inclined to accept working with the South Africans, given that they offered to provide information he desperately needed. He was told that an operative, going by the name of Coors Ravenhoof, was due in London the next day to compare notes.

WHEN JEFFERY TALAMADGE met with Coors Ravenhoof, he wasn't sure what to make of the man. The large, middle-aged South African looked more like an old-school veteran policeman than an educated intelligence officer. Further, he was a white Afrikaner and seemed marginally suspicious.

Talamadge had expected a former ANC type black man now working in government service, or a younger man who had little real connection to the old regime. But, meeting in a secure room offered at Scotland Yard head-quarters under lights designed to assist in interrogations, Talamadge shook hands with a man who could have performed violent activities in the service of the Apartheid for decades.

Ravenhoof was silent as he let the young, sandy-haired fellow sitting across the room continue to look him up and down. He understood the natural suspicions held by those who worked in the clandestine world. He would have to let a measure of trust evolve before he could expect much else. What he was also prepared for was the proverbial wall of silence, in which one agency's idea of cooperation was milking another for all viable information while revealing none themselves. It was a game the old cop had dealt with many times in the past and expected no different now.

"The Dark Chamber," Talamadge opened, breaking the icy silence. "Why don't you tell me who they are? What do you know?"

Ravenhoof remained stoic, taking in the room. He was in no mood to be interrogated. "Well, I'm a little interested in who they might have had contact with working up here."

The older man's evasiveness left Talamadge disgruntled. He wanted a thorough debriefing, not a tit for tat information exchange. But this Ravenhoof was not going to be so obliging. "I was under the impression you were here to be forthcoming about your country's intelligence activities in Great Britain. That starts with answering my questions."

"No," replied the Afrikaner. "It starts when we share information to achieve both our goals. That requires we work with each other. If that's not your intention, then mine is to go look up the cops and see if they'll be less difficult."

"My dear sir, they wouldn't have your answers," Talamadge glared. "We handle counter-intelligence, not them."

Ravenhoof chuckled. "Well, that's what I'd expect a spy to say. But, cops often have a closer ear to the streets than most might be inclined to admit. They also seem to care more about catching criminals than playing politics and posturing."

"One who denigrates his own profession, I see."

Ravenhoof rose from his chair. "I was a cop long before I was ever one of you. Life was better then. So, I'll stick with the people I like more." He started to leave.

"Wait!" Talamadge snapped. "Please sit." He motioned to the now empty seat.

Ravenhoof studied the younger man for a moment. Deciding he had made his point, he sank back into his chair. "I know we live in a world, you and I, where trust is a rare and precious commodity. But we both want the same thing — to bring criminals to justice."

"Very well," Talamadge sighed reluctantly. "I'm authorized to exchange certain information."

"Then, okay, as long as we're exchanging. If it helps me as much as you, I can be open about what we have," Ravenhoof agreed. "I can explain the Dark Chamber in a general context. Our agency will supply more detailed files by diplomatic pouch to our embassy in the next few days. But, what my country chooses to reveal is at my discretion."

Talamadge nodded. "For now, that will suffice. If you could begin with what you can discuss, I will try to help fill in the blanks."

Ravenhoof folded his hands under his chin and took a deep breath. "The Dark Chamber was a unit created by the

Civil Cooperation Bureau to operate as an independent element. A group that took their orders directly from Pretoria. The Chamber was designed as a means of waging clandestine war against anti-Apartheid forces operating in Great Britain. The mission was to disrupt any attempts to forge strong relations with your political left. This meant targeting British citizens up to and including assassinations and other forms of terrorism."

The MI-5 archivist shifted, and Ravenhoof gauged his reaction. Black-Ops groups were not unusual, but the full-blown campaign he was suggesting would give any counter intelligence man indigestion. Ravenhoof cleared his throat. "The unit was drawn up of whites who possessed British lineage. We recruited largely from the pool of Rhodesians streaming across the border. Many already had a significant background from working in the security services of Rhodesia. Some were kids, young adults who possessed the necessary traits for good covert spy work. We later cultivated them to help infiltrate white radical groups operating on the English-speaking campuses."

Talamadge sat quietly. It wasn't a ghost story. He was intrigued. It was simply extraordinary.

Ravenhoof stopped for a moment, giving Talamadge a chance to speak. The MI-5 officer motioned to him continue. Not wanting to be tapped for too much, Ravenhoof studied the young man and decided he needed to divulge further information before demanding reciprocation. "Eventually, as the more established nationalist movements expanded their operations into Europe, it became necessary to follow suit. As you know, many of the activities my government carried out in the late seventies and eighties were not very well managed or concealed with many tracing right back to the South African embassy.

The CCB leadership decided to establish a deep cover penetration unit, the Dark Chamber. Run by the military, it was cut off almost entirely from the South African intelligence community. It was not even run through any offices in Pretoria but, instead, through a secret headquarters established just outside of the Fort Doppies military base in South West Africa. All funding was entirely off the books. Instead of receiving logistical and financial support through the embassy, Dark Chamber was supported through a network of black market types in Africa who were connected to Dark Chamber through the South African Police."

"This is why nothing is known of them." Talamadge shook his head. "Unbelievable."

"Precisely," Ravenhoof agreed. "They infiltrated into the country illegally, were given names and identities of British citizens and blended into deep cover. From there they engaged high priority targets in the ANC and PAC, as well a few organizations of lesser influence. They also infiltrated leftist political groups here in Britain to collect intelligence on their relations with the Black Nationalist organizations and the potential impact this could have on your country's greater political climate. They eventually expanded this mission to active disruption of any political alliances that could prove damaging over time."

"It didn't stop there, did it?" The MI-5 officer was now leaning forward in his chair, listening intensely.

Ravenhoof resumed. "In the end, they were targeting British citizens deemed potential threats. Dark Chamber already conducted sabotage assassinations in addition to other activities judged necessary by their team leader, one Devon Williams."

Talamadge dutifully took dictation as Ravenhoof continued to enlighten him to the phenomenon of Dark Chamber. He was finally getting something tangible about this elusive operation. When Ravenhoof paused, Talamadge set down his pen. "This brings us to your needs. The question of Sauwa Catcher. She is so important that you have a unit designated entirely to bringing her in?" The MI-5 operative was incredulous.

Ravenhoof took a deep breath, which he then exhaled in a slow, deep sigh. "We are tasked with bringing down all the members of Dark Chamber. However, Ms. Catcher presents the highest priority right now. In the circles of South African intelligence and the military wings of the Black Nationalist organizations, she is quite infamous. Her informal title, dubbed by both sides is the Angel of Death for the degree of violence she has carried out."

"Including here? On British soil?" Talamadge returned to jotting notes with some excitement.

"Your government has only received a little information as to her activities here," Ravenhoof replied adamantly. "Your police have only been apprised of one killing she committed in your country. She is responsible for so many more."

"I trust the 'more' will be outlined in the documents you plan to show me when they arrive at your embassy." Talamadge leaned back in his chair and eyed his counterpart.

The South African stared back. "The documents I might show you if you are as free with your information."

Talamadge reached for a metal case placed next to him and turned the combination. Opening the case, he produced a manila folder. He perused the contents briefly, then returned his attention to Ravenhoof. "The South African intelligence network did rely on certain right-wing political groups for various forms of support. Many of them were far right Skinhead types offering muscle for basic rough stuff. Other groups were comprised of prominent citizens who assisted politically. These groups lobbied for the Apartheid cause and kept abreast of the talk within the circles of Parliament and more influential political parties. Nothing dangerous and certainly not illegal, per se. Ultimately, very few have the means to run a complex network capable of spiriting highly sought fugitives out of the country. That's assuming Dark Chamber operatives have indeed left Britain, or they've had dealings with of these groups."

Ravenhoof folded his arms and moistened his lips. "They're gone. I am sure of that. Before the Apartheid fell, word passed to our operatives abroad warning them of what was about to happen. Those who could return home were recalled. Superiors informed those most likely to face criminal charges from intelligence leaks that they would be subject to war crimes if they returned to South Africa. The Dark Chamber leadership knew both countries would pursue charges against their people and instructed them to go into hiding."

"What makes you think they would work through any of these groups? Or that they had any connection with them whatsoever?"

"We gave them no direct support from their government. They had to rely on the underworld and domestic political movements sympathetic to their cause. They would have chosen carefully who they reached out to though. That would mean a very short list of groups that could deliver the support they needed. Criminal groups are less trustworthy than well-organized political groups."

Talamadge tapped his fingers. "In that case, it narrows the field considerably. For a long time, South African intelligence enjoyed a cozy relationship with Loyalist paramilitaries from Northern Ireland. These groups helped with a great deal of logistics and operational support for some of their operations. If your Ms. Catcher was going to reach out to anyone, the Ulster Defense Association or the Ulster Volunteer Force would be the most likely suspects. They have the resources to protect your fugitive and move her out of Britain undetected."

The MI-5 operative handed the folder to the South African, confident that he had gained his needed information.

11

Sauwa's first plan was to stage Donovan's killing to look like a suicide, but on closer analysis, the idea was unfeasible. For the good of both herself and her employers, the police, hunting for vengeance, would need someone else to hold accountable.

It took several days of patient observation for Sauwa to determine Donovan was most vulnerable outside the Sherrfield Café. If she could walk up in the crowd carrying a sharp object, she could stab deep into a lethal area and coolly walk away. The trick was making sure the kill was guaranteed.

She decided the best method was a breakable knife. Not wanting to go through Banker, she combed the warehouse district for materials to build a variety of trial weapons. Her latex gloves fit her hands snugly so she could work with precision. With the meticulous eye of a craftsman, she worked at the small desk in her room, manipulating pieces of glass and hard plastic to determine which weapon would work best.

She sifted through thrift stores to acquire necessary materials, props and clothing to carry out her plan. She collected a variety of bits and pieces in different stores to prevent someone from remembering her. From a flea market, she scavenged a large canvas bag.

It took a few days of experimentation before Sauwa settled on a seven-inch piece of glass — a roughly triangular shape that had been part of an office window. A centimeter thick, sharp and jagged on both sides, it was perfect for stabbing someone, penetrating the outer skin and tearing deep into the soft tissue and organs. Just as important was her ability to break it off from the handle, so the blade couldn't be retrieved or the wound plugged to prevent bleeding out. She would need a grip sturdy enough to allow her to perform the job, but weak enough at the base to cleanly separate, permitting her to escape unnoticed. A thick, semi-cubicle, plastic rectangle from part of a small table served that function.

After having honed both objects to specifications, she attached the plastic cube to the glass shard with airplane glue. It was a cheap, simplistic contraption, but one that would serve well for her purposes. She had learned in her training that simplicity often worked best in a complex operation. Her humble knife was unpredictable, untraceable and a means of assassination resembling methods used in the underworld giving the police a focus for their anger.

The glue dried in an hour, then she was ready to practice. Banker had supplied her with a collection of sandbags partially filled with whole chickens from a butcher shop. The nightclub owner had been confused by her request; however, he knew better than to ask needless questions.

Sauwa stuffed the chickens into the bags until they were deeply submerged in the thick sand. She tied them off tightly, lined them up on a table and leaned them against the wall. The whole exercise would test the weapon's ability to stab through clothes, flesh, and finally soft tissue. Gripping the makeshift knife firmly, she took a deep breath and drew it back from her hip. With a quick thrust, she plunged the knife fiercely into the bag. It tore through the thick burlap into the sand and boney chicken meat.

It seemed her weapon was a success until three inches in, a jagged tooth along the blade caught on a piece of burlap causing the handle to break off prematurely. If her target wore a durable shirt, the blade would have been stopped too early to guarantee a lethal strike. The glass needed to penetrate deep and leave rescuers no way to extract it.

Returning to her work desk she set about redesigning her weapon. She repeated the routine throughout the day. Each time she tested the knife, she examined it for mistakes and made necessary changes to the weapon or the strike pattern. When a bag had been used up, she cut open the top and discarded the contents into the sea water outside her window — the fish and currents did the rest. It was near nightfall when she completed her rehearsals. After five successful stabs in a row, she doused the blade in a thick coat of oleander residue to provide a lethal toxin and wrapped the weapon in sandwich wrap.

She ended the evening by dropping the remaining sandbags into the water, then enjoyed a light dinner and a shower. Her bed, a lumpy, industrial mattress used in military barracks, seemed like heaven as she drifted off to sleep. Both her body and mind had been hard at work the past few days not just planning for the assassination but mulling over the inevitable, unpredictable future that awaited her. When the job was completed, and she was packed onto whatever means of transport Banker would arrange for her, she would be on her own again. The UVF and Banker would wash their hands of her, and she would have to find a way to fend for herself.

SAUWA ROSE the next morning before the sun had come up. No alarm clock was necessary. Her natural instincts seemed to take over. Rising from bed, she exercised, showered and ate. She packed up all her belongings and stashed them in a hard to find location but convenient for retrieval in the event she had to make a fast getaway.

Removing the blade from the plastic, she coated the blade with a fresh layer of oleander and wrapped it in a paper bag. At first glance, it would look like a purchase from a local shop — one extra level of cover as she got in close.

She paused for a moment looking out into the ocean. She took several deep breaths as she prepared herself for what was about to happen. Even the most seasoned operatives, if not mentally prepared, lost control of their faculties when adrenaline and nerves took over. One last breath, a last look around, and Sauwa turned toward the door.

Dressed in her thrift store clothing — a pair of jeans and a long-sleeved undershirt over a black T-shirt and covered in a grey tweed overcoat — she made her way out to her motorcycle. Like everything else, Sauwa had taken the precaution of hiding the bike in the far-off corner of the warehouse under a plastic cover and added debris.

Tucking the weapon into a large canvass bag she had bought at a local flea market, she mounted her vehicle and rode out ready to carry out the mission.

THE SHERRFIELD CAFÉ was quiet this morning. Sauwa counted three young waitresses rushing about serving a scattered collection of older people enjoying their morning get-together. All chattered happily over large mugs of coffee.

Having conducted numerous recces over the last several days, she had decided the best to staging point would be the bookshop a few buildings down. The shop was run by an elderly couple who kept to themselves unless approached by a customer; otherwise, they stayed at the counter hidden deep in the far back of the store. A shabby, overstuffed chair near the bookshop entrance was a perfect place to wait and watch for the opportune moment. It was close to the target location, gave her ample cover, good visibility and a quick way to leave at a moment's notice. Plus, the shaded glass and natural darkness of the shop ensured she was not likely to be seen by anyone outside.

Settling into the chair, she adjusted its angle for the perfect view out the window and waited. A copy of William S. Burroughs' classic, *The Naked Lunch,* served as both a cover and entertainment. As expected, the elderly couple remained behind the checkout counter unaware of what was going on. Her eyes shifted lazily between the pages of the 1950s classic and the entrance to the Sherrfield. She was just another bookstore beatnik.

A half-hour later, the procession of cars pulled up to the curb, one and two at a time. The detectives followed their routine: they emerged from their vehicles, made pleasantries to colleagues out on the street, then shuffled into the coffee shop.

Sauwa caught sight of Marston Donovan's blue Nissan as he drove it up the road and slipped, with precision, into an opening along the curb. Sleek as always, the car gleamed in the sunlight. The well-dressed figure of Marston Donovan popped the door open and hopped out onto the sidewalk, met by two other detectives. The three exchanged warm greetings before moving toward the entrance of their favored establishment

It was now just a waiting game for Sauwa.

An hour later, true to form, the detectives began to leave, crowding out the Sherrfield front door, laughing and engaging in playful antics.

Nestling her book amongst a disorderly collection, she tucked her hair up under a grey knit cap to better camouflage her appearance and strolled out of the bookshop onto the street. She took her time slipping on a good pair of latex gloves not only to prevent leaving fingerprints but also to allow her a tighter grip on the weapon handle.

By now, the mid-morning brought small crowds of tourists and everyday shoppers. Sauwa walked slowly up the street pulling the paper sack with the weapon from her side bag. With one hand in her pocket, she carried the bag and looked around like an indecisive shopper. She took a few deep breaths as if feeling the results of a great deal of walking. In reality, it was to help calm her nerves and control the rising adrenaline rush.

At the edge of the Sherrfield, she stopped and glanced at her watch. A common act. The detectives gave her no notice. It gave her needed time as she waited for her target.

Donovan came through the door of the café enjoying a light-hearted laugh with another set of detectives. He was now in place. She watched him maneuver through his colleagues, talking and back-slapping, while shoppers intermingled around them

Sauwa moved toward him almost within an arm's length, turning and shifting as he addressed different people. She planned to hit Donovan's right side from behind to pierce the liver. She removed her free hand from her pocket and repositioned the canvas bag behind her.

With a small collection of firecrackers she had asked Banker to obtain, along with a lighter, she lowered her hands to her waist, hidden under her coat. Tucking the paper sack into her coat pocket, she lit the party favors throwing them to the side into the crowds.

As predicted, the crackling explosions set the crowd into a panic.

Detectives shouted, "Shots fired?"

Several onlookers shrieked with fear. A passing car clipped the back of a detective's parked car, creating an even bigger diversion. This served to distract the policemen even more, and Sauwa moved in for the kill.

A veteran cop, accustomed to the sound of gunfire, Donovan smiled as he watched the crowds reacting with confused hysteria to the party favors. Taking the sack from her coat pocket, Sauwa closed the distance between her and the detective. He turned, leaving his sports jacket wide, providing an opening. She lifted the bag at an angle and, as she had rehearsed, drove the blade into his torso. The skin and stomach lining were tougher than the burlap and sand she had practiced with, but the sharp blade sliced into it easily. She could feel the blade cut through the soft tissue of the man's organs. Half a second later, she felt the grip of her weapon against his shirt. At once, she snapped the cubed handle with one quick jerk and continued moving casually up the street.

She shoved her hands back into her pockets and walked at the same pace as the rest of the crowd that had not been stunned by the firecrackers. It was not easy. Her adrenaline and basic instincts told her to run—everything that would draw attention to her. She breathed deeply through her nose calming herself. Eventually, her system returned to some normality, and she followed the flow of fleeing pedestrians.

Sauwa was two shops past the Sherrfield when she heard shouts from detectives for someone to call an ambulance. They had discovered their comrade's wound. Again, she maintained control and did not turn around. Behind her, the chorus of shouts grew louder as the detectives began to comprehend what had just happened.

Resisting the urge to duck into an alleyway, Sauwa crossed the intersection. Behind her the detectives, having regained their professional alertness and attention to detail, would be scanning the area for signs of the assailant.

It would be foolish to rush into the first side street. She had planned out the route of escape and two contingency plans beforehand. At the far side of the intersection, she turned and made her way down the road, picking up her pace.

A few blocks down, she stepped into a side street and disappeared from view.

Away from the crowds, she quickly removed her coat and knit cap, stuffed them into her canvas bag and dumped the bag and its contents into a grease collection tank along the way. The tank wouldn't get emptied for another few days. By then, everything would be submerged in the oily substance and would be too stained for police to use for evidence.

She came back onto the main road, crossed the street and was soon in another alley heading toward a large green dumpster. Removing a stack of greasy, discarded boxes, she pulled down some additional cover to find her motorcycle where she had left it earlier that morning. Revving up the machine, she kicked it into gear and sped into the crush of traffic, every second putting greater distance between her and the body she had left behind.

12

Banker didn't need to be a psychic or a genius to figure out what he had gotten himself into. It couldn't have been a coincidence.

He received a sudden call from his contacts telling him to go ahead and pay the mysterious young woman and organize her transportation out of the country immediately. The call came only hours after the announcement of the slaying of veteran Garda Detective, Marston Donovan, by an unknown assassin.

Fetching the money from his secret apartment office, he crossed the complex parking lot toward his car, his mind awash with thoughts and concerns. He wasn't scared. He had been in the business long enough to understand such affairs. Even an extreme like assassinating officers of the Garda did not necessarily surprise him. Given the excessively cryptic way the whole operation was being handled, coupled with the amount of the payment involved, it had to be something big.

Everything was falling into place. His concern lay more

with the after-effects about to transpire. The police would devote serious resources to this investigation. This meant they would be pressing contacts all over the city and casting their net far and wide. It was also during something like this that the perpetrators and their masters would be inclined to do their own evaluation of the affair and determine what loose ends may exist.

Banker had provided all the support and logistics for Sauwa. He need to play out the rest of the job intelligently and ensuring he was protected from both sides.

The police had nothing that could connect him to the killing or even make him a suspect. Neither the assassin nor her employers saw anything that would make him a liability. Professionals in the underworld tended to avoid killing unless it was absolutely necessary. After all, dead bodies were a complication and violence tended to bring unwanted attention. Only idiots who had seen too many movies or had something to prove killed without a pressing reason.

Sliding into the driver's side of his car, Banker turned the ignition and drove out of the parking lot. He eyed the knapsack he had shoved on the floor; it would be just his luck if he were to get robbed or pulled over. He'd be relieved to finally be rid of the responsibility of playing banker to a hitman.

SAUWA GATHERED ALL the clothes she had used over the last several days walking the neighborhood of the Sherrfield Café while conducting her recce. She had taken the precaution of changing her appearance for each visit to avoid people getting used to seeing her and be able to provide a description.

The mission was over, and she needed to destroy all evidence immediately. She'd collected everything pertaining to the mission in a single location in another room, keeping her covert world well apart from her normal life, so as not to accidentally keep any trophies or mementos that tied her to her previous operations. This had been the downfall of many operatives who had neglected to properly dispose of operational materials and wound up leaving evidence for police or other intelligence agencies to trace or help build their case.

She was alerted to someone entering the warehouse by the sound of glass bottles skidding across concrete. As a security precaution, she had bits of glass and bottles arbitrarily laid about. In the darkness, they were hard to see and easy to run into. This make-shift alarm system gave her ample warning of would-be attackers.

Gripping her Browning 9 millimeter pistol, she moved against the wall opposite the door opening. The Browning was a favorite of military and police units around the world. It was a very good weapon in a gunfight and existed in abundance making it easier to obtain.

Sliding down to one knee she took a tactical position, waiting. If it were assailants, they wouldn't know where she was and would have to search rooms randomly. Over time fatigue and stress would set in. Hopefully, they would be less alert when they finally got to her room.

She heard the sound of a door cracking open and figured it was her living quarters. Whoever it was, they apparently knew exactly where she was staying. The footsteps continued toward her. By the sound of shoes on concrete, she deduced it was either one man or, at best, two.

"Anyone home?" The familiar voice of Banker called out gently.

"I'm here," Sauwa replied as she slowly rose to her feet. She still kept her weapon ready to fire in case this was an ambush.

The door opened all the way. Banker entered. Seeing the weapon in her hands and the serious look on Sauwa's face, he knew to tread lightly. He stepped to the side to give her a visual of the hallway and show her no one else was with him. From her position, she looked out to verify there were no signs of anyone else. She still kept the man in view through the corner of her eye.

Sensing she was on as much of an edge as he was now that the mission was done, Banker lifted his sports jacket and turned around slowly to show he was not armed. Only when she was convinced he was no threat did she lower her weapon and tuck it into her waistband.

"I brought your payment," Banker opened the conversation. "Your employers called me a few hours ago and told me to go ahead and pay you." Carefully, he slid the knapsack off his shoulder and lowered it to the ground.

"Open it, please," she commanded in a soft, yet stern voice.

As instructed, he unzipped the bag and opened it wide for her to see the contents. It was the bundles of money she had seen in his apartment. Noticing he wasn't wearing any gloves gave her a sense of relief. More sophisticated organizations were apt to use the less obtrusive method of poison when removing troublesome problems. Such poisons were not always ingested. "Please pull the money out onto the floor."

With a shrug, Banker reached in and proceeded to pull stacks of money onto the floor before her. Sauwa was relieved to find that neither the money nor the bag was laced with an adhesive toxin. Something she had used herself to dispatch targets in the past.

She nodded.

Taking that as a sign that he was okay, Banker stood back up and stepped away from the money. "I'm making arrangements for your departure. I will have your instructions tonight."

"I'll contact you through our usual means," Sauwa replied. "We'll arrange to meet and discuss the details. How long will you need?"

"Right now, for what I'm planning," Banker shifted his eyes from side to side. "You're looking at possibly two days. I'm using a fella I do business with to smuggle stuff in from the continent. I'm reaching out to him to provide a means out of here."

She nodded. "How far do you trust him?"

"My opinion doesn't matter," Banker stated, his voice sharp. "Given the nature of your situation, you don't have the luxury to compare travel accommodations. If it would make you feel better, I would tell you I've done business with him for a few years now. To date, he's always been square with me." He looked Sauwa over trying to guess her thoughts. She was utterly stoic. "I'm not the one resting my unknown future on him. And, you don't know me well enough for my opinion to mean shit to you. I also have every reason to put your mind at ease, because my job is to get you out of this country as quickly as possible.

You would think that I would have vouched for anyone if it made you no longer my concern?"

"Those thoughts have all crossed my mind." Sauwa stared back at the man in an assessing way. "We agree. I'm not exactly in a position where I can shop around for a means of travel. I have to take your recommendation and hope for the best."

Banker shrugged. "You do, and I'm sorry for that. If it is any consolation, I was sincere. The man I'm making the arrangements with has always lived up to his end of the deal."

"I'd like to believe that," Sauwa sighed. "As you've said though, I don't know you very well."

"I'll be waiting for your call around the usual time." Banker started toward the door. "I recommend we meet someplace. I don't want to discuss such sensitive information over the phone."

"I agree," she replied. "But, until I'm gone, I pick the meeting sites."

Banker was almost through the doorway when he turned to face her. "I assume that will be our arrangement from this point forward." He turned and started out the door leaving Sauwa to continue her clean up.

13

Jeffery Talamadge read the collection of documents with all the adrenaline one would get reading a fast-paced spy novel. The archival records brought in from the South African embassy were an astonishing revelation into the depth of the Dark Chamber operation and the missions they skillfully carried out entirely under the nose of Britain's legendary MI-5 organization. What was more unbelievable was the chilling reports accounting for the missions undertaken specifically by Sauwa Catcher.

The documents provided were in both Afrikaans and English, which was rare. Thankfully this dispensed with the need to have them translated. Talamadge rubbed his sweat-soaked forehead for the third time. After reading for the last half hour, he had come to understand why she was such a priority for the South Africans. The accounts documented were astonishing. The asphyxiation of the son of a prominent member of the House of Lords had been made to look like a suicide. The boy had been working as part of a far-left political group trying to lobby the government to supply weapons to the ANC and other anti-Apartheid groups. He had died from carbon monoxide poisoning in the garage of the family cottage. The carefully planned and executed killing orchestrated and carried out entirely by Sauwa Catcher sent chills down the veteran counter-intelligence officer's spine.

Another incident described a fire that killed four people representing the South African Communist Party and three members of the Provisional Irish Republican Army. The fire had allegedly been started by a spark that ignited a basement full of old newspapers and a pile of wool bundles. In the confined and stuffy quarters, the toxic gases from the wool rose quickly beyond the fire itself and managed to poison all attendees of the meeting before the fire was even close enough to be heard or felt. Though ruled an accident by the fire inspectors, the detailed documents described a far different scenario.

The list of atrocities went on. All were attributed to one individual, the one Ravenhoof constantly referred to as the Angel of Death. The Englishman stared at the ghostly looking figure in the small black and white photograph delivered with the file. All he could think about was the report he would have to use to brief his superiors, and the utter black eye it would have on the whole organization. His mind also burned with another thought — she was the Devil, and she needed to be brought down.

David O'knomo ruminated over the report delivered from Ravenhoof after his meeting with MI-5. The conclusion from the British assumed Sauwa Catcher had been given protection from some paramilitary group in

Northern Ireland certainly limited the field. The next question was to predict where she would be hiding. Over the last few days, Dr. Eugene Walderhyn had immersed himself in the study of the Northern Irish conflict known as the Troubles. As if a machine or a hungry beast, he devoured the information obtained discussing the conflict and everything the British offered as intelligence on the biggest Loyalist paramilitaries. He poured over NIS's own documents regarding the past relations these Loyalist groups had with South African intelligence.

O'knomo had been in awe of the way the academic devoted himself to his studies. What was more intriguing were the results Walderhyn delivered. Both the British and Ravenhoof had been of the opinion that their quarry was hiding out somewhere in Belfast or some other city in Northern Ireland where the Protestant radicals had a stronghold. After reviewing the vast sums of information, the academic had a different analysis. "She's somewhere in the Republic," Walderhyn stated with the utmost conviction.

This statement took O'knomo by complete surprise. Sensing his superior needed a better explanation, the academic continued with his report. "As I see it, only two paramilitaries have the resources and organization to both hide and secretly move someone out of the country: one is the Ulster Volunteer Force, the other is the Ulster Defense Association. Of the two, the UVF, as it more commonly called, has a better relationship with South Africa. Reviewing a contemporary history of this group, I've found that it operates extensively throughout the United Kingdom and carries out significant campaigns across the Republic of Ireland.

"Now, two things stick out: one, the UVF is aware of the danger in protecting someone like Ms. Catcher and would not want to keep her in Northern Ireland where the British government has extensive intelligence resources; and two, something I'm seeing captured my attention. I have read quite a few reports discussing a succession of attacks on suspected UVF personnel and safe houses in the Republic by the rival Irish Republican Army. That the IRA would have such good intelligence could only mean they have sources or a source somewhere in the intelligence world. Presumably, Irish intelligence, if I had to place money on it."

"At this moment, a peace negotiation is in the process of being brokered. If the UVF did know who was feeding the IRA intelligence, they would be hard-pressed to carry out any operation at this time; especially, if it would mean working with their own resources and risking exposure. Attacking someone in Irish intelligence directly would certainly have terrible repercussions. The full force of Irish law enforcement and intelligence would be after them. Assuming this possibility, a good strategy to eliminate the IRA's source and protect themselves would be to reach out to a third party. A party that could give their organization distance in what would be a highly controversial matter."

"You think the UVF is hiring Sauwa Catcher?" O'knomo's eyes widened at the revelation.

Walderhyn removed his glasses and rubbed his eyes. "I am making a prediction that Sauwa Catcher is in the Republic of Ireland, not Northern Ireland. And in the next few days, we should be hearing about the mysterious killing of someone connected to intelligence. Furthermore, the killing will be done in a manner that matches the methods known to be used by our little princess."

Detective Sergeant Ryan Youngest stood over the ghost white corpse of what used to be Intelligence officer, Detective Sergeant Marston Donovan. His eyes gazed at the naked body laid out on a stainless-steel tray table. His attention was entirely focused on the words of the medical examiner as he explained the findings of the autopsy. The body looked as if it was a slab of meat being readied for the evening's feast. It was enough to make anyone want to be a vegetarian. The killing of Detective Donovan had created a massive uproar within the Garda, and the examiner's office obligingly gave priority to the case. The autopsy had been conducted and completed within hours of the killing.

The medical examiner, a frail, skeletal figure of a man, stood against an identical table as he spoke. "The good detective died from a punctured liver." The examiner's voice was rough and gravelly. "The object entered into the body through here." He lifted the body slightly to show an inch wide incision into the liver. Afterwards, the object, being a device made of glass, continued to carve through the soft tissue as the detective squirmed and twisted about in pain."

"Glass, you say?" Detective Sergeant Youngest inquired.

"I pulled fragments of glass from the liver and a few other organs," the examiner explained. "It appears to be ordinary window glass that could have been obtained anywhere. It was a solid object that, as near as I can tell, had been forged into a knife-like weapon. It seemed to have had sharp, jagged edges on both sides, which explains the fast insertion into the body. What was really interesting was the strong traces of oleander. The killer must have smeared the blade with the stuff — probably to ensure he died."

Youngest shook his head in amazement. "Oleander? That's not usual, is it? I mean for a gang-style killing, they generally don't take the added step of lacing their blades with poison?"

"Not something I've seen much of in my years," replied the examiner. "What really is surprising is that it wasn't just poison, but oleander in particular. This plant can be purchased at nearly any nursery and has highly toxic properties. A perfect tool for a professional killer: highly lethal, easy to obtain without raising a lot of attention and very hard to trace."

The detective sergeant leaned over the cadaver. "The weapon — were you able to draw any fingerprints from it?"

"There was no handle." The examiner's eyes cocked slightly as if he were on the trail of some great mystery. "Looking at the base of the injury, I found large traces of what turned out to be airplane glue. It looks like the killer constructed an easily disposable weapon with a grip designed to be broken off after impact. All of the material used could be obtained anywhere making it completely dispensable. We have virtually nothing that could narrow down the investigation."

"So, whoever our killer is, he is a highly skilled and seasoned professional carrying out an assassination to look like an everyday underworld slaying." Youngest rubbed his thumbs under his chin as he pondered the matter.

"That would be my guess," the examiner agreed.

"Detective Sergeant?" A voice was suddenly interjected into the conversation. Officer Hilter Dagden, a lean figure of a man in his early-thirties, marched into the examiner's station. He joined Youngest. "Sir, I've talked to the witnesses standing next to the deceased when the incident occurred."

Youngest was slightly amused at the younger man's determination to be so proper and professional. "Go on, what were your findings?"

"Well, sir," Dagden began. "The killer struck with lightning precision. I mean, there must have been fifteen to twenty veteran intelligence detectives standing around, and no one could tell me much of anything. It was as if a ghost did this and disappeared."

"Not a ghost," Youngest sighed as he turned to face his subordinate. "A killer who bides his time and plans methodically." He had long believed it was foolish for the detectives of Ireland's most elite police intelligence units to gather in the same public place at relatively the same time. But, it was in such an upscale section of the city and frequented primarily by tourists and wealthy shoppers. The police were sure it was a place they could meet safely. To the mind of the veteran detective, it was only a matter of time before something like this was destined to happen. "This was certainly a planned killing and done by a professional."

Exiting the examiner's office, the two detectives started down the hall. Dagden was scratching his head. "This case is high profile alright. Before I came down here to meet you, I stopped by the office. People are inquiring all the way up the chain of command, including the Superintendent, about this investigation." Dagden tried to mask his emotions. He was vacillating between nervous anxiety at the thought of getting so much attention from the highest levels of power and excitement at being part of such an important investigation.

The veteran detective could understand his subordinate's mixed feelings. Dagden came from County Cork, where he had begun his career. His first seven years in the Garda was spent working in a small town station in the farmlands. Despite having years of seeing his own share of crimes and emergencies, he felt his big-city colleagues looked down on him as if he came from a mud hut. This had caused Dagden to feel the need to compensate; the need to always try and speak in formal police vocabulary to prove he was every bit the caliber of a policeman as of those in the big city.

"We'll navigate as we have to," Youngest said. "I won't let them slow up the investigation. We'll have to find an alternative place to work, so they don't keep harassing us with demands for the latest information. More high-profile investigations are blown because investigators spend more time in briefings than working the case."

Dagden nodded in agreement. He respected the senior detective — a man he had come to view as the epitome of an investigator. "Sir, what do you think so far?"

Youngest's eyes remained focused as they walked. "It's too early to assume anything. From what I see, someone recruited a skilled professional to target and kill Donovan. We need to be looking into what Donovan was doing to see who would target him."

"By professional, you mean this was no ordinary underworld killing?" the younger detective inquired.

Youngest's eyes remained focused straight ahead. "We have a veteran policeman of the Crime Special Surveillance Unit. A man who collected intelligence on the biggest threats to the country. He lives in a world full of dangerous people. By all accounts, Donovan would not be an easy target. Our assassin took him completely by surprise and used a means of killing him that's nearly impossible to trace and then simply disappeared. No, the one we're looking for is very capable and has killed professional operators like Donovan before."

"It sounds like it will be an adventure." Dagden tightened his lips with a slight sense of dread. He did not relish the idea of chasing phantoms at a time when the power brokers of the force were watching him closely.

CORK REGAN FANCIED himself a veteran soldier of the IRA, even if the totality of his combat service amounted solely to administering punishment to those who ran afoul of the organization. The Lucky Seamus Pub rested in a working-class neighborhood on the north side of Dublin. Apart from being a favorite watering hole for the working-class crowd, the Dublin brigade of the IRA used it as their headquarters.

Regan entered the establishment. He was sure he was going to be given another job — some local hood who had defied the command's edicts. Strolling through the door, the barkeep immediately waved him to the far end of the counter. The pub was nearly deserted. There were only a few pockets of retirees scattered about enjoying their daily pint. Aside from the low murmurs of conversation, a soft version of 'Oh Danny Boy' playing over the audio system was the only other sound breaking the silence. Casually, Regan made his way down the lengthy bar. He stopped beside an elderly fellow in his mid-sixties taking up a stool in the corner. The man was armed with a tall mug of Blond ale and an Aging Room brand Meduro Toro cigar. The man's attentions were fixed entirely on the newspaper resting on the table in front of him. Sliding onto the stool next to the man, Regan folded his hands and waited to be acknowledged.

"I've got a bit of a job for you," the older man began; his attention remaining focused on the newspaper.

"That's the usual story," Regan sniffed, indifferently. "Who am I setting straight? And is this just punishing the lad, or am I sending a message to everyone?"

For the first time since the conversation started, the older man looked up and faced the bear-like figure next to him. "This is a different type of job."

Regan's eyes cocked slightly. "I'm listening."

"We've suffered a serious setback." The older man stated in a stern businesslike manner. "You've heard about the recent killing of that Garda detective?"

"I heard something about some copper biting it yesterday," Regan replied.

"That copper was working for us," the older man stated. "He was helping us dismantle the Loyalist network here in the Republic."

"Oh shit!" the bigger man was astonished.

"Bad enough he was a loyal man to the cause, but his death has crippled an essential operation we've had going on." The older man continued, "I'm sending you and your crew to look into this matter. This order is coming from the highest level. We need to retaliate to show that the IRA can and will protect their assets. Find out who carried out the killing and eliminate them. A message must be sent."

Regan contained himself, though inside he was feeling the pride of being assigned a task with such a serious mission. This was not the usual mindless beating delivered to some local drug dealer or a professional informant getting his jaw smashed for talking to the police. This was a real operation that needed to be carried out. "Who am I tracking then?"

The older man took a drag off his cigar and exhaled a thick cloud of smoke into the atmosphere. "Our people in the north have it on good authority that a rogue commander in the UVF might have orchestrated this. If so, we think the killing wasn't carried out using local resources. Instead, if it was a commander acting on his own, he must have reached out to a freelancer to do it. We think the UVF is working through contacts they have here in Dublin's criminal circles to augment the operation. This is very much your territory, and I told my superiors that you could handle this."

"And, I will sir," Regan replied confidently. "I know some folks who have done business with the Loyalists. I can shake some trees."

"Shake gently," the older man cautioned. "This is a high-profile killing of a decorated police hero. The Garda is putting a lot of resources into finding the killer themselves. Don't draw attention to yourself and get caught in their crosshairs."

Regan shrugged his shoulders and waved his hands in

a subordinate manner that indicated he understood. The older man returned to his paper. "We don't need an interrogation. Find and eliminate the problem on sight are your orders."

"Will do," the bigger man replied, as he rose from his stool.

14

Sauwa cautiously progressed across the street toward the Oriental grocery store. The cold chill in the air brushed across her exposed neck with an icy touch. Turning up the collar of her flannel, she tried in vain to cover up. Inside the store, she was hit by a gust of warm air that came as a much-needed relief. However, it came with the added price of a powerful aroma that burned her nostrils. The icky smells common with foreign foods, spices and herbs of the eastern world were strong, and she needed some time to adjust.

Walking to the checkout counter, she saw a heavy-set, middle-aged Asian woman. "Ma'am?" She spoke quietly as she approached.

The woman turned from her black and white television featuring some Chinese soap opera. "What do you need?" Her English was lightly accented, while her manner was cold and snobby.

"I'm looking for Victor," Sauwa replied. "I was sent by a mutual acquaintance, James Clark."

The older woman viewed the young lady across the counter carefully. "Wait right here," she said sternly, as she rose from her seat and marched into the backroom. A few minutes later, a tall, beanpole of a man emerged. He looked ragged, wearing a long, scraggly beard, with soiled skin from working with God knows what and a highly stained collared shirt.

"I'm Victor." His voice was heavily accented in Russian. Though his features made him look like he came from one of the Central Asian countries that made up what used to be the Soviet Union. "You know Mr. Clark, James Clark?"

"Yes, he's a dark-haired man of medium build, in the business of providing markets for special products and services." Sauwa was, of course, describing Banker, who was either James Clark or used the name as another alias when dealing with certain people.

"If I called him at his place, he would know you?" Victor asked as he reached for the phone.

"He's on personal business right now. He should be at the Rory Club in about an hour." Sauwa remained stoic as she stared at the tall man. Her eyes darted to the phone as he made his call.

"I believe you," Victor said, satisfied the young woman was genuine. "You are then in need of my services?"

"I might be. But first, I want to talk to you about it," she replied.

The man smiled, revealing a row of nicotine-stained teeth. "I like you already. Come." He waved her to follow him into the back room. Sauwa came right up behind him just as he was about to go through the entryway. She figured if he was leading her into a trap, being right up against him would leave an assailant little ability to strike without hitting Victor. Pressed against her stomach, she held a long knife tightly in hand, ready to stab anyone coming at her from either direction or from the tall man himself. It was unlikely she would be accosted from both sides in such a narrow passageway that would offer little room to maneuver.

They walked through the doorway into a room that functioned as a supply room, office, and living quarters. To Sauwa's relief, aside from the middle-aged woman, the room was deserted. The woman, seeing the two enter, returned to her post at the checkout counter, leaving Sauwa and Victor alone.

Victor turned to see the partial end of Sauwa's blade, hidden loosely under her flannel coat. "I trust you are confident that this is not a means to harm you." He sank into a worn couch, entirely unconcerned.

"Just taking precautions," Sauwa responded as she tucked the weapon into her belt. "You know how it works."

Victor smiled. "I've been in this business a long time. You're not the first, and you won't be the last."

Sauwa remained standing and kept her back to a near wall as she carefully scouted for any other entry points or exits. The fact that Victor had no security made her a tad nervous. She had found those in his line of work always had someone nearby in case things went bad.

As if reading her mind, Victor spoke up. "I imagine you expected to see some type of protection for a man in my business. Well, I should tell you my protection is a very well connected and extensive network that handles its own affairs. I don't need to have the unwanted complication of armed men hanging about when many of my clients, and the network I belong to, gives me considerable means to track down and punish those who would rob me or otherwise disrupt a highly essential system used by very powerful people. I also don't do business with those who are not vouched for by trusted sources. James does not recommend clients who are of dubious ethics."

"Most of your clientele is of dubious business ethics I should think," Sauwa stated, her tone thick with the sarcasm of suspicion.

"Like any business culture," Victor shrugged, "the black market is no different. There are those who try to maintain a sense of honesty when conducting their dealings because they see the greater benefits of it. There are those who are too consumed by greed and cannot see beyond the immediate prize. It's, again, a matter of choosing who you to do business with carefully."

Sauwa studied the man for a long time. This was not the first time she had been involved with the Walhalla network. But, it was a network that was hard to properly understand. She was about to make a big decision with a man she didn't know, in a world where she had no recourse. Victor said nothing. He sat quietly as he let the young woman make up her mind.

Finally, with a sigh, she slipped the knapsack off her shoulder and placed it on the coffee table in front of Victor. Victor made no move for the bag; he sat still studying the woman's face. She was hesitant but eventually nodded slightly acknowledging she wanted to do business.

Victor reached over and opened the knapsack. He began pulling out the stacks of money. Carefully he counted it with the meticulous eye of an accountant as

Sauwa watched silently. After about an hour he stood up, stretched and looked at his client. "I count one hundred thousand pounds."

"That's correct," she replied quietly. After expenses, she still had six thousand pounds left over from the money Simon had given her back in Northern Ireland.

"Very good," Victor sighed. "I take five thousand as my fee for making the transaction."

"Thank you," she responded.

Victor took his payment from the collection of money, and then gathered the rest into a cardboard box that looked like it had been used recently to store donuts. Placing a lid on it, he looked up. "Where is this money supposed to go?"

"Sydney, Australia," she said as if fighting to hold back the words.

Victor slid the box off to the side. "That will take some time."

"I'm in no hurry," Sauwa said quietly. "It will be some time before it can be retrieved. At least six months, if not a year."

"That will work then for both of us." Victor folded his hands under his chin. "Such a large sum will have to be arranged." The two said nothing as they stared at each other trying to assess the other's thoughts. Victor's eyes locked on the box at the edge of the table containing her money. She took his actions as a last chance offer to take her money back and pull out if she was still unsure about proceeding.

Though the urge to retrieve her money swam in her head, her rational mind realized that if not this man and not now, her only other option would be to carry all the money she had in the world with her to be smuggled out of the country by criminals she didn't know and were taking her to an unknown place. The idea that she would be robbed and killed instantly was all too evident. As far as she knew Victor, or the man who vouched for him, was her only alternative to move her money.

She nodded her head and turned away. Taking this as a sign she wanted to go through with the transaction, he picked up the box as he rose to his feet. He walked back into the adjoining office, away from where she could see him. He returned several minutes later with a folded piece of paper in his hand. Handing it to her, he raised his finger in a warning gesture. "Once you leave here, the deal is final. Your money will no longer exist in this country. You will have to go to Australia to retrieve it. Here is the address of the location in your requested city to which your money will be paid."

Taking the piece of paper from him, Sauwa took a quick peek to see what was written. She folded it and placed it in her pocket. Victor handed her another small piece of paper. This time it was a receipt from his store with a few scribbles written across it.

"Hand this to the proprietor of the store in the address," Victor said, as she took the receipt. "It will be your means of identifying yourself to him."

Sauwa reluctantly took the receipt and slipped it into her pocket next to the address. This was the point of no return for her. She was trusting a complete stranger operating out of a low-end store with all her money. She could only hope it would be at the designated location when she got there. With a nod, the business transaction was concluded.

15

Jeffery Talamadge was intrigued and, at the same time, dubious. Ravenhoof had explained the conclusion his people in Pretoria reached; they presumed Sauwa Catcher was hiding somewhere in the Republic of Ireland. The MI-5 officer thought it rather brash that some intelligence service in Africa should be advising him on the actions of a group his own organization had been investigating for years. He was quite familiar with the workings of Loyalist paramilitaries like the Ulster Volunteer Force. He didn't need some South African intelligence types dictating to him about what the UVF might have done. However, his vanity aside, his professional instincts told him he could not simply dismiss their assumption entirely.

Though the Loyalists quite proudly took credit for their exploits — they certainly had their own legion of hardened, professional killers to call upon. Yet they possessed the common sense to know when to employ the means to distance themselves from the nastier or more politically compromising affairs. Similarly, the Ulster Defense Association tended to use the extended arm of the Ulster Freedom Fighters to engage in the more brutal and controversial operations the UDA itself avoided. It wasn't unreasonable to think the UVF would be any different by using a freelancer to carry out a killing that would be difficult for them to do personally.

Still, the UVF didn't shy away from much. Whatever they would need a freelancer for would have to be big and controversial. This was all just a theory that may or may not be true. Talamadge was anxious to bring this up in his meeting with his counterpart, Ravenhoof. To be safe, Talamadge had opted to stay focused primarily on Northern Ireland. Probing his people working the Northern Ireland beat, he tried to find out what intelligence traffic they were getting regarding mysterious folks suddenly materializing in close-knit Protestant neighborhoods, or UVF types becoming secretive all of a sudden. At the same time, to appease the South Africans, he had sent a request to the Garda asking about any recent killings of prominent Republicans, IRA sympathizers or any other high-profile types.

The South African theory began to take on substance when he was notified that a high-ranking veteran Intelligence officer of the Garda had been assassinated by an unknown assailant the day before. He and Ravenhoof thought it a long shot but requested more information from the Irish government. As the details came in from the Garda, the handiwork was becoming clearer. Though he had read of multitude ways Sauwa had dispatched her targets, the calculated, methodical way this assassination was carried out was all too familiar. For Talamadge, it was as if reading a continuance of the files he had been pouring over the last few days. When he conferred with Ravenhoof to ensure he was not getting tunnel vision, he was thankful to find that Ravenhoof was of the exact same mind. Both men believed the signature tactics used were that of their young assassin or, at the very least, it was a good possibility.

With lightning speed, Talamadge was on the phone to the Garda asking about the investigation and who was running it. Ravenhoof was, at the same time, jetting to the embassy to contact O'knomo and make arrangements for his possible travel to the Republic.

CORK REGAN KNEW the underworld of Dublin like the back of his hand. He explained that the Prod (Protestant) terrorists had possibly used a freelancer to kill Donovan, and they would have probably worked the deal using intermediaries. Regan figured out who the Prods would use immediately. The UVF was particular about who they worked with in Ireland. That narrowed the field considerably. There were even fewer black market facilitators that had the intelligence to be involved in such an operation; this fact narrowed the field even more.

Not wanting to let word get around that he was trolling the streets looking for whoever helped the UVF, the IRA heavy opted to work more discretely. Instead of working the usual informants the way the police did, he decided to make the rounds of the establishments these men used as their fronts. Since black marketers needed ways to be approached that didn't require suspicious meetings on darkened street corners, they all owned businesses that made discussion with all types of societal elements look casual and above board — that meant pubs and nightclubs. It was a simple science really. Regan was a known IRA enforcer. His showing up for a drink automatically elicited certain reactions. The uninvolved parties would be inclined to exploit any potential business opportunities. They would talk him up, trying to intimate what goods they had access to or services they were in a position to offer. The man he would be looking for would have his hands full hiding the assassin and would be less inclined to have the IRA hanging about his business. He would be evasive in wanting to open any dealings until his current client was gone.

The Rory Club was packed when Regan and four of the toughest members of his crew entered. This establishment had been the third on their list; the previous two suspects had been cleared relatively quickly. Low set neon lights, coupled with a song from the Cranberries coming over the loudspeaker gave the place a trendy futuristic atmosphere. Keeping the group tight, the five men strolled over to the bar. A gorgeous redhead in her early twenties manned the bar. Seeing the men seat themselves at the far end of the counter, she hurried over to take their order.

"Can I help you lot?" she asked, smiling pleasantly. Her accent was clearly British, which irked the IRA men.

"Just some whiskey. Some Tennessee stuff, if you've got any?" Regan opened, forcing a smile on his face.

"Of course, hold on," the bartender smiled pleasantly as she moved to fill the order.

"Is Rudy Sheehan in by any chance?" Regan asked before the girl had a chance to walk away.

"No, he left a couple hours ago," she replied.

Regan's interest peeked. "I'm trying to find him. You know where he might be?"

The girl shook her head. "Na, I'm afraid not. He's been popping in and out all week."

"Really?" the IRA man's eyes widened. "You've got no idea where he's been off to?"

The girl again shook her head. Waving her off to continue fetching the drinks, Regan looked over at the other men.

"Figure we've found our man?" one of the men asked.

"Maybe," Regan replied. "I want to have a wee chat with him before I make any judgment."

DETECTIVE SERGEANT RYAN YOUNGEST was surprised, if not perplexed when he found himself sitting in the office of his commander, opposite a man from British MI-5. There was also another man he understood to be from South Africa in the office; he still wasn't quite clear on his position. The commander, Ian Rose, barely heeded the pleasantries of introductions before attempting to take control of the conversation.

"These men are here regarding your Donovan investigation Detective Sergeant," Commander Rose said. "They think they may have information pertinent to your case."

"Well, it's all still speculative at this...," Talamadge tried to answer before being cut off.

Rose quickly interrupted. "They see parallels between your case and similar killings carried out by a person they are looking for."

"You must have come here in quite a hurry," Youngest replied, shifting his head between his commander and the two men. He was not quite sure whom to address.

Sensing the moment, Talamadge quickly took up the conversation. "Just to be clear, we're not exactly sure this is the person we're chasing. However, the information we've received regarding your victim seems to fit the methods used by our killer. It further narrows the field that the analysis our researchers have done presumes our killer is most likely here in the Republic and is probably being protected by one of the larger Loyalist paramilitaries."

Youngest sat back; his interest heightened. "And you think this person would have been contracted by the UVF to kill Detective Sergeant Donovan? Who is this person and, if on the run, why would he expose himself by carrying out an assassination that would be guaranteed to bring him a lot of police attention?"

"That is why we want to discuss the matter with you," Ravenhoof, the South African suddenly interjected. "It is a theory and one we need to investigate further. But, as you have said, the killing of a high-level police officer in your Counter Intelligence unit would be a big prize for a group like the UVF."

"It would also, as you have pointed out, bring down a powerful response from your organization," Talamadge spoke up. "Using a freelancer you can distance yourself from would be a logical decision, especially if that freelancer is a highly skilled, professional killer who is beholden to you for her safety."

"Still," Youngest replied, "I mean, this seems like wishful thinking on your part."

"Possibly," Talamadge nodded, "which is why we want

to discuss our theory with you."

"Of course, you need to discuss this," Commander Rose interjected abruptly. "Our department wants to give you our full cooperation."

"Provided you're equally forthcoming in sharing your information," Youngest retook control of the conversation clearly irritating his superior.

"Of course," Talamadge smiled. "Provided we have control over who sees it, we can offer you what we have to assist you in your own investigation."

"Good, then it's settled." Rose was up and walking about. "We will move your meeting to a secure briefing room, where you can continue your discussion. I will stay involved to ensure good cooperation between our agencies."

The meeting ended with Youngest, Talamadge and Ravenhoof being shown out of the office. Left alone in the hall to speak amongst themselves, the mood shifted and became more suspicious in nature.

"You really think my case is connected?" Youngest, was not sure he liked the idea of working with spooks. His experience with the shadowy world of espionage and intrigue had left him with a foul taste for the whole business.

"That is why we want to speak to you first," Ravenhoof replied.

Talamadge pointed his thumb toward the office they had just left. "Your boss seems rather anxious for our help."

The trio began to walk. Youngest pursed his lips. "This is a high profile case alright, with the highest echelons of the department paying close attention to it. If you can offer us a viable suspect, he'd be dancing on his desk. If that suspect is a highly sought professional assassin wanted by someone as prestigious as British intelligence, then it's even a bigger prize for us."

"Assuming we're right, and this was something orchestrated by a terrorist group," Ravenhoof rubbed his balding head, "it all becomes predicated on why they would go to such great lengths to assassinate Detective Donovan?"

Making it to a deserted conference room, Youngest ushered the two visitors inside. Shutting the door, the Detective Sergeant turned to them. "I have a theory. Now that you're here telling me all this, it is starting to make sense. Donovan investigated a lot of different things including terrorist groups, both Republican and Loyalist. He largely focused on their activities south of the border. Quiet comments have intimated he had sympathies for the IRA and the Republican cause. I've also heard that certain people known to be working with the UVF here have been assassinated, and the assailants were thought to be IRA. Suspected safe houses and other facilities used for UVF operations have also been attacked, and IRA forces were suspected."

"You're saying Donovan may have been passing intelligence to the IRA about Loyalist operations in your country?" Ravenhoof took a breath, as he processed what had just been said.

"I'm saying, I thought my theory was wild at best. It is starting to sound more like a logical consideration after what you've been saying." Youngest was beside himself. The idea of a respected and decorated detective of the Garda being an informant for a terrorist group was not something any policeman wanted to consider.

16

Rudy Sheehan didn't know what to make of the situation. When he got back to the Rory Club, Kella, his new barmaid, was quick to explain about some rough looking types asking about him. Kella had no interest in Rudy's business affairs. She was simply working the bar to pay her way through medical school. Still, she had good sense and street instincts. She instantly figured the men for some hardened criminal types.

Kella's instincts had proven fairly accurate in the past when she was concerned about someone. Since he was currently hiding someone who, he was sure, had committed a serious crime in his city, he was already concerned about who might come around asking questions. The problem was, who were these guys and what were they after? Was it even related to his charge or to some other affair he'd been embroiled in?

His questions were answered when Kella's face went blank with concern as she raised her hand and pointed. Turning, Rudy felt a cold chill suddenly crawl down his spine. The image of Cork Regan was a familiar one in the Dublin criminal world; he was someone everyone feared. Regan never went asking for someone unless they had run afoul of the IRA. Regan walked from the far end of the club and made his way toward Rudy at the bar. Regan's men fanned out to surround him.

It wasn't hard for Rudy to deduce that his club had been watched. Someone shadowing the place called Regan the moment he returned. That the IRA's top enforcer in the city was so interested in speaking to him gave him definite cause for concern.

"Rudy Sheehan," Cork greeted in a manner sounding like an old friend but came across in a more sinister manner.

"Tend to the boxes in the back," Rudy commanded Kella. "And, take your time about it."

Kella looked concerned as she nodded and slipped quickly into the back room. The IRA men did not chase after her. Hopefully, they had no interest in her or saw her as a potential witness to anything they intended.

Cork took up a seat at the bar. "Ah, Rudy, he began. "I was just driving about with the lads when we thought we'd stop by."

"I understand you were looking for me earlier."

"I was, to be certain," the enforcer cracked a sinister looking smile. "You see, a few days back, a detective with the Garda was killed — assassinated is a better word. Marston Donovan worked for the intelligence boys, you know — the Crime Special Surveillance Unit."

"I heard about it. Nasty business." Rudy kept his composure, though he could feel a cold pool of sweat forming.

Regan continued, "It is indeed. Especially, since the killer hasn't been caught. Hell, a suspect hasn't even been identified. This makes certain types whom I answer to kinda angry. Such a decorated lad working for the service of his people gets offed by some piece of shit, and no one knows who he is."

"I can imagine. Bad stuff all around." Rudy kept his words minimal as he listened intently. The message was being received loud and clear. Donovan had been the IRA's guy, and now someone had to answer to them for it.

"True," Regan continued. "So, as a favor to some friends, I said I'd look into it. You know, ask around, and see if anyone knows anything."

"Then, that's why you're here?" Rudy asked innocently. "Asking around."

Regan nodded his head as he raised his eyes slightly. "Something like that. See, from what I've learned about the killing, I'm inclined to think it wasn't some punk off the street. No, I assume a professional was called in since a detective with criminal intelligence wouldn't be a job for local talent. And, that professional would need someone for support. Someone who could set up a safe house to work from and obtain needed materials and supplies."

Rudy shrugged. "And, you're wondering if I know anything about it?"

Regan remained silent, as he nodded his head.

"I don't know a thing," Rudy stated as he leaned casually up against the cabinets displaying alcohol and feigned a look of ignorance. At this point, he felt his nerves jumping. He couldn't tell if this was all a fishing expedition or a grace period to save his own ass. In either case, admitting that he had assisted in killing someone important to the IRA could only end with him dead.

The other consideration running through his mind was, who should he be concerned about from the other side? He had not forgotten that powerful forces had dispatched his young charge to Dublin and forced him to assist in her operation. Even if turning her over granted amnesty from the IRA, it could very well place him in just as dangerous of a position from her employers.

Reviewing his options carefully, Rudy determined his best play was to protect his charge. He had made all the arrangements for Sauwa to depart the following night. She would be gone and so would the liability. Any other option, as he saw it, only ended with him as a corpse.

"You sure you haven't heard anything or been approached by anyone looking to acquire your services and what not?" Regan studied the club owner carefully. Rudy maintained a casually innocent pose and seemed to be completely unfazed.

Shrugging his shoulders, the enforcer rose from his chair. "Well then, sorry to bother you with all this. Thanks for the time." He started off, his entourage following in tow.

Rudy kept his pose until he was sure they were gone. Only when he saw the doors to the club open and close did he finally take a deep breath. He had figured the mysterious young woman he knew only as Bridget, or by her nickname, Swan, had been involved in the detective's killing. He had not wanted any of this. He was determined to find a way to survive.

Not sure what to think, he ran through every possible angle. Rudy tried to figure out the situation in order to plan his next move. The IRA might be pursuing wild theories to flush out a lead to the assassin, or they were onto him? Had some word gotten out that had brought the IRA to him? Cork Regan had a reputation throughout the Dublin criminal scene as a violent enforcer. Rudy decided that if the IRA knew anything for sure, the visit he had just suffered would have had grossly different results. His suspicions were confirmed. He was protecting a hired killer — a ruthless, professional killer at that. It could prove equally deadly to consider any plan of betrayal.

Deciding the IRA was still unsure of anything and grasping at straws, he felt the safer route was sticking to his current plan — protecting Sauwa and getting her out of the country. He would be rid of her in a day's time along with any connection to the whole sordid affair; something he definitely wanted.

After waiting a few hours to avoid attracting attention, or any IRA heavies lurking about, Rudy jumped in his car. He headed immediately to the warehouse where Sauwa was staying. With the IRA looming, he felt it wise to alert his charge to take additional precautions. He pulled out of the club parking lot and headed down the street. He was oblivious to the figure on a motorcycle following him. Rudy drove carefully as he navigated the streets of the city. It was mid-afternoon when he pulled up outside the warehouse. He walked up to the doorway and waited. That it was a surprise visit to the safe house was not lost on him. He wanted to make sure Swan was aware of his arrival before entering.

"Hello, Swan!" he bellowed. "It's Banker. I'm coming in." With that, he gingerly stepped inside. The darkness was mild, but still dark enough to mask any traps or setups that might be around. He made it to her room to find it empty. It still looked lived in, but all the clues suggested she had only just departed. Banker remained standing in the doorway unsure of his next move. He entered the room and heard a click that sounded like the hammer on a gun. Raising his hands, he began to shiver slightly as he waited.

"Why are you here? This is not part of our protocol." The cold stern tone of Sauwa's voice was too familiar to him by now.

"It's important, or I would not be here." Banker defended himself listening to the slight sound of muffled feet.

Turning around, Banker was looking at a frizzy-haired woman who had been resting when she heard him come in. He thought how most normal women would kill a man if he saw her in such a state. "I need to warn you about a recent development."

Sauwa remained silent; her cold stare said everything. "The IRA is giving me trouble about some business issues. While they're hanging about, I want to limit our dealings. So, here is the information regarding your departure tomorrow night." He walked over and slipped Sauwa a piece of paper. She opened it to find a pier number, a ship name, a code name to use for her contact on the ship as well as the code name she was to use. It also had written the passwords that were to be used upon meeting. "When will you have your documents?" Banker asked nervously.

"I went this morning to where you told me to go. A woman took my photo, and said she was putting a priority on my documents." Sauwa sighed, as she brushed her long hair over her shoulders. "My understanding is that I should have them by tomorrow evening around six."

"Good." Banker was pacing nervously. He was walking a thin line. He didn't want to tell a professional killer that the IRA was looking for her. Such an explanation would invariably mark him as a liability. Still, he needed to take more precautions with her and couldn't operate as if it were business as usual. If he could get her to handle the remaining things without his assistance, then he needn't deal with her anymore after this meeting. "Then you're all set. After you get your documents call me to let me know if there are any problems. If I don't hear from you by six thirty, I'll assume everything went well."

Sauwa nodded. She could tell the man was more on edge than usual, and his dealings with the IRA affected him more than he was letting on. However, she didn't ask anything; he would probably lie to her if she did. She studied him for a minute trying to ascertain whether this was a lead up to betrayal or the actions of a nervous man who couldn't wait to be rid of her. Eventually, she determined it was the latter. She also agreed with his advice that it would be safer to carry on without him. The less he knew of her activities and movements the better. What she got from Banker's disclosure was the IRA was looking for her. What they knew of his involvement was still uncertain. Still, he hadn't seemed to betray her by his mannerisms, and he had quickly come to warn her.

She reminded herself that men like Banker survived by assessing the odds and going in the direction that gave him the best chance of survival. In this case, her benefactor's attempts to veil the true story while providing a warning indicated he wasn't sure if it was the IRA or her that presented the most danger.

Thanking Banker for bringing the issue to her attention, she carefully pulled out the Browning automatic she kept under the bed. He watched, as she carefully fingered the piece, explaining details of the weapon, its make and abilities. All of it was done as an indirect reminder to the club owner that she was a rather dangerous person in her own right — there could be deadly repercussions if he had thoughts of giving her up.

Banker was awash with sweat as he exited the young woman's room and then the warehouse. He had gotten the message of both parties loud and clear. Leaping into his car he pulled out from the parking lot and onto the street heading back to the club. As he left, he was oblivious to the motorcycle rider parked somewhat hidden just across the way.

Regan's plan had worked like a charm. He had suspected from the beginning the owner of the Rory Club had been the man involved in Donovan's death. The idea of beating a confession out of someone often proved a waste of time and prone to faulty information. Instead, just watching where Mr. Rudy Sheehan went all the time seemed more practical. It had been his experience that throwing a scare into a man tended to make him desperate and take poorly thought out actions. In this case, he went straight to the location where he was hiding the assassin.

He was enjoying a round of pool at his favorite pub when the barkeep reported a phone call for him. It was the motorcyclist; he gave him the address of the warehouse. Regan jotted the information down and ended the conversation with a few words of gratitude before rounding up his men from various places in the establishment. With the team assembled, Regan called over to the barkeep — a thin, frail man of elderly years — who proceeded to lead the enforcers into the back room. Through the storage area and down a hall, the barkeep pushed passed a collection of old boxes before pressing a lever hidden inconspicuously behind some old pipes. Everyone watched as the wall in front of them cracked open. The barkeep pushed the wall all the way back to reveal a hidden room.

Moving inside, the men found themselves standing in an office. It was used at times as their headquarters to plan missions and conduct business. With the help of Regan, the barkeep removed bricks from the floor and dragged a large canvas bag out from a hole. Bringing the bag to the center of the office, Regan unzipped it and removed some plastic protective sheeting. He then began pulling out an assortment of weapons — mostly handguns — and laying them on the ground along with several boxes of ammunition. As a rule, Regan, like most operatives, carried guns only when they were on a mission. Otherwise, getting caught ensured both prison time and the loss of already scarce weapons.

Each man chose his preferred weapon and the correct box of ammo. They carefully loaded the magazines and cylinder chambers before stashing them in their belts under their coats and sweatshirts. When they were finished, the barkeep handed Regan a set of keys.

"This car's clean?" Regan asked as he pocketed the keys.

"Untraceable," the barkeep replied with an expressionless face. "The car has papers, license plates, no warrants or tickets."

"Good," Regan nodded. "Then we're all set. We'll call you when it's finished. Once it's done, call the boss and let him know."

The barkeep nodded silently as the enforcers exited the room.

SAUWA WAS ENGROSSED in her book when she heard the sound of a glass bottle being kicked across the concrete floor of the warehouse. It was part of her informal security system. At night, she had scattered cans and bottles on the floor in the main area. People prowling about tended to overlook such innocuous things as simple debris and did not get concerned. Quickly, throwing off her shoes, she padded over to the bed where she retrieved her gun and two additional magazines of ammo. In her stocking feet, she padded quietly out of the room and down the hall in the direction of the shower area.

A little way down the hall she stopped. When she was sure she was immersed in darkness, she slid against the wall and knelt down. Earlier, she had taken the additional precaution of killing the power to the hallway lights. Figuring that in a fight she would likely be the defender, she wanted to deny her aggressors any advantage. The only light offered in the hall showed from her room. She had shut the door on her way out, leaving the hallway nearly pitch black except for the illuminated sliver outlining her door.

With weapon in hand and hammer cocked ready to fire, she waited silently. Even in the distance, she could clearly make out the sounds of several people walking about in the building. That noise became clearer as she heard them entering at the far end of the hall and heading in her direction. At the late hour and the number of people, she could assume whoever she was dealing with had violent intentions.

The footsteps became louder as the group started up the hall. They moved with confidence. That told her they were men accustomed to violence. No timidity or hesitation as they strode up the hall. However, by their movements, it was easy to tell they were not professional soldiers, police or trained guerrillas. They all wore footwear that echoed with each step on the concrete — workers or tactical boots, maybe even cowboy boots. Professional operators would have chosen sneakers, or some other form of soft footwear, just as she herself had gone to her socks to mask her movements.

Instead of spreading out and moving along the wall to prevent someone shooting at all of them, these invaders were moving in a tight group right down the center of the hall. Sauwa guessed she was dealing with gangsters or heavies sent for some purpose yet unknown.

Readying her weapon, Sauwa began taking deep breaths as she felt her adrenaline rise. Each footstep brought the impending battle closer. She wasn't scared, but she had been in enough gun battles to know what could happen to someone when their nervous system took over.

In the scant light, she began to make out the outlines of a few of the men. She waited until they opened the door. They had been in the darkness so long that the sudden burst of light would temporarily blind them and destroy their night vision. She would need every edge if she were going to survive. She lowered her eyes and raised her weapon slightly and prepared.

With a powerful kick, the door to her room flew open. In that moment Sauwa raised her eyes to clearly see the figures of five men standing close together just outside of her room. She lifted her Browning automatic until she was seeing through the rear sights lined up with the front sights pointed directly at the men ahead of her. Pressing the trigger, the hallway was soon exploding with thunderous echoes as she unleashed rapid fire on the stunned gathering.

Even over the cannon-like booms of .45 caliber bullets, she could hear the screams of the men as the lead tore viciously into their bodies. As they fell away from the door, she could see splashes of blood flying through the air letting her know she was hitting her targets. With the trained instincts of a seasoned combat soldier, she carefully rotated her weapon a few centimeters from side to side trying to hit as many as she could in the short time available.

Bodies briefly entered and exited from the wall of light as the assailants hysterically moved about not knowing what to do. While they had administered plenty of violence in their time, they were virtual strangers to being in an actual gun battle and being on the receiving end. Men fell to the ground screaming in horrific agony, as others tripped over each other and themselves trying to get away.

The whole episode lasted less than a few seconds. But, it felt as though it had been hours when the shooting stopped, and the Browning's upper receiver was in locked back ejected position signaling she had exhausted her magazine. With her weapon silenced, she could now hear the howls of injured men lying on the ground.

Ejecting the spent magazine, she quickly inserted a fresh one. She held her ground as she heard the voice of a man, she presumed to be the leader, attempting to call out orders. "Get to cover! We're under a fucking attack! Get to fucking cover!"

She could make out three bodies flopping about on the floor as she heard the sounds of two more stumbling in the darkness trying to get away. Rising to her feet, Sauwa slid against the wall as she moved up on her assailants. The one she assumed to be the leader crawled into her room. Coming to the first two, still in the hallway, she fired two quick rounds into the upper torso and head of each of the injured men. Staying just outside of the doorway, she peeked into the room to see a large, bull of a man trying to turn over enough to reach the waist of his pants. Blood oozed from his arm and leg into thick pools on the floor and his one good arm was working to stabilize himself while trying to reach for what she presumed was his gun. He was entirely oblivious to her peeking through the doorway looking at him.

She turned back to the two other men lying in the hall. In the clear light, their eyes were hollow and staring into the darkness. One, a pool of blood and brain matter encircling his head like an aura; the other, a defined hole in the chest cavity shielding the heart. Both were dead.

From her place in the doorway, Sauwa now turned slightly to angle herself and sight in on the other man. He turned just in time to see a young girl, looking like a ghostly figure staring back at him from behind a gun. He attempted to speak. Before he could get any words out, she fired a shot that landed directly through his left eye and exploded out the back of his head spraying the floor behind him.

As if on robotic programming, she darted down the hall past the three bodies. She could hear the sounds of glass bottles and cans as the other two men stumbled in the darkness. At the end of the hall, she dashed through the doorway. The main room of the warehouse was pitch black, except for the faint light coming in through the windows. She could hear the sounds of the terrified men tripping and uttering a litany of curse words as they tried to navigate the darkness.

With her night vision destroyed, Sauwa made her way to the power box. Cracking it open, she flipped a switch and instantly the warehouse lit up. The two men were standing feebly in the middle of a large room blinded and debilitated. She didn't wait for them to get their bearings before she sighted in and took her first two shots. They tore through the torso of the first man, who dropped to the ground and began crying out. Confused and still partially blinded, the other man turned to try and see what was happening. He looked back just in time to see the flash from a corner and the horrifying sound of a gun being fired before he felt a powerful force explode through his stomach with another following right through his throat.

With both men on the ground bleeding out, Sauwa maneuvered her way to them. Moving within a few feet she raised her weapon. The first man attempted to make a plea for mercy before a bullet punched through the soft skin of his chin. The other man was gasping and choking but said nothing as the final bullet exploded through his head.

Satisfied both were dead, Sauwa turned and ran back to her room. Looking down the hall, she could see the bodies of the first two men lying motionless. She moved carefully, watching for any signs one of them might still be alive. The blood splatters were uninterrupted from where the corpses lay. They hadn't moved since they fell. Sliding around the door frame into her room, weapon held at the ready, she came in to see the third gunman lying on his side exactly as he had died.

The immense thundering sound of .45 caliber gunfire echoing loudly in the concrete corridors would have been heard by anyone within the immediate vicinity. She was aware of the night watchmen who hung about in some of the other nearby warehouses. It was easy to surmise that they had heard the entire gunfight and had already reported it to the police. The clock had started ticking when she fired the first shot.

Satisfied her assailants were no longer a threat, Sauwa felt her energy drain. She had been on an emotional adrenaline high during the entire fight and now her body was crashing as it receded. Still able to function, though now operating with the faculties of someone slightly intoxicated, she threw on her shoes and reached for her bag. Thankfully, she had been prepared for a quick escape since she had assassinated Donovan.

Changing out of her flannel pants, she quickly threw on a pair of jeans and her flannel coat. Within a minute she was dressed and packed. Her last act was to hurdle the Browning far out into the sea. She had taken the precaution of loading her magazines with rubber gloves to limit any fingerprints. Police may find them throughout the room but not necessarily on the bullet casings.

Flinging her bergen over her shoulder, she raced out the room for the last time. Retrieving her motorcycle from under a canvas cover in the far corner of the main room, Sauwa wheeled it out the entry door. Leaping onto it, she revved the engine until it roared to life before riding into the darkness.

17

Detective Sergeant Ryan Youngest pressed his fist to his lips as he absorbed the information from the two intelligence officers. The story he was hearing was crazy — almost absurd. It sounded like a weird plot from a cheap spy novel. At some level, he felt foolish even entertaining the idea. However, the South African, Coors Ravenhoof, continued to explain about Sauwa Catcher; this professional killer who was previously in the employ of his government. The MI-5 operative, Jeffery Talamadge, discussed her extensive history carrying out acts of assassinations and terror throughout the United Kingdom.

"If Donovan was forwarding information to the IRA about Loyalist groups and their operations in the Republic, it would make perfect sense to have him killed," Youngest finally spoke up. "You're right. The blowback on all of this, especially during the peace talks, would be serious. If they had hired an outsider they could trust to carry it out that would be a logical deduction. This Catcher woman, from what you're telling me, seems like the ideal candidate."

"Quite," Talamadge quipped, "and she's likely being protected by them. Now, your people probably have a good pulse on the UVF and its activities around here. We should start shaking the trees to see what falls out."

"Not so fast," Youngest interjected as he turned to Ravenhoof. "You mentioned your analyst people concluded that the UVF would want to keep their distance and work through intermediaries."

Ravenhoof nodded.

"That makes sense," Youngest continued. "Why use a freelancer, if you're supporting her with your organization's own organic resources. It would make no sense to go shaking down the local boys. If this affair was made somewhere between England and Northern Ireland, chances are they wouldn't have involved anyone around here."

"Someone has to be helping her," Ravenhoof stated. "Who would they reach out to as an intermediary for this?"

"Do they work with any other radical groups?" Talamadge leaned back in his chair as he tapped his thumbs.

Youngest rubbed his hand on the lower part of his face. "No, they don't have those kinds of connections to anyone here that I know of. But, that's a question for the intelligence boys, not me. Let me reach out to them and see who they would recommend."

"Would it necessarily be a radical group though?" Ravenhoof chimed in. "I mean, we're looking for someone who would have the network and resources to hide a highly sought after killer effectively, aid them in this type of assassination and, ultimately, arrange an exit out of the country." The South African looked about the room as the two other men were staring back at him with a look expecting further elaboration. "I mean if it were me, I would reach out to some criminal type. Someone the UVF does heavy business with and who could be trusted to support such a plan."

"That's certainly a good point," Youngest replied. "I know a few types who could pull off such a job."

At that moment, Officer Hilter Dagden entered the room. "Sorry to bother you, but I thought you might want to know. You asked me to keep an eye out for any violent homicides that took place in the last several hours and appear to be gangland related. Well, I just received word about a gun battle at a warehouse down at the dockyards. Five dead so far, all gunned down."

Youngest looked back at the two intelligence officers. "In the absence of any other immediate leads, we should possibly check this out."

Dagden stepped out of the room as the three other men moved to get up.

"Given my suspicions about Detective Donovan's involvement with the IRA and your assumptions about a freelance killer, I presumed that whoever it is, the IRA would be looking for them too," Youngest explained as he reached for his coat.

THE SIGHT at the warehouse was the result of what could only have been one hellacious gun battle. Detective Sergeant Youngest and the two intelligence men looked about in amazement at the carnage sprawled about in thick pools of drying blood. As seasoned policemen, neither Ravenhoof nor Youngest was the slightest bit fazed at the grisly sight. They studied the scene with detective-like instincts. For Ravenhoof, it had been years since he had actually investigated a crime. He felt a tad bit of excitement getting back to his roots. Talamadge, by contrast, was a counter-intelligence officer who had little exposure to actual death and carnage. He tried hard not to disgrace himself as he held back the urge to vomit.

At the scene, the trio found a stout little man with a glowing, bald head directing the investigation. As if a general commanding an army, the stout man waved his arms about constantly demanding answers from a multitude of people working different aspects of the case. When Youngest approached, the bald man was incredulous with the initial assumption he was being usurped by another detective.

A few quiet words of diplomacy quickly calmed him. The thought that his investigation was connected to something of significant importance, such as the Donovan murder, excited the bald detective. Youngest introduced both Talamadge and Ravenhoof as foreign police officers from their respective countries. They were investigating crimes that might be related. All of which made the bald man even more interested.

"Detective Glenahaughan," Youngest began, "what do you have so far?"

Looking at the two foreign detectives waiting for answers, Glenahaughan beamed with a certain amount of pride. "For starters, we have five bodies, two in the main area here and three more in the back hallway. It looks like a deal or hit gone shitty. From the looks of things, the gunfight started in the back with the first three getting ambushed and continued out here with these two." Glenahaughan waved at the two corpses sprawled out. "They tried to escape and got caught by whoever they were running from. They took bullets from someone firing from a distance, with what looks to be a .45 caliber model. We found .45 casings all over the place."

Ravenhoof and Youngest looked closer at the bodies. Their trained eye quickly picked up the wounds that were clearly inflicted by bullets fired at a distance that landed in the torso. Then the headshots that finished them both off could only have been fired from a few feet away.

"Your killer or killers were pros alright," Ravenhoof said, as he looked back at Glenahaughan.

"Can we see the other bodies?" Youngest asked.

Glenahaughan eagerly ushered the three toward the back. As they walked, Youngest took note of the distance between the shooter and the bodies. Coming to the entry of the back area, he saw the flags marking the spent casings. He turned to look back, noticing that the initial shots were taken from a considerable distance, well over thirty meters. Realizing it was done under what was obviously combat circumstances and limited time, the shooter was incredibly skilled. He also caught sight of various cans and bottles lying arbitrarily on the floor. At first glance, it looked like debris left by lazy workers. However, he soon noticed that the arbitrary debris was not so arbitrary. He began to see an informal pattern to the way they were laid out — close together but with a few feet between them.

"We found the lighting in the back hallway had been disabled," Glenahaughan said as he led the men through the door into the back hall. "The only light that worked was coming from this room here." He pointed down a hall illuminated by a collection of standup lights. They had been brought in to compensate and lined the pathway displaying two more bodies sprawled out in front of the room.

"You think the gunfight originated in here?" Youngest asked as he looked at the grisly scene and then further down at more flags noting the location of more shell casings.

"Yes, I do," replied Glenahaughan as he pointed out what Youngest and the others had already noticed. "From the looks of the bodies and where the shots initially struck along the side, I'd say these boys got taken by surprise. From the look of it all, it was someone hiding in the dark down that way. The shooter got these two and this one." At the base of the room, Glenahaughan waved the men to look inside, where they found an additional corpse." Ravenhoof and Youngest took turns peering inside to limit their foot traffic across the crime scene. Talamadge, becoming ever more nauseous at the sight before him, opted to remain in the hall looking the other way.

Youngest studied the body further. Though it was lying on its side and the back of the head had been destroyed, he couldn't quite understand why he felt he should know the dead man. Then, it hit him. He turned to Glenahaughan. "My God, is that Cork Regan?"

Glenahaughan nodded. "Oh yes, it is to be sure. We were just as surprised when we made a positive identification on him."

The action of Youngest caught Ravenhoof and Talamadge by surprise. "What is it?" Talamadge asked. "Who is this Cork Regan fellow?"

"He's the top enforcer for the IRA here in Dublin," answered Glenahaughan. "In fact, all these boys are known IRA heavies. They call Regan out when they want to send a message and lay down the law with the Dublin criminal world." Glenahaughan was trying to hold back his glee as he saw the growing interest of the three policemen before him. The thought that he was investigating something much more than the originally suspected gangland shootout filled him with excitement. "Whoever they were after has angered some seriously powerful people," he couldn't help adding.

"That's true," Youngest concurred. "Regan's well known in Dublin streets as the last man you want coming after you."

"Did any of them get a shot off?" Ravenhoof suddenly interjected, as he looked around and noticed there were no nearby bullet casings next to them, and none of the dead men had drawn their guns.

"Not that we can tell," Glanahaughan replied. "That's what makes this so concerning. This mystery shooter, or shooters, took out the city's most dangerous enforcer and four of his guys without them getting off a shot. I mean disposed of all five men like they were nothing."

Ravenhoof and Talamadge were looking at each other with concurring glances. This was sounding more and more like the work of their assassin. Youngest walked into the room followed by Ravenhoof and, eventually, by Talamadge, who had to work up the courage to navigate past two bullet-riddled corpses.

Inside, they saw the basic accommodations of what was obviously a person's living quarters. Someone had been living here secretly. Walking about slowly, the detectives realized that the room had been well cleaned. It looked strangely devoid of any personal items. Something highly unusual for a person leaving in a rush, after being in a deadly gunfight. Even at a quick glance, it was obvious that the person who had once lived here had been meticulous about keeping the place free of anything that might provide any information about him that someone might be able to use for tracking.

Normally, in a situation like this, police could find boxes from restaurants they frequented or receipts from places they had shopped at recently or just hung out. There was none of that. Looking out at the open window, it became apparent to all, that their mysterious squatter had been quite careful in ensuring the sea devoured any information.

"Did your men find anything so far that could allude to the identity of our killer?" Youngest turned to face Glana-haughan.

"A killer?" Glenahaughan looked back in surprise. "You think one person did all this by themselves?"

Youngest rubbed his jaw for a moment. "It looks like our victims were ambushed by a single person who heard them coming from outside. The shooter moved into a planned position and waited until they could be seen in the light before opening fire. This whole hallway was set up to be a kill zone."

"Are you sure?" Glenahaughan responded with utter shock.

Youngest continued. "You said the lighting in this hallway had been deliberately deactivated. The only light came from this room and the shooter knew exactly where to position himself to attain maximum concealment while retaining a visual of the area. The light from this room would have covered the hallway. The shooter didn't fire until the victims were visible by the light after they kicked in the door. With the light destroying their night vision, they had no means to even see who was shooting at them or where the shots were coming from. They were caught in an ambush."

"That seems a little elaborate," Glenahaughan replied.

"He's right," Ravenhoof interjected. "Looking at where the shots were fired from, the shooter took a clever position far down the hall and stayed close to the wall. At that distance, it would have made it difficult to get a clean return shot without it bouncing off the wall first. These boys looked to have foolishly stood in the middle of the hallway making them easy targets."

"Let's not forget the makeshift alarm system we all seem to have initially missed," Youngest said, as he pointed his thumb behind him. "In the main room, if you look closely at that debris outside, it looks random; however, they are sprawled out in such a way as to cover almost the entire floor. Furthermore, they are arranged in close proximity to ensure that someone walking around in the dark would eventually trip or kick something. In this concrete structure, the sound would have echoed and alerted anyone back here, giving him ample time to prepare. Detective Glenahaughan, am I correct in assuming the switches up front entering the main room from outside were also disabled?"

"Why yes," Glenahaughan replied with a bewildered look on his face. "We had to make our way to the back of the room to get to a switch that would work." Glenahaughan's eyes lit up at the sudden revelation of what his colleague had just assumed. "In fact, now that I think about it, one of my men almost injured himself on a board of nails that was positioned at one of the side doors. The board was hidden under a dark burlap cover and was set right up against the door."

"It's her," Talamadge's voice caught everyone by surprise.

"Who?" Glenahaughan asked with the tone of a child being left out of the big kid's game.

18

Sauwa could feel Rena struggling in her arms. The little girl had wanted to be free of her sister since they had gotten in the back of the truck. Sauwa held her baby sister firmly not wanting to let go out of fear she would be lost if they suddenly had to escape. In the darkness, she could hear the sobs of the other terrified women and girls as they hunkered down. The only sight she could make out was the silhouette of the two men standing guard at the back of the vehicle. Their weapons were held firmly in their hands ready to fight at any moment.

"I want mommy," Rena whined.

Sauwa had no means to respond. How could she tell her that her mother was dead? She tightened her arms around her combative little sister and attempted to rock her to sleep. Then, she saw the flash of light hitting the end of the truck and the terrifying growl of the explosion that followed. She pressed Rena's face into her chest as she watched one of the men clutch his chest and fall forward onto the road below. The other guard had drawn his weapon and began returning fire. Another burst hit. It was. It came crashing down close enough to lift the back of the truck that left all the occupants in pain.

SAUWA WOKE to see the face of a thin, elderly man looking at her with an expression of concern. "Are you all right, Lassie?" he asked pleasantly.

"Yes, yes I am," she replied nervously as she sought to get her bearings. Lifting herself from the sofa she had been sleeping on, she took a few deep breaths to calm her nerves. She found her shirt soaked in the usual cold sweat that was common after a nightmare. She looked around the small coffee shop as she struggled to gain her faculties and remember where she was. Anxious to find a place to get out of sight, she had stepped into a small bookshop. With the crisis over, her adrenaline high had begun to dissipate, leaving her drained of energy. She found a refuge and was lulled into a deep sleep.

The old man was still looking at her with concern. "You looked like you were having one serious nightmare little one."

"How long was I out?" she asked.

"You came in here about five hours ago," he replied as he helped her finish sitting upright. "You looked at some classic books for a few minutes before you sat down and fell asleep. You looked completely worn out. I haven't had any customers, so I just let you sleep. It was when I heard you calling out that I started to get concerned."

"I'm fine, thanks," she said as she gradually moved to stand up.

"Are you sure?" the old man pressed. "I mean, if you need to, you can continue to rest here. You looked like you needed the sleep."

"No, thank you. I need to get moving." She gently waved the old man off as she started out the door.

THE APARTMENT COMPLEX where Banker maintained his secret office may have been a good location to hide from prying criminals who dealt with the seedier side of town. However, it offered little in the way of good security from a more professional threat. The vegetation surrounding the estate had grown to almost jungle-like levels with thick, leafy bushes that had not been trimmed. Trees grew too close together and had many low-hanging branches providing a thick wall of concealment. They also provided the ability for someone to navigate the perimeter of the entire estate. Most of the parking lot dipped into various side streets remaining hidden from view making it easy to ambush someone without a lot of eyes watching or ways to escape.

Sauwa remained hidden in the bushes, just outside the complex where Banker kept his apartment. The setup of the complex was such, that she had no trouble finding a favorable vantage point allowing her to see anyone entering from either direction. She had no guarantee that he would show up anytime soon, if at all. Short of risking herself by going to the Rory Club, this was her best avenue. It had been dusk when she had arrived and snuck inconspicuously into the bushes. Now, it was sundown and, as darkness fell, the street lamps and the open shops became the only source of illumination.

It had been nearly two hours when she caught sight of Banker hustling into the apartment complex. Slipping out of the bushes without disrupting the vegetation or drawing attention, Sauwa came out into a shadowed patch in the parking lot. Rising to her feet she began walking toward the door Banker had just gone through. In her head, she played out three possible scenarios: 1) Banker had anticipated she would come looking for him at his apartment and called the police in hopes they would apprehend her. 2) Banker came as a decoy to draw her out for another hit team to make an attempt against her. Looking around, she saw no one in the distance or any vehicles that suggested such an idea. 3) Banker may indeed be on the level and had nothing to do with the intruders at the warehouse.

Banker had gone into the complex with no sign of any additional people nearby. Confident she was safe to move, Sauwa crept to the entrance Banker had entered. Opening the door, she slid in to find Banker standing alone down the short hall waiting for the elevator. Moving slowly, she drew back her coat and produced a long, sharp piece of metal she had procured from one of the scrap buckets at another warehouse. She made her way down the hall, keeping watch for any possible surprises. Less than a few feet away, she drew the weapon she had kept low to her side to avoid attracting immediate attention.

Banker suddenly felt a sharp object against his spine. At first, he thought it a muscle spasm or some nervous system anomaly. But, the sharp tightness grinding into his back told him this was something different.

"My knife is pressed against your lower spinal cord," a feminine voice he recognized said. "If you attempt anything you'll be paralyzed from the waist down in seconds before you can strike me." Her voice was cold and serious.

Not wanting to exacerbate the situation, Banker stepped forward with his hand away from his pockets. The elevator opened, revealing an empty compartment. With a nudge, she nudged him inside. They turned simultaneously so he could face the control panel. Pressing his floor, the doors were about to shut when a striking blond woman came darting in. Her hands were full of some shopping bags. "Oh, thank you," the blond said with a tired sigh as she leaned over to catch her breath.

Feeling the sharp object grind warningly into his back, Banker only nodded as he returned the pleasantry. The blond woman hardly took notice as she seemed lost in her own world.

"Could you press the second floor, please?" she asked.

Banker obliging smiled as he pressed the button for the second floor. The elevator doors finally closed with the low vibrating hum of the car going up. The blond hardly took notice of the young girl standing in the corner behind the handsome man. The car reached the second floor. The doors opened, and the woman disappeared out into the hall.

After a few seconds, the doors closed again, leaving Banker and Sauwa alone. "What's this all about?" he demanded. His tone was angry and confused. His anger was further exacerbated by the woman's dead silence and tightening of her weapon against his back. The doors opened at his floor and with a sharp jab, Sauwa directed

Banker outside. They walked down the hall slowly trying not to draw any attention. Banker thought about calling for help and running. But, between the blade and her hand held firmly onto his belt to ensure he didn't try anything, he understood his best option was to cooperate. If she had wanted him dead, she could have killed him more easily downstairs, or outside where she could have gotten away.

Arriving at the door of his apartment, he carefully reached into his coat pocket for his key. One bad move would have meant death or a wheelchair. Unlocking the door, he no sooner had it open when she pushed him forcefully inside. He heard the door shut, leaving them alone.

Sauwa looked Banker over. Assessing the location, she saw nothing that assumed recent occupation. Satisfied the apartment was empty, she relaxed a little. "Tell me about the hit team." she snapped.

Confused, Banker's head shook, "Hit team? What hit team?"

"The one at the warehouse today." Her voice was low and calm, but her seething anger was all too apparent. "Some very dangerous men paid me a visit this afternoon. At my safe house, no less. They came looking for someone with the intent to do unkind things. They came looking for me."

"I know what you may be thinking," Banker began, choosing his words carefully. "But I don't know anything about a hit team. I certainly didn't sell you out."

"I know," she cut in. "If you had you wouldn't have warned me about the IRA poking around. You would have just told them about me and stayed far away. You would have kept your ear to the ground wanting to know the outcome. You certainly wouldn't have come back here when you found out they were all dead and I was gone — not alone anyway,

Banker's face displayed a look of confusion. "So, why have you accosted me like this, if you didn't think I set you up."

"Because," Sauwa looked at him coldly, "you were the only one who knew where I was staying. The people in the neighborhood are out of the way. There is no other avenue in which they could have been tipped off about me. It all points back to you. Who did you talk to?"

Unsure of what to say and aware his life may very well end at any moment, Banker raced through his memory trying to think where he could have made such an egregious mistake. The only thought that came to mind was his meeting with the IRA enforcers. "Cork Regan, a strong arm for the IRA, dropped by asking questions. I didn't tell him anything, and I sure as hell didn't take him to you. All I can think is he must have followed me or made a logical deduction and went from there."

Satisfied with the answer, Sauwa lowered her weapon. "Well, I tangled with about five men; they looked like enforcer types. They appeared to be led by a big fellow."

"Sounds like Cork and his boys," Banker explained. "You obviously got away. But Regan's dangerous and determined; he has connections all over the city. If he's still after you, Dublin's definitely not safe anymore."

"He's dead. They all are." Sauwa's tone was cold and firm.

Banker dropped to his knees at hearing that Regan was dead. It certainly wasn't sympathy that drove this reaction. It was shock. Regan was a dangerous man. To hear that he was dispatched along with his crew was difficult to comprehend. That it was done by a young girl was even more unbelievable. It also made him realize fully who he was dealing with at this particular moment. He had worried about this girl and played the odds between her and the IRA. It turned out he had backed the right side. He also comprehended fully that this little girl was much more dangerous than she appeared. "If you don't think I set you up, what was it with the knife to the back?" He asked looking at the menacing steel object in her hand.

"A man like you survives by playing the odds," she responded. "You informed me about the IRA but didn't tell me about your entire discussion with these guys. My guess is you calculated the situation and decided that it would, in the long run, be very dangerous to cross me. You tried to navigate both sides as best you could and try not to be a liability to me or be punished by them. I figured you would have assumed I was coming after you, once you heard about the shootout. You had either gone to the police to turn me in or taken your chances with the IRA and gave them a second chance to come after me. I wasn't going to take any chances either."

"So, what now?" Banker felt strangely out of his league at the moment. "I mean if you killed five men like you say, the coppers will be all over this by now."

"The IRA will be. too," Sauwa cautioned. "And, they'll be the real danger."

Banker was confused. "You just killed one of their top operators. I'm sure they'll think twice before striking again so soon."

Sauwa shook her head with a cold, deadpan look on her face. "I got lucky this time. They sent street enforcers to get me not professional operators. That was because they underestimated what they were up against, and it gave me the edge. After this, they'll know what they're dealing with. Who they send next won't be gangsters. I assume it will be an Action Service Unit. They won't make the same mistake twice."

Banker cringed at her words. An Action Service Unit, an actual IRA commando team wasn't the street tough heavies he was accustomed to dealing with. These guys were the real deal. Highly trained, these people carried out missions against Protestant Loyalist paramilitaries, RUC police and the British security forces. All at once, it became apparent to the club owner just how deep he was in this situation. "With all this heat surrounding you, are you sure they'll really escalate this?"

The woman sighed. "There's no need to be secretive anymore. I killed a ranking intelligence officer with the Irish Garda. A man the Loyalists believed was serving as a key intelligence source for the IRA. By eliminating him, I virtually crippled their intelligence system and operations against Loyalist activities in the Republic. In addition, I just killed five of their men. No, if anything, finding me will become a priority."

"Shit sakes!" Banker exclaimed. "If that's true and Regan was on to me, he probably reported his suspicions to his bosses. After this, they'll know I was the one helping you."

"It's not safe for you in Ireland," Sauwa cut in. "Not now. It was a horrific gunfight at the warehouse. One that ended in a bloodbath. By tomorrow it will be all over the news if it hasn't already gotten back to the IRA."

"I know it's not in my best interest to bring this up

right now," Banker leaned against the wall. "Why do you not believe I wouldn't try to save my own ass and turn you over to them?"

For the first time, the cold look on Sauwa's face changed into a smile. "Because you have no angle to play with them. After this, you're a dead man no matter what. If you try to make a deal, they'll kill you once they've got me. If I get caught, you run the risk that I'll have enough information to help them eventually find you. Then, there is the police who will make all of this a big priority. Your only play is to try and get out of the country. Since you have given me the information for my escape and all has been arranged, it's in both our interests to see I get on that ship and out of the country safely."

She was right; he was trapped. Either way, he was a dead man or one destined for prison. "Well, your ship leaves tomorrow night. We just have to keep you under wraps until then. But, I can't get you a new safe house, not now. Between the cops and the IRA, I have nothing that wouldn't be discovered quickly."

"I'm staying right here tonight," Sauwa stated, making it clear the issue was not open for discussion. "So are you. In the morning, I'll leave and find somewhere else to go to ground until it's time to meet at the pier. I suggest you don't go back to work and spend tomorrow transferring assets to whatever fallback location you have set up. We'll meet at the pier an hour before my departure."

"What makes you think I won't double cross you and leave you stranded?" Banker couldn't help being inquisitive.

Walking past him down the narrow hallway, Sauwa responded. "Those who hired me picked you because you play it straight in your dealings. Even in this dark hour, I don't believe you would be any different. Besides, those who employed me to kill the informant did so to distance themselves. My getting caught automatically connects them to the killing. They have a huge vested interest in getting me out of the country. Do you really want to have more enemies after you with a distant reach and a penchant for violence?"

With nothing more to say, she headed into what looked like a spare room, leaving Banker to digest all that had just happened.

19

After having explained to Glenahaughan about the ghostly female assassin who now had the combined intelligence and law enforcement agencies of three countries involved, the bald detective took quick notice of a recently discovered long black hair found in the shower area. It hadn't been there long in a warehouse that hadn't been active in months. He eagerly contacted Youngest and his foreign colleagues.

The report of having a possible suspect in the killing of Detective Marston Donovan was well received given the pressure the department had been under — not just by Youngest. The announcement that the killer may, in fact, be an internationally wanted assassin and had actually killed five known IRA members in a spectacular shootout whetted the interest of Commander Ian Rose. Ever the politician and media whore, he salivated with alacrity. The idea he was currently commanding what was turning into a case with such international ramifications was mind-blowing.

His subordinate, Detective Sergeant Youngest, watched his superior calculate the political capital to be gained from such an event — a case that had become a joint effort with two other countries and was supposed to be a secret operation. The idea of having a highly sought after professional killer be a suspect and wanted by both Britain and South African governments was too enticing to simply pass up.

His commander was talking about how he had convinced the top brass they should hold a press conference, address the newspapers and enjoy the moment. Youngest was cautioning him to the contrary; however, Rose blatantly ignored him. The idea his department could be the agency apprehending this person would be the pinnacle of his career and perhaps garner world attention. For Rose, there was a massive opportunity, and he was determined to exploit it as much as possible.

Youngest reminded his superior of the sensitivity of the case. He stressed they would be working with foreign intelligence agencies who were assisting with sensitive information. This affair needed to be handled with delicacy.

The respective governments agreed that the existence of Sauwa Catcher could be publicly disclosed, as it was already a matter of record for the British police. The British were forwarding existing information on Sauwa Catcher from their records plus photos and her recorded fingerprints sent to them from South Africa's state archives. Unfortunately, the photos were all black and white, so grainy, and dated they were almost useless. Youngest hoped she'd been at the warehouse long enough, they might be able to obtain some fresh, viable prints.

Being proactive, Youngest proposed dispersing copies of the photos to police along with all possible exits out of the country. He emphasized ports and harbors as well as the boating docks. He figured their suspect wouldn't risk trying to corner herself by boarding a plane. She had somehow slipped into the Republic totally undetected, which meant a private boat crossing the Irish Sea, or entering through the unprotected border of Northern Ireland. Ravenhoof promised to contact South Africa hoping to obtain better pictures.

"The question we have to answer is who's been protecting her? She's been in this country for at least two or more weeks and has managed to stay well off our grid even though she's never operated here. That doesn't happen without resources and assistance from someone." Youngest asked.

"The UVF must be protecting her," suggested Hilter Dagden. "We should check with the intelligence boys and shake some trees."

"That's a good idea," Youngest replied.

"Just a minute," Ravenhoof stopped him. "That may not be the avenue we wish to pursue," he cautioned. "Our analysis presumes that a disconnected intermediary may have been brought in for this."

"What do you mean?" Youngest asked. "If you and the British are right and this is a UVF orchestrated operation, logic suggests they would want to play this close to the vest and ensure the mission's success. Why would they risk using some disconnected outsider?"

"Because he is disconnected," Ravenhoof replied, capturing the room by surprise. "I know we're dealing with terrorist organizations. They generally don't trust their political business outside of their own circles. I have extensive experience dealing with these types. History would point to the idea that we should be looking at the Loyalist network here in the Republic to find answers. But, this job is different. They didn't use their own people for this. They used an outsider — a contractor to assassinate your comrade. They either didn't trust their network, or they wanted to make sure they were well distanced from the killing. In either case, it would only make sense they reached out to a third party to provide the necessary support."

"Politically, it makes sense," Talamadge interjected. "For several months now, peace negotiations have been underway in the north. A killing of this magnitude would only complicate things. Not to mention that the full weight of your organization would be brought down in reprisal. No, it wouldn't be enough to bring in an outsider for this job. They would have to be completely disconnected."

"You're right," Dagden admitted. "Having Sauwa Catcher caught in a Loyalist's safe house or being helped by a Loyalist agent could only lead right back to their door."

Youngest sat rubbing his chin as he digested the information. He hated the bizarre universe of espionage. For him, the world of smoke and mirrors turned everything upside down. He was a brilliant detective who enjoyed the hunt offered in a criminal investigation; the logic of following the evidence before him. Spies and intrigue, of which everything seemed poised to mislead only served to irritate him. He felt he was immersed in some conspiracy theory. They were all in a room working on a theory to an unsolved murder trying to guess and second guess the strategy and mindset of some group.

"So, then what?" Youngest asked. "We look for someone the UVF would trust with this business and not have it get leaked back to the IRA who, I might add, is very well connected to this city's underworld."

The room was silent as minds began to grind. The detectives and intelligence officers were desperately trying to figure out their next move. While no one said it out loud, it was understood that they were racing against time. Their killer was not going to linger in the country and would soon try to escape.

Finally, Youngest seized the phone and dialed. The voice at the other end sounded like it belonged to a rather energetic young man. "Crime and & Security, Detective Reardon speaking."

"Detective Reardon. I'm Detective Sergeant Ryan Youngest..." Youngest was quickly cut off.

"Aren't you the one investigating the murder of Detective Donovan?"

"Well, yes, I am…" Youngest attempted to reply.

"Donovan was well respected and liked. He didn't deserve to get it the way he did. We all are hoping you catch the piece of shit responsible. You should know if there's anything we can do to help, we're all here."

"That's why I'm calling," Youngest said. "I need to speak with someone in your Crime Special Surveillance Unit. I would like to get some information about the underworld in Dublin that's connected with the case…" He was again cut off.

"I can put you in touch with exactly the guys you need to speak to. Detectives Ian Galligan and Harry Curly know the crime figures in this town like they were family. Let me patch you through to them," Reardon said energetically. Youngest barely had time to thank the young man before the phone began ringing.

Youngest looked around the room at the assortment of confused faces wondering about the strange conversation.

"Detective Sergeant Curly," the voice answered.

"This is Detective Sergeant Youngest with Homicide."

"Yes?" Curly asked.

"I'm investigating the murder of Detective Marston Donovan, and I was wondering if you could perhaps assist me?"

"Anyway I can, of course," Curly replied.

"We're working on the theory that the killer may have been a hired professional. Someone from outside the country brought in to do the job. If that is the case, they would need support and protection from someone local. Who would come to mind that could offer such services?"

The phone on the other end was silent except for some light breathing. It went on for several minutes. The homicide detective was about to say something when Curly spoke up. "This is a big city, and there are a lot of folks in the business of providing such services to anyone who has the money and connections to pay for it."

Youngest hesitated for a moment. He didn't want to divulge too much information and open the door for rumors to start circulating; he didn't want another problem to emerge. When a respected policeman is killed, it isn't uncommon for their comrades to seek revenge. Giving away a potential suspect to a victim's former colleagues opened up the possibility of reprisals. Curly pressed for more information, and Youngest could see no other way.

"This person would be inclined to do business with the UVF and would be someone they would trust to aid in this type of job." The homicide detective looked up to see a disapproving look from Dagden.

"Really?" Curly responded in an almost sinister way. Youngest cringed slightly. "That narrows the field. Not many do business with Loyalist paras. It could lead to serious punishment from the IRA lads if they found out. I can think of a couple boys they could reach out to if they wanted to keep their distance and needed something done." Curly gave Youngest four names along with a brief personal assessment of each one.

Youngest thanked him. "No, Detective Youngest, thank you very much." It was the same sinister tone that made Youngest cringe before he hung up.

"Are you sure that was a good idea?" Dagden asked.

Youngest looked at all the faces and said nothing. His deep frown and slight shaking of his head said quite enough. Jotting down the names and addresses of the people Detective Sergeant Curly had given him, Youngest stood up. "We have only four names to check; unfortunately, we don't know how much time we have; we need to make quick assessments."

"We can probably make this faster," Ravenhoof spoke up. "We have one thing going for us — the IRA."

All attention was now turned to the South African. Ravenhoof, his understanding of radical groups and police instincts kicking in, continued. "Remember, the IRA is looking for this guy, too. We have five of their men dead at a warehouse. We presume this was a hit team sent to kill

Ms. Catcher. My guess is they are already onto whoever is helping her. With six of their people dead, whoever that person is, is now living under a death sentence and trying to get out of town quickly. We just need to see who on this list has suddenly become hard to reach."

"You're right," Dagden agreed. "We're not interested in anyone who's doing business as usual. We need the guy who's trying to close up shop."

WHEN RAVENHOOF WAS PREPARED to give his report to South Africa, he hadn't been entirely confident of the investigation. Though a great deal of evidence alluded to the idea, he still wasn't sure it led to Sauwa Catcher. It was only in the minutes before he was set to leave for the embassy in Dublin that a report came in from the warehouse solidifying he was on the right track. He was now positive they were on Sauwa Catcher's trail.

Through the embassy, Ravenhoof made contact with O'knomo. Ireland wasn't a high priority for South Africa, which meant it was complicated getting time on the communication system. His boss had been waiting nervously for an update. When the Afrikaner apprised him of the details of the warehouse killing, O'knomo also became convinced it had to be her.

The request from Ravenhoof to find better photos of their fugitive was accepted with some difficulty. Both men knew, without saying it, that time was of the essence. They were asking for something that would take days to find — assuming any family she had would be at all cooperative. Regardless, O'knomo conceded this was their best chance of catching Ms. Catcher at a time when they had the full resources of the Irish police to assist them. Any sign of sincere cooperation would go a very long way to cement the relationship.

SEAMUS NALLY DIDN'T RELISH the phone call he was going to have to make. It was already a tense enough situation, because one of the IRA's best intelligence assets was now lying on a slab. More, the men sent to adjudicate the matter were now lying right next to him. This did not help the image of the Dublin unit, who were looking hopelessly useless in the eyes of the higher command up north.

Stepping into a remote phone booth on the north side of the city, Nally dropped several coins into the coin slot and dialed a number to someplace in County Cork. "Rittery's Bar and Grill, Mickey speaking." A voice heavily flavored with an accent indigenous to the county of Cork answered.

"I'm looking for Ivan. He's an old boy of the country. I'd like to speak with him," the old man spoke as if looking for an old friend.

"Ivan's out," the voice replied. "He's fixin' the pipes at home, he is. I'm holding the place."

"Oh, I just thought I'd check up on an old chum," the old man remained pleasant. "Just tell him Paddy thought he'd give'm a hand."

"Hold on," the voice commanded. The phone went dead, leaving Seamus listening to his own breath in the receiver. To anyone snooping, it sounded like old friends trying to keep in touch. In actuality, it was a code that was used to initiate a meeting. It was difficult to make phone calls over the border. Most of the places used for business by the IRA north of the border were quite well known and usually monitored by either British Intelligence or the Royal Ulster Constabulary. When communicating from the Republic to the UK, an elaborate network of remote houses and establishments were used to mask the network in the south. A call made to a place in the farmlands of Cork would be relayed to another remote establishment in a county near the border. A messenger would be dispatched to make physical contact just over the border. It sounded complicated, but after decades of using this operation, it was actually quite fluid and sophisticated.

A few minutes later, a voice, distinctly different from the one who answered came on. "What's your update?"

Seamus struggled for a moment. "We've had a problem."

"What kind of problem?" the voice asked in a commanding tone.

"Our attempts to find the killer of our loyal comrade… well, it ended with more deaths; more of our people."

"And the killer?" the voice was now growling.

Seamus sighed deeply as he prepared to answer the question. "The only casualties were ours."

For several minutes there was silence. Then the voice spoke up. "How did this happen?"

Seamus found it hard to speak. This only served to anger the man on the other end further. "I asked, how did this bloody thing happen?"

"We're not sure yet," Seamus answered weakly. "What we have understood so far is they were ambushed by professionals. My people were dealing with totally different operators than normal." He knew the answers he was giving made him sound weak and incapable. He couldn't find a better way to explain himself; he didn't have all the facts yet. They probably wouldn't have helped if he did.

"This is fucking bullshit!" the voice growled over the phone. "Someone kills an important man to the cause and makes mincemeat of your people. What the hell is going on over there? Is there a fuckin' new force in town challenging us? Are the Loyalists trying to set up in your city? Are you in over your head? Are your men so pathetic they can't do more than fuck up junkies and low-lives?"

Seamus didn't know what to say; apparently, he didn't need to say anything. The voice on the other end didn't seem interested in answers to any of his questions. He just continued speaking. "I'll send word across the way. I can tell you already what the answer will be."

Seamus didn't bother responding. There was no point. His superior had apparently made the decision and was only interested in giving orders. "We have a place in the farmlands where we have the right men for this job. Assume they'll be leavin' tonight. When they get there, they will find you. Make yourself entirely at their disposal."

"Understood," Seamus replied, trying not to sound nervous.

The voice continued, "In the meantime, press your police sources for all available information, so our people know who they're up against. I'm sure you can accomplish that much, at least."

"Yes sir," replied Seamus. He could feel the beads of sweat trickling down his forehead.

"Do you have any pertinent information that can assist us in finding this team of assassins? From what you've told me, I'm sure there has to be more than one." The voice wasn't even trying to mask his contempt for his Dublin subordinate.

Ah, well yes," Seamus struggled to try and redeem himself. "My operative, reported he was looking into Rudy Sheehan, club owner and a known trafficker in the black market. He was being looked at as someone who might be working with this hit team."

"Good. At least, you aren't completely worthless," the voice growled bitterly before hanging up.

20

Sauwa awoke to the sound of the shower running across the way. Banker had chosen to stay the night after realizing he had nowhere else to go. She stretched lightly before reaching for her jeans. Though she should have had a stomach full of butterflies with all the concerns that plagued her, Sauwa was feeling somewhat serene.

Perhaps it was the temporary lull in the frenzy she had endured over the last few days. She had been continuously looking over her shoulder for the ever-growing list of enemies pursuing her. She was able to enjoy a slight break. Banker's apartment was a secret he guarded closely — one he kept even from his closest associates. It was not in a part of town that lent itself to the local criminal elements who would inform on him.

Sauwa stepped outside the bedroom. The shower was still going. She could hear Banker thumping about as he washed. It was good to know he was still there. She was sure her talk with him the previous night had sunk in. He was aware of the need not to neglect her at a time when he was likely to be caught up in his own affairs and trying to prepare for his own escape from the country. Banker was now a desperate man and, in her experience, desperate men often made dangerous mistakes.

Either way, Banker's usefulness was coming to an end. While she was confident he hadn't sold her out to the IRA, she was sure they had found her through him. Now that he was a fugitive himself, his resources were going to quickly dissipate. It was good that she was leaving tonight — any longer would be too hazardous.

Banker stepped out of the bathroom in a pair of sweats and rubbing a towel across his head. He saw his Sauwa working in the kitchen. Between the refrigerator and the cupboards, she had been able to find enough to make something of a breakfast.

"You're still here?" were the first words out of his mouth.

"We needed to talk and finalize our plans," she replied. Her eyes were darting about as she continued to explore his kitchen. "Besides, with everything going on, this is the safest place to be at the moment. I'm in no hurry to be out on the streets with everyone chasing me."

"That's reasonable," Banker slunk into a nearby armchair. It was obvious the events of the last several hours had drained him. "I'm in no hurry either. I am a fucking target, too. Both the London firm that sent you or IRA, if they know I helped you, will probably consider me a liability."

Sauwa continued making breakfast. "I'm sorry that you were forced into the middle of this. Right now, the focus should be on preparing for the next step. What we previously planned is no longer viable with all the added complications. The ship that's supposed to take me out of here is not due to leave until 2200hrs tonight. Has anything changed that has altered that plan?"

"No," Banker shook his head. "Everything is still good with your arrangements."

Sauwa was hesitant. "With the IRA creeping around your organization, is there a chance they may have discovered anything about it?"

Banker again shook his head. "No, I keep my operations compartmentalized. Aside from you, me and the contact on the ship, only one other person knows anything; an additional person I use as an insurance policy. They're random people I hire for jobs from time to time. They know the details of the job and have instructions. If they don't hear from me by a certain time, or if they get a call from me and don't get the message and code, this person will start making phone calls and alerting everyone, from the cops to rival interests, who might be interested." He looked at Sauwa with a cold stare of sincerity. "So, if you are looking at me as a liability to your own self-preservation and have considered killing me, I would caution you against it."

She said nothing as she continued making breakfast. She would have been lying if it hadn't crossed her mind to do exactly that. The professional in her saw a gangster, a racketeer whom she barely knew and was being hunted by some very dangerous people. He owed her nothing and even his walking around brought the possibility of danger directly back to her. On one hand, her more human side appreciated not having to kill someone needlessly. Contrary to what this man and others thought, she was not some sociopathic killer who was entirely indifferent to it all. In any case, her practical side remembered he was the only person resembling an ally. Things could still go terribly wrong between now and 2200hrs, and Banker was still more valuable alive than dead.

Banker continued, "I'll meet you there, and see you off just to ensure all goes well."

Sauwa was again hesitant, "You have a lot of your own problems right now. The least of which is making your own arrangements to get out of the country. I'm a little concerned you might be taking on more than you can handle under the circumstances."

Banker shook his head slightly. "I've been in this business awhile. I knew a time like this would come, and I would have to beat a hasty retreat. In my line of work, a quick retreat has always been a consideration. I've had things in place for just this sort of moment. I'll be gone soon after I've taken care of you. My chief concern is what you pointed out last night. Whoever you work for clearly has a lot of pull of their own. Having you in this country dangerously exposes them if you get caught. That would only earn me the wrath of another dangerous organization, and that I can't afford."

Satisfied Banker was still with her as near as she could tell, she responded. "Then let's plan our moves for tonight. We meet an hour ahead to finalize any last-minute issues. I want ample time to make changes in the event something unforeseen occurs."

"Only an hour is cutting it close, don't you think?" Banker gave her a questioning look. "I mean, if something goes wrong, it's a narrow margin to make any modifications."

Sauwa was now looking at him directly. "But, the alternative is to be lingering in a place that will be crawling with security, not to mention anyone else looking for us. Ideally, I wouldn't want to show up until it's time to board. An hour is a good medium between the two."

Banker sighed, "There's a place called Pikeys. It's outside the port area and is secluded. It's a good place to meet and finalize arrangements."

"I've seen it. We'll meet there. The next step is communication. Because of the threat of the IRA looming over our heads, and because we don't know what the police know yet between the killing of the police detective and the more recent shootout at the warehouse, things are likely to change considerably between now and tonight when we meet. It will be unwise for you to go anywhere near your club or any other place you're known to conduct business. It would be better for you to call me. Here is a number." Sauwa walked over and handed him a piece of paper.

"We'll set a time when we walk out of here. From that point, you will call that number every three hours, so we can apprise each other of any developments that might complicate things for tonight."

"A little elaborate don't you think?" Banker asked as he took the paper from her.

"Not at all," she replied. "We are operating with several unknown variables, and we need to remain as flexible as possible if we intend to survive."

"The IRA should be simple enough," Banker said. "Word travels quickly when they're after someone. It's the cops that'll be the problem. With a case this big, no one will be talking this early in the investigation. When it's one of their own, all the interdepartmental rivalries that would normally work so well in our favor come to an end. Everybody in the Garda comes together to solve the case."

"We don't even know if they've tied the cop and the warehouse incident together yet." Sauwa suddenly realized, "We don't even know if they know about you."

Banker shook his head. "It's doubtful. I covered my tracks well. There's nothing that connects me to the warehouse, and you've never set foot in my club. There is nothing that would put us together in a surveillance picture."

"The IRA was onto you in about a day," Sauwa reminded. "If the Garda is stomping the grounds with their intelligence departments who know all the same avenues, they could be onto you as well."

"Shit," Banker replied, despairingly. He hated admitting this novice oversight. He was a master of the criminal world in dealing with racketeers and other types of gangsters. His experience with the police tended to be more with vice cops and those investigating robberies than with high-level intelligence. It was terrible to admit that while he had provided services to paramilitaries both Republican and Loyalist, it had always been on a limited basis, providing safe houses for meetings or house operatives on the run, or helping fence the goods from heists the IRA or UVF committed in the name of the cause. He had never been directly involved in the military affairs of these groups before. Being embroiled in the world of high-level terrorism and intrigue placed him well outside his element.

Sauwa emerged from the kitchen holding two plates filled with poached eggs, toast and bacon. It wasn't the healthiest meal but, given the circumstances and the day they still had ahead of them, it would suffice. The two ate their meal as they finalized the remainder of their plans. With her bergen all packed, Sauwa prepared to leave. The metal object she had used the night before was carefully tucked into the loops of her pack's shoulder straps. It was hidden nicely between her back and the bergen with only the small handle slightly protruding at the small of her back for easy access.

"Isn't it a bit risky walking around with that?" Banker asked as he pointed at the object.

Sauwa was a bit preoccupied adjusting her bergen as she responded. "It's a necessary risk given what I'm up against. While a gun or knife would be an instant flag to any policeman, a cop would presume a hunk of metal like this would be just something I found rummaging through the trash and decided to bring home. I'm more likely to be relieved of it with a stern warning."

21

Nash Emery made no attempt to hide his fueling anger over the whole matter. The idea of working with Dublin made his stomach churn. He was an operative, a man who fought the British and the Loyalists head-on in combat in both the streets of Ballymurphy in Belfast and in the wild countryside of County Armagh. To him, the IRA of the Republic was little more than a crime syndicate, masking its business behind the thin veneer of still fighting for the cause.

While he had heard all the excuses from his superiors trying to rationalize their actions as generating needed funds for the cause, he saw gangsters who spent more time engaging in violence over criminal behavior and punishing people who ran afoul of them on the streets. In his eyes, they were racketeers, pure and simple. "They'd piss their nappies, if they ever saw a real fight," Emery would often quip.

His cab pulled up to the curb just beside the wharf. Exiting, Emery paid the fare and casually walked down the street. He had deliberately chosen the location for its strategic advantage. The wharf was quiet this time of day with only a few old pensioners and some young couples wandering about enjoying the sea air. This made it hard for a surveillance team to go undetected, especially since so little time would have been given to prepare.

Emery had phoned Seamus Nally's pub only a half hour before. It had been his experience that short time frames to establish meetings guaranteed that any watching security agencies would have little advanced warning. As a result, they often wound up arranging an amateur setup that was easy to spot.

It also helped that if the meeting party had any dubious intentions, as was common in his world, an ambush would be impossible to arrange in such a short time or be adequately concealed in such an open area. Emery was quite an experienced hand at such arrangements. He had no illusions about how the world he existed in worked. Even when dealing with allies and comrades, betrayal was common — awareness and some preparation was always needed.

The wharf had the benefit of being lined with an assortment of small shops with large windows. While it allowed someone inside to have a wide view outward, it also made it easy for them to be seen from the outside. Emery casually walked the line of shops, carefully looking for any sign of trouble.

He saw that with the exception of some ferry boats heading out toward England and Wales, the waters were virtually empty of any other sea craft. This was also a good sign that there were no surveillance teams operating and waiting to catch sight of the meeting. His disdain for the IRA in the south also extended to his belief that in addition to being corrupt, they were also amateurish in the way they conducted their affairs. The idea that the police would have knowledge of this meeting due to the local IRA's poor security was a strong consideration. If he had spotted anything that remotely looked like the police were expecting this meeting, he was ready to walk away immediately. If it did happen, it would ensure Seamus Nally met with a bullet in his head.

It wasn't long before he saw an older man with a crop of salt and pepper hair. He had a thickly lined face under a neatly groomed beard. His long brown coat and floppy plaid hat played well to the image of an elderly gentleman enjoying the sea air.

Seamus Nally strolled up to the pier railing and looked out at the waters of the Irish Sea. Seamus was a good thirty meters from Emery and gave not the faintest hint of knowing or even being interested in him. He had seen from the younger man what he needed, the green army field jacket and a copy of the sports section of yesterday's paper, folded to a Canadian hockey article that was facing outward.

The two enjoyed the view for another ten minutes before Nally started to walk away. Emery waited as he turned casually and leaned against the railing while looking out at the people on the wharf. This continued for another three minutes as he watched everyone who was walking in that direction carefully for earpieces with wires running down the side of their necks, speaking into their hands or to themselves, or just working to keep close to the old man to see if there was anyone tailing him. When the minutes had elapsed, he started walking in Nally's direction.

Nally was about fifty meters ahead, keeping a slow, leisurely pace with no more than a handful of people between him and Emery. Emery was now convinced his contact was not being followed. At a nearby turn, he pulled into a side alley and pretended to discard his newspaper. All this Nally caught while he turned slightly to look at a storefront. To anyone walking by, it was two separate actions. In reality, it was one, well-coordinated.

After every alleyway and road turn, the one being followed would stop momentarily at the first logical storefront they came to. He would use the moment to discretely look back and see what his pursuer was doing. If the pursuer, once eye contact was made, stopped and turned directly around, it was a sign of a surveillance detail having been spotted. If so, the meeting was canceled and new arrangements would have to be made for another time. If, after eye contact had been made, the pursuer turned into an alley and then turned around, it meant that he was confident there was no surveillance detail in pursuit.

Now it was Nally's turn to reciprocate the courtesy. Though it had been some years since he had lived in the world of intrigue, he still remembered his operational craft. It was while going through these procedures he understood just how far he had gotten from everything. None of his men, even Cork Regan, would have considered taking such precautions. He waited at the storefront looking out the corner of his eye as Emery began walking. After about three minutes, Nally began casually walking back the way he came. This time he was the one keeping watch for anyone possibly surveilling them. Like Emery, he watched for all the signs and saw none. When they found themselves back at the wharf, Emery turned to look out at the water. Out of the corner of his eye, he watched as Nally walked over and slipped onto a bench along the railing several meters away. It was his sign that all was clear.

Emery still gave one last look around to see if anyone was showing any signs of curiosity. Though the measures taken would have thwarted any amateur team with little preparation time, a more professional operator — like the British 14 Intelligence Company — would have understood the exercise being conducted between the two men and reacted differently to keep from being detected. Confident that they were alone, Emery started over to where the older man was sitting. Slipping next to him, Emery sat down tentatively on the bench.

"It's good weather we're having today," Nally began, his eyes focused toward the sea.

"Stop wasting my time. I didn't come all the way here on such short notice to engage in bullshit, idle conversation." Emery commanded. "Now follow me." Emery rose from the bench and straightened his coat.

Nally was beside himself. He was not used to men speaking to him in such fashion. However, the man standing seemed unconcerned with being insubordinate. Under the circumstances, pulling rank seemed the worst possible thing for him to do. He rose to his feet and followed as Emery started walking. "It's good to see you," the older man began. "I understand you've been briefed on the situation."

Emery shrugged. "I've been told some. What I've heard, I don't like."

Nally continued. "We've had a serious attack against the movement."

"A guy was feeding you information on the Loyalists here in Ireland," Emery cut in. "I know he was a great help in weeding those bastards out." Emery had been on a few of the operations that had been launched based on Donovan's intelligence. He was well acquainted with what devastation the detective's death had been to their operation. He was even more irritated that the boys in Dublin had done such a shitty job protecting such an asset. They were supposed to have a good ear to the ground when it came to the underworld. And yet, they couldn't catch a word about a low life with a grudge or about a professional hit team or assassin operating in their city. He imagined they were so careless because it didn't coincide with their criminal enterprise.

"It's become more serious." Nally was sounding slightly nervous. It was clearly obvious to Emery that the old man was way over his head. "We lost five more comrades. This team seems very good. That's why you're here. Six good men have been lost to the cause, and we need to strike back."

"One good man has died for the cause," Emery replied, incredulously. "I'm here after the person or team that killed Marston Donovan. As for your band of street enforcers, they died as they lived, men of the streets. As far as I'm concerned, that's not my problem."

Nally became agitated at Emery's cavalier remarks. "You're awfully callous about this. Men died for the cause."

The two men proceeded down the walkway they had previously been on. Nally couldn't help but notice the lack of windows along the building sides. It was probably the reason this route was chosen. It was another reminder that he was dealing with a world he had not seen for many years.

"No!" Emery was now looking straight at the older man with a glare that could have burned through rock. "They were racketeers; their service to the cause amounted to shakedowns, collections and punishing anyone who ran afoul of your business ventures. I was training true soldiers to go north and fight for the cause — to go across the border and engage in real combat with real enemies — an actual war."

"I was getting ready to go north myself to continue the fight when I was suddenly pulled out to come here. So, understand me well. I didn't come to Dublin to avenge a bunch of lowlife gangsters masquerading as soldiers. Nor do I care in the slightest about protecting your credibility. I came because whatever is happening, it looks like a whole new front in the conflict is about to break out. My guess is the UVF is looking to rekindle the old campaign of waging war down here. As I see it, I'm here to fight that."

Nally shied away. He wasn't sure how to answer any of these comments. He knew he was in a bad light with the brigade command in Belfast and would be pressing his luck dearly to try and argue back. All he could do was hold his tongue and meet the man's needs as best he could.

The look in the older man's eye told Emery everything he needed. "I need to get a picture of who I'm dealing with. You have good contacts on the Garda."

It wasn't a question, but Nally nodded anyway

"Are they good enough that you can arrange for me to visit the scene of the shootout?" Emery pressed. "I need to know who I'm up against."

"I can find someone to sneak you in," Nally responded feebly.

"I need to see it today; in the next few hours." Emery was stern in his demand.

"You will get it," Nally replied. "It will take a few phone calls, but I should have an answer for you in the next couple of hours."

At Emery's direction, the two men changed course as they started down the docks toward the marina. It was a strange detour the older man thought. But it seemed like another intended component of Emery's plan. The old boards of the wharf creaked in an eerie sort of way as the men continued walking. Soon they were alone on the pier lined with old weathered fishing boats.

Emery moved on to his next demand. "I also need you to start pushing your sources and connections on the street. Someone is working with this team. You gave me a name — Rudy Sheehan. You thought this person may be the assassin's benefactor? Find him. I want to know where he is within the next few hours. I want to deal with him immediately."

"That could prove difficult," Nally quivered slightly. "Since yesterday, he hasn't been seen at his normal places of business."

The look Emery gave the older man was chilling and sent the unspoken message that he didn't want excuses; he wanted results. Nally nodded submissively. "My people are working on it."

"Here's a number where I can be reached." Emery handed the older man a piece of paper. "Call me when I have access to the crime scene. I believe it's a warehouse on the waterfront."

Nally nodded as he read the paper handed him.

"Until then, I want as much information as you can get," Emery commanded. "I'll move when I have something to move on. In the meantime, my team and I are getting prepared. I expect I'll be activating them by tonight."

"As I said," Nally responded, "I'll start making calls to get your access to the warehouse arranged. We still have some people in the ranks of the Garda who help us from time to time." He finished reading the number, confident he had memorized it. Then taking a lighter from his pocket, he set fire to the paper and the ashes dropped it to the ground.

He turned to see Emery already walking away leaving him alone to collect his thoughts. It was certainly a bad situation all around. The thought that entered his mind was the notion that this man may be right. If this was the act of a Loyalist paramilitary, it was signaling the start of a new campaign of violence. The very idea was disconcerting. It also made him realize how little he really knew about what was going on.

22

Detective Sergeant Youngest looked up at the neon lights of the Rory Club as he prepared to enter. He had heard about the place in conversations with officers working vice and narcotics. It wasn't the type of place that would necessarily interest a man who preferred a quiet drink in a local pub surrounded by men wanting nothing more than the same. He had just finished his interview with Rodney Madge, the owner of the Thrift store — one of the names mentioned by Detective Curly — when he received a call from Dagden telling him he should come to the Rory club at once.

When he got there, Youngest found his subordinate standing outside waiting. Dagden walked over to his boss, his hand waving back in the direction of the club. "I thought you'd want to hear this," he said as he walked up. "The club's owner is a Rudy Sheehan. He was on the list you gave me to check out. I came here asking about him and found he's not here. I mean, he hasn't been seen since he left last night, and no one has been able to get ahold of him all day."

"That's interesting," Youngest replied. "What else do we have?"

Dagden shrugged. "I got that much and a little more when I figured this was probably our man. After that, I figured you'd want to take the lead."

"You thought right," Youngest nodded as he started up the steps. "Who've you been speaking to?"

"The barmaid — she opens up in the morning," Dagden replied, as he trailed after his boss. "Also, sir, I should tell you. There's another detective in there."

Youngest stopped his ascension and turned to face his subordinate. "Who?" he asked.

Dagden's eyes darted from side to side as he struggled to remember. "Ah, a Detective Ian Galligan from one of the intelligence units. He showed up just after I did and started asking for Mr. Sheehan as well."

Youngest's eyes widened at the sound of the name. He began hurrying up the steps at a much faster pace. He burst through the doors and walked into the main room. Looking over at the bar, he saw a large bull-like man in a cheap, grey suit. He was leaning over the bar and appeared to be having a conversation with a young redhead. He was rapping his fist against the bar — a sure indicator he was getting exasperated.

Youngest strolled forward. The young woman was cognizant of the larger man's growing anger and was trying to mask her concern. "Forgive me for intruding," Youngest opened, pretending not to notice the tense situation. "Detective Sergeant Youngest, Garda homicide investigations."

The large man turned to face him. "Detective Galligan, Garda Crime Special Surveillance Unit."

Youngest observed the situation carefully. "I don't wish to bother you, but I'm looking for someone, and I need to speak with this young lady."

"I need to speak to her as well," Galligan said in a tone denoting he wasn't about to leave.

"Might we speak quickly in private, since I can assume we're looking for the same man — Mr. Rudy Sheehan?" Youngest was trying to be diplomatic as he navigated the tense situation. Dagden had come up behind him and was waiting to see what happened next. The burly detective followed Youngest to a more private area of the nearly deserted club leaving Dagden to stay with the woman.

"Detective, I'm in the midst of a murder investigation," Youngest began. "If that woman knows where Mr. Sheehan is, I need to speak with her."

Galligan folded his arms in an attempt to look intimidating. "I'm also here on business. We have reason to believe that the UVF might be trying to reorganize. We think it's for the purpose of starting a new campaign here in the Republic. We believe Mr. Sheehan may be helping them."

It was all nonsense, of course, which Youngest saw from the get-go. As he had predicted, Donovan's old friends, hearing about paramilitary involvement, were looking to make trouble as they embarked on their own investigation. The excuse of acting on recent intelligence gave them the proper cover to do so.

Youngest nodded his head as he thought out his next words. The future of this conversation would determine if this situation would be amenably concluded or turn into a rivalry between departments. "Detective, I believe we are close to finding the killer of Detective Donovan. I believe Mr. Sheehan has been shielding his killer. My concern is that time is running out. Can I just have a few words with her?"

"I've been talking to her," Galligan snapped. "She's been evasive. Not giving me shit."

Galligan was an intelligence officer who dealt with threats and terror organizations. It was obvious to Youngest the man he was speaking to had no real experience solving crimes. "Well, do you mind if I have a word with her anyway and see if I might try a different approach? She may not realize what she knows."

The large detective held his intimidating pose, unsure what to do. Youngest continued, "At least give me a chance to try, since we're both after the same thing."

Finally, Galligan capitulated as he dropped his arms and waved the Detective Sergeant forward. Youngest approached the bar where the young woman was working. She was clearly nervous having all these cops around.

"What's your name?" Youngest asked in a soft friendly tone, as he took a seat at the bar like a patron looking to order a drink.

"Kella," the redhead responded quietly.

"I'm Ryan Youngest. I'm sorry if we're bothering you," Youngest said warmly.

"You're a cop also, I reckon?" Kella asked.

He chuckled a little. "Yes, yes I am. And I'm wondering if you could help me out?"

"Like I told your friend over there, I don't know where Mr. Sheehan's gone off to." Kella was nervous as she tried to prove her innocence.

"I believe you," Youngest replied. "I just wonder if anything unusual has been happening with your boss the last few days."

Kella paused. "Well, it's been weird the last few days."

"How so?"

"He's been disappearing a lot. Putting me in charge and then stepping out for a few hours here and there with no reason at all. Then yesterday, those men came by asking about him." She stopped as she started to wipe the counter.

"What men?" Youngest continued.

"Never saw them before," Kella replied. "About five of them, looking real mean though — rough like. The kind you send to collect money or send a message. They seemed interested in my boss as well. They were really interested when I told them what I told you."

"Kella, it's important we find your boss. I know you don't know where he is, but can you think of any acquaintances he has or names he's brought up in the past? People who seemed to be important to him when he mentioned them?"

Kella stopped her wiping as she turned and looked about as if trying to find the answer among the bottles of booze. After a few moments, she turned toward the detective. "I remember him briefly mentioning a Mr. Larky. He didn't say anything else. Only the few times the name came up, it seemed really important to my boss. He made sure he kept whatever appointment they had planned." She shook her head. "That's the only name he mentioned."

Youngest nodded. "Thank you. I'll let my friends back there know." He nodded to the large detective watching from the distance. "I don't think he'll need to talk to you anymore."

The girl smiled with a look of relief at hearing that. Youngest rose from his seat and started back to where Galligan and Dagden waited. "Well it's a cinch he's either dead or in hiding." Youngest opened as they joined the intelligence officer.

"That's all you got with that wee chat of yours?" Galligan said in disgust. "I'll deal with this." He started back toward the bar but was stopped by Youngest, who quickly stepped in his way.

"She's just an employee, and she knew better than to ask questions," he counseled the bigger man. "Questioning her further would be a waste of time. Besides, she gave me a lot more than that."

"What?" Galligan had now stopped and was looking at the homicide detective intently.

Youngest hesitated. He didn't like the idea of sharing information with a cop who had pointedly inserted himself into such a sensitive investigation. However, he also liked the idea of this intelligence cop going off and working his own angles even less. "She mentioned a Mr. Larky. It could be a nickname or an alias. But, according to her, he's someone who's very important to Mr. Sheehan."

Galligan ruminated for several moments. "I've heard the name come up from time to time in certain contexts and discussing certain circles of organized crime. I know some fellas who would have a better finger on this. Let me check with them and get back to you." He started to leave.

Youngest stopped him, again. "But, you will be getting back to us?"

Galligan confused. "Of course, I will. We're all after the same thing."

"I just want to make sure that we are." Youngest stood his ground in preparation for a fight. "Seeing you here asking about the same man we're looking for right after I discussed it with your colleague, I'm just inclined to want to make sure that we keep each other informed and working toward the same agenda."

The burly detective said nothing. Instead, he folded his arms as he presented his same intimidating expression. He looked both detectives up and down as if debating whether to answer their concerns or punch their lights out. He would have been quite capable of both. Youngest stood his ground waiting, displaying a look that demanded an answer.

Finally, Galligan conceded. He dropped his arms and scratched his head. "Look, I understand how this looks to you both. On the eve of losing one of our own and seeing us talking up the same people, you're probably wondering what exactly I'm about. Maybe you're all wondering if perhaps this isn't some kind of vigilante revenge thing masked as police work."

"Since we're being honest," Youngest replied with a tone that made his suspicions clear.

Galligan continued, "You've got it all wrong. When you called us and explained possible UVF involvement, it got some powerful people in my branch in a hell of a panic. We still have several old timers who remember those dark days of the seventies when the Loyalists were carrying out a terror campaign here in the Republic. They specifically cringe at the memory of the dark day in seventy-six when the UVF detonated three car bombs along a busy thoroughfare during rush hour. Some three hundred people were seriously injured and sent to emergency. It's still a haunting reminder."

"After your call, our bosses got worried we were being caught off guard. When they started asking around and heard of the warehouse shootings — where those five IRA men got killed — it looked like these murders may actually be connected to your case. My superiors were sure we were seeing the beginning of a war between the UVF and the IRA here in Dublin. This is our own follow-up to make sure we're on top of it before the next bloodbath."

Youngest licked his lips as he stared at an equally confused Dagden. Neither one had fully understood how much of a life this case was taking on beyond their control. Reluctantly, Youngest turned back to the intelligence officer. "I think you need to come by my office later. If this is becoming a concern for your department, then we should probably disclose our current findings to head off any further paranoid theories."

Nodding, Galligan extended his hand. "I'll do that. In the meantime, I'll talk up my people about your Mr. Larky and see what they might know."

"Thank you," Youngest replied, as he took the brawny man's hand in a firm handshake.

23

The atmosphere of the warehouse resembled that of a mausoleum. The bodies had not yet been removed, and detectives were still busy finishing up the last of the crime scene walkthrough. With the help of a young constable working the security perimeter and sympathetic to the cause, Nash Emery, along with a young sandy-haired fellow in his early twenties, slipped inside and began walking around. Everyone was preoccupied trying to capture any last photos or details before the crime scene was cleaned up. People had been coming and going throughout the day. It was like the platform of a train station. This meant that with little more than a few snagged visitors' badges, the two IRA operatives went unnoticed.

From the very moment they entered and saw the display, it became apparent what had happened. With the years of experience both men had in combat, they could easily replay in their minds how the whole fight went. Neither man spoke as their eye contact said enough. They continued through the main area and headed toward the back corner following a darkened hallway. As with the detectives before them, both saw the only light offered was through the setup of police work lights. The hallway was deserted at this point, so they felt comfortable engaging in verbal conversation.

Seeing the blood splatters and the bodies clumped closely together in front of the lit doorway with the third body just inside the room, the sandy-haired man spoke first. "This wasn't a fucking team. This was one person against five idiots."

Emery looked back at his cohort, Ewen Callaway. The young man was a deceiving vision — he definitely looked younger than his twenty-two years. Yet, as Emery well knew, he was a seasoned fighter from the streets of West Belfast. He had inadvertently become involved in the movement at the age of sixteen — when his twin sister was abducted off the streets by a Loyalist kill squad out trolling for Catholics. Somehow, the girl had managed to fight free and escape from the car. The Loyalists tried to give chase but were thwarted by IRA gunman coming to the rescue from a nearby bar.

The Loyalists took off after a quick but violent gun battle. The twins fought back against the attackers. When it was over, an impressed Nash Emery decided to take the youngsters under his wing. He trained them and found them to have a natural instinct for the work of an active service soldier. Likewise, grateful to the men who had saved them from certain death and Emery for his training, the twins became ferociously devoted to him. By seventeen, they were accompanying him on missions where they proved their abilities on several occasions.

Callaway continued his observations. "These idiots walked right into a bloody trap; a dark hallway, an echoing concrete structure and a killer who had firsthand knowledge of the setup." He turned to face his mentor. "Why the fuck didn't they just wait outside and ambush their target when he came out?"

Emery shrugged. "They underestimated their mark. They expected to find some street hood and got careless. Whoever they were up against has done this sort of thing before and been doing it for a while."

"It looks it," the young man agreed. "This whole place was set up as one big ambush spot."

"What do we do now, is the question?" The older man stated as he looked about. "Someone like this doesn't make themselves easy to find."

"Have they been able to find the man who they think is helping him?" Callaway asked.

"They're working on it," Emery responded. "My concern is that this person will be gone by the time we find him."

The younger man peered into the room off to the side and saw the blood-soaked corpse of Cork Regan. "This killer laid in wait in the shadows down the hall. When they appeared in the light, the assassin opened up with a large caliber automatic, a .45, I'd say."

"You're absolutely right." Emery couldn't help playing the role of a mentor when it came to his young protégé. "Then the assassin moved up and executed the three right here at close range with headshots and chased the two survivors down. They were taken in the main room. What does that tell you?"

The younger man thought for a moment. "Even in the

heat of the fight, he was smart enough to know they were dangerous as liabilities and had to be taken out. This assassin has been in gunfights like this before."

"Several gunfights from the way he was able to think under such pressure," the older man added.

Callaway shook his head. "I'll say it again. I don't like this. The cops are all over this case, and we're putting ourselves at great risk. Even you agree that this looks like a gangster beef. Why don't we let the Dublin boys eat their own shit?"

Emery placed a calming hand on the angered youth. "Because we're soldiers, and we follow orders. And because, if this is the work of the Prods (Protestants), then it means it's part of the war, and we fight wars. Make no mistake, lad. When we catch up to this assassin, if we do, it won't be an easy mission. Expect that a war is what we'll be fighting."

IT WAS NEARLY six o'clock when Sauwa found herself standing outside an old apartment building. She leaned against the wall of the building directly across the street and innocently looked about. She was checking for anything that looked remotely out of place. With the police combing the city, it was a sure bet that someone like the man she was about to see would be a person of interest.

The streets were quiet with the exception of a few older folks who seemed local. There were none of the signs that indicated any surveillance was on the ground. As an added precaution, she walked up the sidewalk a short distance before crossing the street and doubled back until she was, again, facing the apartment building.

Armed with a cup of ice cream she had picked up at a shop around the corner, she pretended to be just another bohemian traveler visiting the different pockets of the city. It was an answer that readily explained her presence to the locals and made her easily forgotten. It also explained the strange act of her leaning up against the wall and staring up at the window sills of the apartments across the way. To any observer, they would assume she was just enjoying the historical architecture. In actuality, she was studying each room to look for signs that someone was watching the street — either the police or the local old battle axes with nothing better to do. Satisfied that no one seemed interested in the slightest, she finally entered the building.

It was a different location from where she had gone when she first met Mr. Larky a week and a half ago. The first location had been an office building on the other side of town. It had been professionally set up with photography equipment and other machines needed to make documents. The whole operation offered quality goods but could be taken down and, if necessary, destroyed in a matter of seconds.

The building she was in now was a sharp contrast to Larky's previous location. This structure dated back to the nineteenth century, and looked like something out of a historical movie. On the lower floor, there was a creepy display of lights from the early age of electricity against dark wood paneling.

All Sauwa saw was the perfect location for an ambush, if this turned out to be a betrayal. The darkened shadows lined the hallway and nestling next to the stairwell would make it hard to see anyone hiding, even with the use of a torch. She aware that someone could shoot or stab her through the open slits of the stair railing as she ascended. She had learned through her training and personal experience that when working at night or in the dark, it was best to rely more on hearing, smell and touch than on sight. She closed her eyes as she listened for any alien sounds alerting her to someone lurking.

Proceeding down the hall, she kept her hand touching the handle of the weapon wedged between her bergen and her back. Creeping the short distance to the staircase, Sauwa could sense nothing out of place. She believed she was alone as she started up the staircase. Three flights of steps later she was on the third floor looking down another darkened hallway with only a few wall lamps providing minimal lighting. The old warped boards creaked loudly beneath her feet as she stepped forward.

Reaching the door marked Room 314, she knocked. The sound of someone thumping about on the other side was distinctive. Slipping to the other side of the hall, she grabbed her weapon. Concerned about the possibility of a trap, she wanted to give herself every advantage. Standing a distance from the door meant an attacker would have to race out the door and cross the hall to attack her. Bullets fired through the door would be less likely to hit her.

After what seemed like forever, the door cracked open to partially reveal the thick, rounded face of a man. It was Mr. Larky. He stood looking at her for a moment. With the darkness of the hallway and the number of clients he dealt with, it took him some time to recognize Sauwa. By his own behavior, she could only guess he was holding the same suspicions of her. Neither of them lived in a world where trust was a lavish commodity.

Seeing her arm tucked behind her, the old man could guess what she was holding. Flinging back the door, he stepped aside allowing her to have a full view of the room. She could see no viable place for someone to hide. As she prepared to cross the threshold, she looked through the crack of the door's hinges and saw that no one was waiting behind the door. Much like the rest of the building, the place had poor lighting. She was thankful her night vision had returned on her way up the stairs. Reciprocating the courtesy, she lowered her hands to her sides as she prepared to enter.

Inside she turned to keep continuous sight of the man. A heavy-set figure, in his mid-sixties who seemed to have trouble moving about, Mr. Larky didn't pose much of a threat. He shut the door and ushered her into the next room; it was set up as his office space. Again, as a precaution, he entered first with her close behind to ensure he would be protection from any aggressors.

Like the entryway, the office was empty except for a few Spartan pieces of furniture and just enough random items to give the place the appearance of being used. Like the office building, this place was another one of the man's business fronts. If the police or someone more dangerous were onto him, he could walk out the door and disappear. Thinking about it, Sauwa realized the logic of the setup. It was an old neighborhood with a homogenous community of long-established families and older people. It would be hard for anyone to watch the place for long without attracting attention from suspicious and inquisitive locals creating an informal security warning system. His clients were prepared in one location where people coming in for long appointments would not be out of the ordinary. Then they were handed the finished products in this low-key place where someone popping in and out of an apartment could be delivering a package to anyone in the complex or visiting friends and relatives. Short trips could be explained, long-term visitors, not so much.

Mr. Larky waddled his way to an old couch that was sagging in the middle and promptly flopped into it. "Everything's been paid for by your benefactor, so you don't owe me anything," he said as he slid the rest of the way over until he was able to access a weathered cabinet off to the side. Opening the small door, he struggled to bend over and reach inside. He sat upright, giving a deep moan as if he had just run a marathon. In his hands, he held a thick, yellow envelope. He extended his arm in her direction to hand it to her.

Retrieving it, she opened the envelope immediately. Inside was a collection of documents: a passport, driver's license, birth certificate and other viable records all in the name of one Deidra Tory. Flipping through the passport, she saw her picture done up in what looked to be an authentic British passport.

"This should help get you into any country you have to go through," Mr. Larky spoke up. "Included is another set of documents for Australia — the country you asked for — in the name of Carly Renford. These papers should allow you to escape into a new life when you finally get to where you want to settle."

The Australian documents were every bit as professional and authentic looking as the British ones, though she had never actually seen Australian documents. "Thank you," she replied in a quiet tone. She was about to burst into tears. The very idea that she was holding her new life and her freedom in her hands seemed like a dream she never thought would come true. "What about all the negatives and other materials you used to create these?" she reminded herself suddenly, her professional instincts activating.

Emitting another groan as he bent over, the old man reached into the cabinet and came back with another envelope; this one was much larger than the first one. "Everything is here." He handed her the package. "When you leave here today, there will be no record of our ever having done business together."

She took the larger envelope. Checking inside, she saw that Larky had been true to his word. Everything denoting Sauwa Catcher was stuffed into it. She resisted the urge to hug the grandfatherly figure as she maintained her stoic disposition. Folding the package, she tucked it into her bergen. She was about to throw it over her back when the phone rang.

Mr. Larky wrestled to stand up and shuffled a few feet to answer it. The call lasted only a few seconds before he placed the phone back in its cradle.

"We have company," he said. "I'm the only person on this floor. I have a guy just below who I pay to watch the stairway when I'm here and let me know when someone's coming up. He just told me two men are walking up the stairs. You go and hide. I don't want to have anyone catch you here."

Sauwa took up her bag and hustled into the kitchen and heard a pounding at the door. Placing her bergen in one corner, she lowered herself to her knee in the shadow of the wall, peeking to see who was there. Mr. Larky waddled his way to the door and opened it. Two grimacing men — a large, brawny man, and a smaller, bullish man with red hair — pushed Larky back, forcing their way in.

"I'm Detective Galligan. This is Detective Curly of the Irish Garda," the larger man said gruffly. Both produced their police credentials. "We need to speak to you, sir."

Sauwa watched as Mr. Larky retreated into a nearby chair. She heard him flop down with his all too identifiable groan. "What can I do for you gentlemen? I don't normally get calls from the police."

"We need to ask you some questions, sir," the red-haired detective said as he tucked his credentials back into his jacket pocket. "We understand that you are known to be somewhat of an associate of one Rudy Sheehan."

"Rudy Sheehan?" Mr. Larky asked, confused. "I'm afraid I don't know that name."

"Really?" the bigger cop cut in. "You see, we have it on good authority he has had serious dealings with you. Serious enough he dropped everything while running a very high-end nightclub just to make his appointments with you."

"I have no idea who you're referring to," Larky gushed. "Do I look like the sort of man nightclub owners come to visit?"

"Well, let's ask this a different way," the larger detective was curt. "We're also looking for a woman — this woman." Sauwa watched as he pulled a picture from his coat pocket and handed it to the older man. "She's in her early twenties, sounds British but is South African by nationality, and goes by the name of Sauwa Catcher."

Instantly, Sauwa's eyes lit up. She had hoped this was an entirely unrelated issue. At the very least, if she were discovered, she could have played the role of an innocent girl looking to use the bathroom or visit an old man she knew. That these policemen were here looking for her and had a photograph of her, the peaceful option was no longer available. She wondered how long Larky was going to hold out. From the sounds of his incredulous response to the cops, it seemed he was not one for cooperation. However, their intelligence seemed thorough.

"You mind if I look around?" Galligan asked as he started to move into the adjoining office. Larky didn't have a chance to respond before the cop was through the door. Galligan was casual, as he sauntered into the office.

Preparing for the possibility of battle, Sauwa slowly slipped her shoes off leaving her in stocking feet. She looked about and saw a cutlery holder on the counter a short distance away. The soft padding of her socks masked the sounds of her movements across the hard kitchen floor. Retrieving one of the longer cutting knives from the holder, she crossed the room quietly and climbed onto the counter located next to the doorway in order to give herself some height against her much larger opponent. The dismissive nature of the detectives made them oblivious to any slight creaking she made mounting the counter and took up a fighting position. As the apartment was very dark, she still enjoyed the concealment of the shadows. Her immediate hope would be that with his attitude, he would pass right by her.

"Hey, you're starting to sweat some," the red-haired detective remarked as he spoke to Mr. Larky. "You got something or someone around here you don't want us to know about?"

"Ah, no," Larky responded. His nervousness was becoming quite apparent. "By all means look away. I have nothing to hide."

At that moment Sauwa could see Gallagan perk up and become more alert. She watched as he took a more tactical stance and drew his firearm from his holster. He began to move more cautiously.

Though they were police officers who carried guns, they were detectives and went for long periods without firing them. Normally, they were more focused on interrogating witnesses and writing reports. She guessed that most of their weapons usage amounted to shooting on controlled ranges at paper targets and cleaning the weapon afterward.

For Sauwa, it was easy to tell the man was out of his element as he moved around. His tactical movements were unwieldy and academic — not instinctive and natural that came with the experience of one who belonged to a military Special Forces unit or police tactical squad. That his partner opted to stay with Larky in the next room as opposed to joining in a search of the quarters further demonstrated their inexperience. Neither man even considered trying to find more lighting, further displaying their inexperience. Instead of keeping the weapon tightly to his chest or his hip, Galligan extended his arms well in front of his body.

The way the larger detective entered the darkened office showed he still was only partially concerned. Lowering herself as he neared her position, she clutched the kitchen knife and the sharp steel blade she had retrieved from her bergen. A few deep breaths had calmed her as she closed her eyes and concentrated on the creaking boards. She opened her eyes when she could hear him on the other side of the wall.

Her eyes had adjusted to the darkness. She watched as the weapon appeared around the corner, extended arms gradually following. With her weapon raised, she waited. Somehow she fought back the pounding of her heart as she took deep breaths. She saw the elbow as it crossed into view. With her arm raised enough for the needed momentum, she thrust the steel blade down with all the force she could muster driving it deep into the meaty, muscle and tendons of his elbow joint.

Even in the dark, she could see blood spurting profusely. She barely heard the man's screams of pain and terror before she robotically grabbed the carving knife sitting next to her. Rotating the blade in her hand, she thrust the knife deeply into the soft tissue of the man's jowl. It had all taken place so quickly, the detective barely had time to register what had just happened before he felt the sharp blade cut through his jowl line. Sauwa drove the blade through layer upon layer of tissue. She could feel it hit the hard bone as she made the kill.

Releasing her hand, she leapt catlike to the ground as she heard the gun drop. She lost her balance and fell when she tripped over the flopping leg of the detective thrashing about in his final death throws. She landed on her side with a painful thud, feeling a lancing pain in her shoulder. She could hear the shouting of the other detective, who realized what had just happened. He began delivering a litany of obscenities in her direction. She knew she had only a short time to act.

Detective Curly forgot everything in his astonishment. The shock of seeing his partner suddenly drop to the ground after howling wildly left him confused. His mind raced in all directions as he struggled to think. He had never drawn his weapon in such a circumstance. Frantically, he was trying to remember his weapons training. He fumbled for his sidearm and clumsily fought with the snap on his holster.

It took Sauwa a few seconds of muddling in the dark before she could feel the cold steel of the gun's muzzle and then the warm rubber of the grip where the Galligan's hands had been. She turned back over on her side just in time to see the other detective as he tried to process what had just happened and fumbled for his own gun.

Carefully, she gripped her weapon, her fingers feeling around for the trigger and the safety. As she was steadying herself, she heard the explosion of a shot echo in the hall. It was immediately followed by the intense velocity of a bullet whistling by. It passed near her, and she could hear it crash into the wall just above.

The detective had his gun out and had fired the first shot. She continued undeterred and aimed her weapon. He fired two more shots in rapid succession. As with the first shot, they were wild and well away from hitting her. She judged he was making the mistake common in the heat of battle. Though he was holding his weapon in the proper firing position, he had failed to line up his rear sight aperture sight with the front post and was foolishly looking solely beyond his front post causing his shots to go high.

Often a shooter firing under combat circumstances would expend half a magazine firing wildly before beginning to line up his weapon properly. Another two shots fired well above her head hit high on the wall and ceiling again. It was a safe guess that between the low light and his excitement, the detective had no idea where his shots were going.

With the weapon now firmly in her hands, Sauwa was back on her side to stabilize herself with more of her body weight. Her body's endorphins kicked in as she felt the strain on her shoulder gradually subside. Having spent no time on this particular weapon, she was unfamiliar with how accurate it was. To compensate, she leveled the weapon toward the center of the chest cavity which gave her the widest target and margin for error. She found the V of the rear aperture first. From there, she guided the gun until the front side post lined up in front of the V. Calmly, she sighted in toward the center of the detective's shadowed silhouette. She could see he was trying to take up a tactical posture based on his training. It was the common stance of moving one foot far behind the lead leg and stabilizing his arm. This was done both to create a steadier shooting position and to turn the body to limit the silhouette offered to the enemy shooting back.

The detective had tried to limit his silhouette but had not moved as far as he thought. His stomach and chest were still wide and visible to her. If she shot high it would hit his throat or head, low it would hit the stomach and abdomen. She was positioning the shot while trying to dodge the incessant kicks from the larger detective thrashing as he choked on his blood.

Firing her first shot, she watched as the man dropped back and clutched at his stomach. Behind him, the wall suddenly became awash with a massive splatter of blood

— a grave mistake of not wearing body armor. Though in obvious pain, the cop remained standing as he continued clutching his weapon. He was attempting to regain a fighting position but, due to the darkness of the room and from the way held his wound, he ended up shooting too low.

Sauwa fired her next round, this time angling her body as she aimed slightly higher. The gun bucked in her hands as she fired. The detective jerked back as the round struck him with great force and exploded out the back of his head. He dropped first to his knees and then sank to his side motionless.

She held her ground as she listened. The larger detective had finished choking, becoming a lifeless corpse. After several seconds of waiting, she saw no movement in the other room. Assuming she had neutralized her target, Sauwa rose to her feet, the weapon still at the ready. With the deliberate movements of a soldier on patrol in the jungle, she stepped over the large detective's body.

Her gun was lowered but, at the slightest hint of movement, she would have unloaded the remainder of her ammunition into his body; however, he remained completely motionless. Not knowing where the lights were and not wanting to expose herself, if a threat still remained, she had the unnerving experience of stepping into the oozing pool of drying blood as she cautiously continued through the doorway into the office.

It felt as if God had sent her a moment of reprieve when her feet were once more touching hard flooring. Confident the larger detective was dead, she picked up her pace and hustled over to where the body of the second cop lay. There was more natural light from the windows in the main room. The shot had gone through his forehead just above his right eye, the back of his head gone. Sauwa didn't have the opportunity to check, but the signs showed that the first policeman had loaded his gun with hollow point ammunition, a practice used by police around the world. The hollow points mushroom and are said to offer more lethal stopping power.

Sauwa heard grumbling. She turned to see a scared Mr. Larky looking back at her. His face was pale and his eyes wild with the fear of what he anticipated would come next. He was a witness to the murder of two detectives as well as being the only one who knew of Sauwa's new identities. It would be stupid to think he would be anything other than a dangerous liability to her. He began to shake at the thought his death was imminent. He closed his eyes readying himself for the inevitable.

Then he heard a clicking sound. He forced himself to open his eyes as he looked up to see the young assassin before him lowering the gun and tucking it into her waistband. Confused, he attempted to open his mouth to inquire what she was doing. However, he stopped himself. Pressing such an issue at such a moment seemed incredibly unwise. He wasn't dead, and a professional killer who skillfully killed two men only seconds ago was showing no sign of extending her tally to him.

To Larky's surprise, she asked, "Can you walk?"

Still shaken, he could only nod slightly. He didn't dare say he needed help moving at a time when he thought his life was in dire peril.

"I'm assuming this is not your actual home, nor is Larky your actual name," she explained as she moved back toward the kitchen.

Feeling a need to answer, he fought to spit the words out. "Ah, yes, you're correct."

"Good," she echoed from the hallway. "Then once we leave here you can disappear."

"You're letting me live?" Larky could no longer bear the anticipation of wondering if his death was certain or not.

Sauwa returned with her bergen and shoes in hand. "Of course," she replied as she dropped into a chair a few feet from where the detective's body was laying. "I have no need to kill you. And, you resisted turning me over to the detectives when you had the chance. I figure if given the ability to vanish you'll take it, especially since you are now party to the deaths of two police officers. You really don't have much to bargain with, if they catch you."

A sense of relief hit the old man as he saw his survival. At the same time, he also lamented what the girl had brought up. The career he enjoyed as a master forger had come to an end. After today he was retired.

Sauwa finished putting her shoes on. She discarded her flannel as it was stained with splatters of blood. Rolling the garment up, she tucked it under her arm after throwing on her bergen. She saw the old man struggle to get up from his couch and took him by the arm. Not wanting to give her second thoughts about keeping him alive, he began to explain. "You're right, this is not my home, nor is there any means to connect me to it. Further, none of my clients know me by my real name. When I walk out of here, I'll become a ghost in the mist."

Taking his arm over her shoulder, she aided him as he stumbled beside her out the door. It was an arduous journey as the two limped down the stairwell. Strangely, the old man seemed to become more agile as they went along. She could assume much of his invalidism was more an act than real. Possibly, he used this stunt to disarm those he worked with. Dangerous people tended to become less guarded and complacent around those they didn't perceive as threats. It served as a good tactic if one needed freedom of movement in dangerous circumstances.

"Were the acoustics in the room good?" Sauwa asked as they edged toward the last flight of stairs. "I assume several people heard those gunshots and are calling the cops. I also imagine people are watching the building from outside."

"You're right," Larky replied. "It's one of the reasons I chose this location. I figured I would be more victim than assailant if it should come to violence."

"You think we have to worry about anyone in here seeing us?" Sauwa pressed.

"No, most of the rooms are empty," Larky assured her. "The residents that do live here are old and, between their eyesight and the darkness, wouldn't be able to make a good identification. I know a couple of old battle axes in the building across the way who were definitely on the phone to police after the first shot. I can assure you they'll be watching the front. A few are really into crime novels and will probably even have cameras waiting for the first people who come out."

Reaching the ground floor, Sauwa looked about. Larky already knew what she wanted. "There's a back door that leads to an alley, and there are no windows facing it."

"That's where we'll go," she replied.

The two navigated their way toward the back of the building. Eventually, they came to a door that looked like it hadn't been used in ages. "I test this door weekly," Larky explained. "It'll work."

Carefully opening the door, they were confronted by a powerful glare of light temporarily blinding them, but they managed to press on. With the heavy man walking better than when he started out, they were able to get out the back fairly quickly. Outside, they checked and found the alley deserted.

Larky removed his arm from the girl's shoulder as the two gave an unspoken look at each other that said it was time to part. Sauwa watched as the old man started down the narrow street. He was walking slightly faster but still with the shuffle of an old, out of shape man. She turned and went in the opposite direction. She traversed the labyrinth of joining roads and alley systems before emerging onto a residential street several blocks away. It was a quiet road with few people around. When she felt she had no one watching her, she discarded her blood-soaked garment in a nearby dumpster before pressing on.

24

It had not registered with him mentally when the deaths of Detectives Curly and Galligan were announced over the phone. Detective Sergeant Ryan Youngest was in utter disbelief as a commander of the intelligence branch ranted bitterly. Hard pressed to find a viable response that wouldn't sound like hollow sympathy or cold indifference, the homicide investigator remained silent. The only viable information he obtained in the whole dramatic update was the address of yet another crime scene.

A demand for full disclosure of what was known of this mysterious woman assassin was made abruptly. However, the demand was left to be argued between the intelligence commander and Youngest's own Commander Rose, who was enjoying the power of being the center of everyone's attention. The interest the escalating murder case was generating from the newspapers and broadcast stations as well as the growing focus on an ever-increasing number of departments in the Garda was being soaked up by the homicide office.

THE APARTMENT LOOKED like a war zone. Youngest walked about looking first at the bullet-riddled corpse of a man he did not recognize but presumed had been Detective Curly. The man's head was partially gone and the pools of dried blood caked over his body and on the floor told him the man had sustained a nasty injury before the lethal shot was taken.

Moving down the hallway, he followed the crime scene markings and set up lights that led him to the other body. He recognized Ian Galligan at once when he stood over the larger body observing the grizzly picture before him. The arm had a long hunk of sharp, jagged metal embedded deep into the elbow. It had sliced clean through to the point it had nearly severed the appendage completely. As ghastly an image as that was, it didn't compete with the sight of the carving knife entrenched in the jowl and the cut along the neckline leaving the entire inside of the man's throat open for view.

Youngest had seen many deaths in his years on the police force but, somehow, the deaths of other police officers always seemed more real to him than others. Perhaps because it was a reminder of his own mortality. In this case, the savagery displayed only added to the darkness of the moment. Ravenhoof was at the doorway observing as much as he could from his slight vantage point. Upon seeing him, Youngest waved him forward to join him.

The South African looked through the scene as he

walked along. Unlike his Irish colleague or his British counterpart, he was less fazed by it. Death, particularly grizzly deaths, were something commonplace in his world. He didn't like to admit to himself how many times he had been in places exhibiting such terrible displays.

"Your girl is quite the killing machine." Youngest was shaking his head as he remained focused on the body of Detective Galligan. "This was cold and precise — the work of a stone cold killer. I have to admit your people do a crack job creating monsters."

Ravenhoof said nothing. It was not the time or the place to offer defense or sympathy. He was a cop who had played in the shadows of the covert world. As a cop, he wanted to allow his colleague a chance to process it all. As a veteran operative, he knew that wasting time on sympathy was pointless and made a person emotional as opposed to mindful and logical. Looking at the display and the cold precision by which Sauwa had executed the kills, he could tell she had acted on her training and conditioning. He also knew that to catch someone like her meant being able to function decisively and deduce what they could; time was of the essence. "She was here for a purpose," he stated in a curt, commanding tone.

Youngest looked up at the South African, who only looked back with an expressionless face that indicated he was all business. Ravenhoof continued, "We're dealing with a professional assassin. She's not wasting time processing what she just did. She's moving on to plan her escape. If we don't want to lose her, we have to be as clear in our heads as she is right now."

Youngest was beside himself. Part of him wanted to punch the callous South African prick right in the face. The other side of him reluctantly concurred with everything he had said. He had to snap out of it. Ravenhoof had already pressed past him to head into the kitchen. "Why was she here in the first place?" The South African looked about a little while examining the scene.

"From what I understand, this is supposedly the home of a Mr. Larky, a man the intelligence boys tell me is supposed to be a master documents forger," Youngest explained.

"Really," Ravenhoof echoed from the kitchen. "You think your people would have had this place staked out for her already."

The homicide detective rubbed his face. "The detectives were here initially looking for Mr. Rudy Sheehan, the one we believe to be providing all her logistical support. Mr. Larky has done a very good job hiding from everyone. He keeps a low profile and selects his clients carefully. The intelligence units really had to dig to find out about him, and they only got lucky with a tip from a source."

"Where is he now?" the South African asked as he emerged from the kitchen walkway.

Youngest nodded. "We have two dead policemen. This begs the question as to where our Mr. Larky is. What's more, why didn't she kill Larky, since he had to have witnessed everything? Assuming he was in the room when it happened."

"He was, I can assure you." Ravenhoof was once again looking at the Irish detective. "I'm assuming she had no need to kill him."

Youngest gave him a puzzled look. The South African continued. "I've had a lot of time to look over the files of our Ms. Catcher. She's interesting in that she's not as stone cold as we would think. All her kills while in service to the state have either been at the direction of her superiors or against combatants in the course of carrying out an operation. My guess is that the documents were not in her possession and she needs the forger alive to obtain them. The police posed a threat to her, and Mr. Larky did not. I'd wager Mr. Larky is an alias and this apartment, from everything I'm seeing, is not his actual home. That said, the idea that both had a great deal to fear from the police and, therefore, she let him live with the consideration that he would disappear entirely."

"That's a pretty big guess," Youngest interjected. "I mean she had to assume he lived here and that we would find him."

Ravenhoof shook his head. "She's trained to assess environments for situational awareness. She'd have seen the same things I'm seeing and concluded that this was a front, not his actual home."

"Same things?" Youngest had already answered his own question before he had even asked it. Someone had gone to a great deal of trouble to give the impression the place was an actual residence. The place was littered with second-hand furniture that fit nicely with the environment and a few scattered documents were there to make the place look lived in. Looking closer, it was an obvious setup; it was all cosmetic. Mr. Larky was certainly a master of his trade, and everything here showed it.

This left the detectives paralyzed to know what to do next. They had lost their lead. By all accounts, whoever Mr. Larky was, he was gone — most likely forever given the gravity of the situation. Ravenhoof and Youngest did as their police instincts dictated, they continued to investigate the scene.

"What the bloody hell!!" A graveled voice, so familiar to both men, cried out. They looked up to see the bald figure of Detective Glenahaughan practically bursting his way into the room. "Jesus, this is a bloody slaughterhouse in here," he said after looking at the room and the two shredded bodies.

Ravenhoof shot a questioning look at Youngest that demanded an answer. Youngest had learned long ago that the best way to stave off needless turf wars and rivalries was to be inclusive early on with other rank and file investigators. "I had a call placed to Glenahaughan to give him an update; it's part of his case as well."

Glenahaughan walked past the first body and followed the trail of markers until he had joined his two colleagues. "So, this appears to be the work of this Catcher woman?" he asked as he came up and gaped down at the body below. "Christ, she carved this one up like a pig. Who are they, more IRA heavies?"

"Garda detectives," Youngest replied softly. "They were here following up on a possible lead. From what we can tell, they expected to find someone else and ran into Ms. Catcher instead."

"My God," Glenahaughan realized he had placed his foot in his mouth. "The intelligence boys are going to be up in arms."

"We need to consider our next step," Ravenhoof interrupted the Irish detectives who seemingly had fallen into a muddle of despair over the loss of more of their comrades. "As I see it, our best play is to assume she's leaving the country. We should focus on that."

"We don't even know if she has the documents she came here to get." Youngest was irritated. He hated the idea that so many had died on his watch, and he was no closer to finding this whirlwind of death.

"She came here for a reason. There's no camera equipment, but we know Mr. Larky's profession. We all agree that this place is not his true residence. By simple process of elimination, we have to assume she has what she came for. Leaving the country is the logical next step," Ravenhoof summarized.

"You speak as though she's leaving tonight," Glenahaughan interrupted. "Why are you so sure she's not going to simply lay low in another warehouse until the heat dies down?"

"I don' know," the South African retorted sternly. "I do know she has the full weight of the Garda after her and, after today, the pressure is only going to be greater. In addition, there's the IRA that still has a score to be settled — five of their people are sitting in the morgue. Her own handler/support agent is on the run. Plus, if your Protestant Loyalists are behind her activities here. They can't afford to keep her in Ireland — not alive anyway. She has nowhere else to go. If she was planning on leaving in the next few days, you can be sure her departure has been moved to tonight or tomorrow morning at the latest."

"She won't be traveling by plane," Youngest interceded. "It will have to be through the water ports."

"That is where we must focus then," Ravenhoof said, with Glenahaughan nodding in agreement.

CONSTABLE SEAN WILLOCK saw the sign to Garrity's Watering Hole. He beckoned his superior to let him go relieve himself at the necessary. The man he was with, a gruff old sergeant, grunted before pulling over to the side of the road. "Be damn snappy about it," the old man grumbled. "You're not paid to take a piss on the city's time."

"I understand sir," the young constable said humbly as he exited the vehicle and made for the pub.

"And, don't stop for a drink," the sergeant shouted to his fleeing subordinate. "You're not paid for that either!"

Inside, the pub was filled with an assorted collection of patrons; most of whom were divided into groups around the tables in the establishment. The few drinking alone were all deep into their tall mugs and concentrating on nothing else. Even a uniformed policeman went unnoticed amongst such an obliviously despondent lot.

Making his way toward the bathrooms in the back corner, Willock walked calmly not wanting to attract attention. He got to the back and quickly turned into the dingy washroom. It smelled of a horrid mixture of stale urine and marijuana. The washroom offered three stalls and three urinals. As instructed, the constable strolled over to a urinal and began looking to relieve himself. Within seconds, the door behind him was opened by a sandy-haired young man. The young man showed not the slightest interest in the constable as he nonchalantly went about exploring the stalls.

After checking each stall, he walked up to the sink and began running the water. Without facing the constable, he began to speak. "A football fan, are you?" he asked unassumingly.

Willock's eyes sprang open as he stammered trying to get the words out. "Only if the team is Chelsea." It was the response he had been instructed to give.

The sandy-haired man turned to face the door. "What do you know so far?" The conversation became serious quickly.

Again, struggling to find the words, the constable spat, "They're investigating another set of linked murders. As it was explained to me, two more detectives with Intelligence were killed at what looks to be the home of a document forger."

"Keep going," the sandy-haired man commanded.

"Well, they're not looking at Loyalist paras for this. The killings seem to have been done by a freelancer — a South African."

"South African?" the sandy-haired man interrupted.

"Yes, some former spy, or rather," the constable spat, again, "one of their operatives working in England as part of a professional death squad. Now that the Apartheid has lost the war, she's one of the folks that's found herself on the run. She's here because she took a contract to do a job."

"Marston Donovan?" the sandy-haired man interrupted, again.

"That's him," the constable replied.

"What does the Garda know about this South African? Who is he?" the sandy-haired man demanded.

"She," Willock replied.

"A woman?" sandy-hair was shocked.

"Yes," the constable began to get nervous, "she goes by the name Sauwa Catcher."

"A female killer took out a seasoned intelligence officer with the Garda, along with an additional team of five IRA hitmen, and now another two cops?" sandy-hair wasn't sure if he was believing what he had just heard. His reaction to the information unnerved the young constable.

"By herself from what we know so far," Willock stammered, as he reached under his patrol coat and presented a wrinkled, large yellow envelope. "This is the picture given to us by the British. MI-5 is looking for this girl for all the stuff she did back in England. She's a high priority for them. There's also a representative from South Africa, some intelligence guy. Her own people are looking for her."

"Where is she now, do they think?" sandy-hair kept his gaze on the door.

"She's disappeared," Willock replied.

The sandy-haired man ruminated for a moment before speaking. "Tell your handler, the minute the Garda has anything about her whereabouts to contact us at once. This woman is a high priority for the movement." The conversation ended with the sandy-haired man walking out of the washroom leaving the constable alone holding himself.

Ewen Callaway exited the washroom and casually made his way to a table in the far corner. The only occupant was a woman his age and bearing a striking resemblance to him. Ellen Callaway, Ewen's twin sister, looked stunning with her long hair running straight down her back and her trim athletic frame. The twins took their role as soldiers very seriously and, in addition to a strong adherence to developing their military training, they also stayed in peak physical condition.

Sliding into the seat next to her, Ewen placed the envelope he received from the constable on the table before her. They both watched as Willock, the nervous looking constable, made a hasty exit. His eyes forward. He did not display the slightest recognition of the man he had just met.

"I hope you didn't make him shit his nappies?" Ellen asked jokingly.

"Probably did," her brother replied with exasperation. "The piss ant certainly acted like he was about to."

"Well, what matters was the information worth our time?" Ellen asked leaning up to her brother.

"Good enough," Ewen looked over his shoulder to view his sister. "We have a name, Sauwa Catcher."

"One person?" Her voice denoted a twinge of shock.

"And, a woman, no less," he replied in a surprised tone as he tapped the envelope on the table.

His sister patted him affectionately on the shoulder. "My dear brother, it might surprise you to know women do more than cook, clean and get ridden by a man in bed." She picked up the envelope and peeled away the seal. Reaching inside she pulled out a slightly bent photograph of a ghostly looking woman who she considered to be, at best, in her twenties. "She looks like someone who'd work for the secret police."

Snatching the picture from her, Ewen glance at it. "Aye, this is the one the police are looking for from what our friend in there said. He also said she recently killed two more cops."

"Oh shit," Ellen said with a smirk. "She's certainly been busy the last couple of days."

Ewen dropped the picture and began tapping it. "Three detectives — the Garda is going all out to catch this one."

"Makes me think it's perhaps a mistake for us to be getting mixed up in this any further." Ellen leaned back in her chair and looked at her brother. He was still tapping the photo and contemplating something. "You know I'm right."

He nodded. "I know you are. This, however, is well above our pay grade, as they say in the army. It's not our call to make. We need to talk to the boss."

Ellen clicked her teeth and asked, "Do the cops even have an idea where she might be?"

"Not a fucking clue," Ewen gnashed his teeth with irritation.

The twins rose from their chairs and slowly made for the door. None of the patrons showed the slightest interest in them as they normally mingled among their own pocket of friends and tended to their drinks.

25

He could feel his heart racing, though he couldn't tell if it was being driven by fear or anger. He felt both as he sat tied to the jagged stone wall with an assorted mixture of chains and wiring that cut into his body. David O'knomo could hear the screams echoing loudly throughout the different parts of the dungeon-like facility. He hated hearing them; they never seemed to stop. Outside he could hear the footsteps walking up and down the pathway and the creaking of doors as they entered the various stalls where others were being kept. All he could do was wait helplessly for his time.

The door finally creaked open very slowly. It was a practiced action that the interrogators liked to use to add to the agony of anticipation by the prisoner. O'knomo watched as two men, both white, entered the stall. "Well, you going to talk to us today, kafir. Or are we going to have to use persuasion?" asked a tall, wiry-looking man with a pencil mustache. He smiled smugly as he began to unravel a thick plastic bag.

O'knomo said nothing in reply as he started to breathe harder anticipating the inevitable. The other white man — a bit shorter and looking much younger than the first — began to unravel a set of cords that sported two hooks on the end. "No, this one's going to be like the others today. Seems none of them want to do the smart thing and talk to us."

"A shame really," the taller one said. "I was hoping for at least one that didn't have to be given an incentive." Both men spoke with the thick accent of Afrikaners. They spoke English, though it was obvious that it was not their first language or one they spoke often. Still, the blacks understood it better than the whites understood Afrikaans.

The younger man threw the cord over a thick log railing just above him leaving the two ends dangling. Looped through each end was a small, sharp metal hook. O'knomo raised his head and watched as it slid down until it was just past his head. Then, the taller man grabbed the ends and dug the hooks into O'knomo's upper back. The tall man was skillful as he maneuvered the sharp daggers deep into O'knomo's skin to stab into muscle.

O'knomo was tied to the wall and couldn't move. The shorter man, having put on some gloves, grabbed the cords and heaved down on it with all his strength. O'knomo felt the hooks dig and began to pull tightly. At the same moment, plastic sheeting was dropped over his head and pressed firmly against his face. He could feel the air getting thin as the bag tightened around his neck. O'knomo almost forgot about the hooks in his back, as he struggled to breathe. Every breath of life was being blocked. His heart was racing with the terror of knowing he was going to die.

O'KNOMO WAS JOLTED AWAKE. Suddenly, it was all gone. He was looking at the bleak walls of his office and confronted with the ghostly image of Sauwa Catcher looking back at him with her cold gaze. His heart was racing as if he had just run a marathon.

Jamie Nawati entered the room. His boss looked bedraggled. "You okay?" he inquired, not quite sure what to do.

Wrestling his way out of his chair, O'knomo tried to stand up; he felt his legs begin to buckle. He managed to grab hold of his desk to stabilize himself. He could see, out of the corner of his eye, a concerned Nawati racing over to help. O'knomo raised his hand to stop him. "I just need a minute." He walked slowly out of his office and down the hall to the nearby washroom. His head was still swimming as he tried to make sense of what had just happened. He went through the door and made his way to the closest sink. The cold water felt good. He splashed it on his face. It was then that he noticed his shirt was soaked in sweat — a familiar byproduct of the night terrors that still haunted him.

He returned to the office to see Nawati standing by attentively looking concerned. "Everything alright, sir?"

O'knomo waved him off with a slight shake of his head. "I'm fine."

"Ghosts of our past don't rest easy, do they?" Nawati commented.

O'knomo said nothing. He looked back at his subordinate with an expressionless face. Nawati continued, "I have them myself. I wake up in a cold sweat just like you after reliving episodes from my past — neither memory nor my conscience will let me forget. Like you, I spend my waking hours trying to make sense of it all."

Reaching for his shoulder, O'knomo felt the scars where the hooks had been. Years later, even through his cloth shirt, he could feel the marks as if the whole episode had happened yesterday. "My ghosts just won't rest. The war is over, yet the past still lives with me."

"It lives with all of us," Nawati stated. "And, it won't be forgotten easily, not for us, and certainly not for her." He nodded over at the ghostly photograph on the wall.

Leaning against the edge of his desk, O'knomo stared at her picture. He wasn't sure what to think. "You really think she's bothered by any of what she's done? After all, we mustn't forget she's still plying her trade and no longer for her cause."

"She's doing what I would have done in her place," Nawati revealed. "When you're hunted and desperate, you make decisions that cause you to question yourself. When I was alone and hunted by dangerous people, I made my own pact with the devil. With what she has done in Ireland, she's either fighting for survival, or she is a stone cold killer."

O'knomo sighed lightly, "I will let you in on a secret, James."

Nawati turned to face him. O'knomo continued, "I can't let her go. I look at her on that wall and read her file. All I can think is that catching her is the step needed to finally see some peace, some closure. Yet, listening to those smug politicians, both black and white, talk as if they had been in the jungles and the townships fighting and enduring hardships alongside the rest of us was almost nauseating. I feel more akin to her — another fighter in the trenches. I was tortured by ruthless men who enjoyed being sadistic. Many of them used the covert war to justify indulging their sadism. I have no illusions about that. There is the concept that we are giving too much respect to someone who could just as easily be another psychopath herself. Yet, something tells me that will not be her story when we finally have a chance to confront her. I feel strange about all of this."

"As do I," Nawati agreed. "I think it strange that our white compatriots seem more deep-seated hatred for her than we do. I'll admit, she is an assassin — she's killed many. But, so have we. And, like you, it's hard not to be able to relate in some way. We both bear scars from our enemy and people on her side. She survived Rhodesia and coming to South Africa. The Afrikaners despised her but they needed her people for their expertise in counter-insurgency and clandestine warfare."

"At present, I just want to look her in the eye and see her face to face," O'knomo rubbed his eyes; he was tired. The tension of the job was getting to him. "Did you come here to tell me something?" He suddenly wondered what Jamie was doing here when he was supposed to be at the foreign office monitoring communications with the embassies in England and Ireland.

"Yes," Nawati exclaimed. "We got a quick message from our embassy in Ireland. They have informed us that Ms. Catcher is the prime suspect in another set of killings. This time it's two more detectives of the Garda."

O'knomo rolled his eyes. "My God, that woman is littering the streets with corpses."

SAUWA ARRIVED JUST in time to catch the payphone ringing. She raced over and grabbed the phone from the cradle. "Hello?" she answered.

"Swan, is that you?" She recognized the voice instantly.

"Banker?" she replied immediately. She didn't like the idea of not having some sort of security protocol with all that was at stake. However, the code names sufficed. Only the other knew the voice that each had become familiar with.

"It's me," he replied. "We have to meet now!" He wasted no time getting to the point. "Our original plan has been scrapped. Meet me at our first meeting place. I'll be there in twenty minutes." Banker finished his comment with a click and the dial tone signaled Sauwa was no longer speaking to anyone.

It was getting dark. The evening air was gradually becoming colder. Thankfully, Sauwa managed to duck into a secondhand store and obtain a worn but still usable sailor's P-coat. It helped keep her warm as she traversed the streets.

Hailing a cab she was instantly picked up by one passing by. Normally, she preferred buses; they were a more discrete mode of travel. Bus drivers tended to be oblivious to the numerous faces that boarded day in and day out. The patrons on public transportation seemed to possess a similar apathy to those around them as they focused on the issues of their own muddled lives.

However, she was strapped for time, and an everyday taxi cab was much safer than walking around town with every policeman in the city looking her.

Pints was a little busier than the last time she had visited. She proceeded to casually walk along the streets scanning for any possible sign she was walking into a trap. By the sound of Banker's tone, more exasperated than scared or desperate, she accepted this emergency meeting was legitimate.

She had finished doing her little recce when she saw Banker approaching the door to the pub. She caught up with him as he was about to enter. He looked down to see her right behind him. There wasn't time for pleasantries or initial conversation. He took her by the arm and beckoned her to come with him. Confused, Sauwa didn't resist as she was being led down the street. She wanted to ask questions but, by the determined look on Banker's face and the number of strangers walking by who could catch their conversation, she opted to remain quiet.

They continued walking. At the intersection, they turned and walked a few more feet before Sauwa was forcefully ushered into the backseat of a waiting car with Banker following close behind. The car door was barely shut before the vehicle drove away. "What the hell!" she cried out angrily as she moved awkwardly for a better position. "What are you doing?" She still wasn't sure if she was being abducted. The lack of people and the fact that Banker wasn't trying to sedate or restrain her left her reasonably sure she wasn't in any immediate danger.

"A lot has happened since the last time we spoke." Banker was finally talking to her. "The old plan is no good, and we have to make alternate arrangements." Sauwa looked at the burly figure driving the car. She had never seen him before and was hesitant to speak with him present.

Sensing her concern, Banker updated her immediately. "He's an old friend, and one we need right now. He already knows most everything."

"I do, Ms. Catcher," the burly man interjected.

Sauwa was startled these men knew her real name. "When did you find out?"

"You've become a hot item with the police," Banker replied. "They know who you are and somehow have a photograph of you."

"What?" Her eyes lit up.

"That's why we had to change plans," Banker continued. "I was down at the port when I called you. The cops are all over the port right now looking for a female matching your description. They're keeping it quiet, but I have some friends in the department. They explained to me how they're looking for this female assassin who they want for the killing of the police detective and the five guys at the warehouse. She goes by the name of Sauwa Catcher. I'm assuming that's your actual name. My friend said your picture has been floated to the units sent to patrol the harbor. We can't get out that way."

"So, you're washing your hands of me?"

"Of course not," the burly man, again spoke up. "We're going to see this through. We have to."

"Who is this guy?" Sauwa pointed to the driver. "Why are you trusting him?"

"A silent partner," Banker answered reluctantly.

"Someone he comes to when he gets in over his head," the driver chimed in, again. "His interests are also aligned with mine. I want very much to see you gone tonight."

Sauwa was speechless. Everything was going too fast, and she had no control over any of it. She needed an explanation. "We have a connection in Skerries; it's a town north of Dublin. It's an old fishing village that's out of the way. The police don't have a strong presence there, which will make it a safer exit."

"We're leaving on a fishing boat? That means you're shipping me back to Britain!"

"No! No, we're not. It's just we don't want to endanger our source by divulging too much," Banker tried to explain.

"Bullshit!" Sauwa spat. Her bergen was finally off and nestled in her lap. "I don't care about security risks. I have my own concerns. So, fucking tell me what your new plan is, and why I should trust it!"

"You're in no position..." the driver began before he felt her hand clamp around his neck.

"Niceties are over," she growled. "You know what I've done these last few days in your country, and what I can do to you now. I hate threats, so let me speak frankly. Those I work for, as well as the IRA and the fucking British government, will find me just as easily there with the greater resources they'll have available. It would not be in your best interest to think you'll dispose of me easily."

"Sauwa," Banker said sympathetically. "We have no intention of dropping you off in England or the UK. We can't get you onto a ship at the harbor, not now. The fisherman who'll be helping us will sail you down to the Irish Sea where you'll make contact with a cargo ship. It will be coming out of Liverpool and meeting up with you in St.

George's Channel. That's the ship we'll be putting you on; it will take you out of here altogether."

Sauwa's hand was still latched onto the driver's throat. She could feel his body tense. He didn't dare try to fight her not knowing what a professional assassin could do to him if he did. "How do I know I can trust any of this?"

"Because the fisherman would be at your mercy, if he did anything else," Banker replied. "As we've said before, we see our deals through. What's more, your insurance in all this is that we have become far too intertwined with you and your exploits. We can't afford to see you get caught by either the British or Irish authorities. Nor do we need the UVF after us in addition to the IRA."

Banker's answer seemed logical. Sauwa slowly released her hand from the driver's throat and leaned back into her seat.

NASH EMERY HAD NEARLY FINISHED his game of solitaire when the pay phone across the street started to ring. He got up and stretched before walking over to pick it up. "Yes?" he asked gruffly.

"Is this the Cannerman residence?" a voice he recognized as Seamus Nally's asked.

"No," he replied, curtly. "You're off a number. This is the McCord residence."

It was the code they had worked out to ensure each other's identity and verify neither was being held under duress. If either one had been compromised, they would have given a different family name for the residence they presumed to be calling.

"What have you got?" Emery snapped.

"A contact of ours found Mr. Sheehan. Saw him getting into a car with another man we know as an associate of his. Our contact overheard them saying something about a trip to Skerries tonight."

"Skerries, uh? Smart move given the heat that's on them in Dublin," Emery thought out loud. "How reliable is this source?"

"He's good man; I believe him," Nally replied.

"If it turns out to be bullshit, our next conversation won't be so pleasant," Emery growled. He normally wouldn't have been so curt with a ranking IRA officer; however, Nally was in no position to be high and mighty. "Anything else?"

"That's all I've got." The older man sounded quite nervous over the phone. Emery didn't bother with more words. He crashed the phone in its cradle and started back across the street.

Ewen and Ellen Callaway were engrossed in a game of chess when the door was flung open and Emery marched in. His commanding presence alone seemed to call everyone to attention. The twins rose to their feet as did a fourth man, Irial Kerry, who was setting the papers he was reading to the side.

No radios or television were on so everyone could hear what was going on outside. It was an old habit they had learned from years of dodging ambushes.

"We've got a lead. Our people think the targets are heading north to Skerries," Emery snapped as his team collected their coats preparing to leave. "We can assume this is their means of escape. We will have to move fast to catch them."

The team started filing out the door past their leader and headed in the direction of the parking lot. Emery followed them. They were soon piling into a small blue van. Kerry took the driver's seat while the twins piled into the back. Emery was last to slide into the passenger seat. The engine came to life as Kerry turned the ignition. It was a rule to always back in when parking to make it easier to drive out quickly.

In the back, the twins were pulling a large canvas bag out from under a pile of old blankets. Soon, Emery was hearing the familiar metallic sound of guns being racked. The twins were loading magazines and chambering rounds in preparation. He had trained them well, he thought to himself with a fatherly sense of pride. "Finish up and place the weapons back in the bag," he commanded.

"We're going on a mission, aren't we?" Ellen protested. "We should be ready."

"We've got some distance to go," Emery replied. His eyes were fixed on the road ahead. "We're still driving around in a large city in a closed-up van. We don't need to have anything lying about for the police to see if we should get pulled over by an overly suspicious cop."

"Right, we'll finish later. We just want to be ready when the time comes to move," Ewen said as he began loading the guns back into the bag and trying to temper his sister's irritation. She sometimes felt their team leader was a bit too paternalistic.

"Good initiative," Emery remarked, "but wait until we get outside of the city. You'll have a good half hour to prepare the equipment." He felt pride that his training had turned the twins into such skilled professionals. Still, he had to remember they were young. They had more to learn.

Kerry kept the van at a mild pace. He was a seasoned operator with experience going back to the seventies. He knew the validity of his superior's concerns. The twins might not have seen the picture, but he did. Two rough looking men driving around in a suspicious looking van with two youngsters sitting in the back would make them look like criminals exploiting kids. To any cop, the whole scenario would raise questions. For what they were doing though, it was a logical choice.

He looked over at the man in the passenger seat. Emery was quiet; his breathing was controlled and steady. Kerry heard no motion or sound in the back either. The twins may still be somewhat headstrong, but they understood the dangers of what was about to take place. When an operation involved guns, it always had the potential for danger. It was essential that everyone had a clear head. It also wasn't lost on any of them who they were going after. They had seen with their own eyes some of her handy work. She was a well-trained and experienced killer they all knew could not be taken lightly. This mission had to be treated with the same respect of any other mission they had undertaken for the cause.

26

Skerries was quiet when they arrived. It was a small fishing village about twenty kilometers north of Dublin. The town had a small population of long-rooted families who drew their living from the sea. It was late, and the houses and shops along the route were closed. Even the local pubs were clearing out their last patrons.

Sauwa looked out her car window. This route was an interesting alternative, no one awake to notice strangers moving around on the docks at this hour. It was also unlikely to have busy-bodies call the police. She had seen many operations end in failure because this little fact was not taken into account.

As if sensing what was going through her mind, Banker spoke up. "Our man is a bit of a night owl. He likes doing his boating at night. The locals are used to him being out at this hour. You don't need to be concerned about attracting suspicion."

Sauwa began to relax. She sank back into her seat as she looked out at the rows of old houses as they passed.

Like her trip into Dublin, she marveled at the structures in a town that easily dated back to the early nineteenth or possibly even the eighteenth century. It was another reminder of how young Africa was. With another life, she would have worked to become a history major or archeologist.

Everyone had been silent for the rest of the drive. It was hard to tell if it was nerves or the simple lack of anything beneficial to discuss. In either case, it only served to make the trip longer. Though it was only a small town, the ride through the main street seemed to last forever.

The car pulled alongside the road up against the small white concrete bumpers that separated the road from the coastline. Across the way were a collection of big red and white brick houses and shops. On the other side of the concrete bummers was a graveled beach where several small fishing boats were docked. The smaller craft was used primarily by weekend hobbyists. Light came from the few scattered streetlights on the housing side. A few lights were seen from the boats themselves. This left the beach line nearly black, ideal for people looking to move about unnoticed.

Everyone exited the car as casually as possible. Sauwa slipped out the driver's side grabbing her bergen in the process. She pretended to check it while she looked about for anyone prying or any other sign they were being watched. It was a quick sweep and most of the houses and shops were completely dark. No way to see anyone. Deciding she had done her best security check with the time and visibility available, she followed Banker and the other man as they started down the graveled beach. The wind coming off the water was cold.

They were crossing the barriers when a small blue van passed by. Banker and his friend froze. The van slowed for a brief second before picking up speed and continuing down the road. Not wanting to attract attention or look suspicious, Sauwa snapped at the men to keep going.

She had no real reason to be concerned, yet something about the van and the way it slowed made her leery. Reaching into her coat pocket, she felt for the gun she had removed from the dead policeman. Once she had a grip on it, she slipped off the safety. Then reaching into her other pocket, she did the same with the gun she had taken from the second policeman. Both already had rounds in their chambers. Now all she needed to do was draw, point, and shoot.

Like the British, the Irish police did not generally carry firearms. These detectives must have been on some sort of special duty.

In any case, they had been carrying Sig Sauer 9mm's. She had had only a limited amount of time after the shooting to examine the guns and estimated there were fifteen rounds in one and eighteen in the other. She edged one of the guns far enough out of her coat pocket to rest the butt against the pocket opening for easy accessibility. She tucked the other gun into the waistband of her jeans.

Starting down the beach, she navigated the slick rocks beneath her feet. Banker and the other man were invisible in the darkness, but she could hear them only a few feet away. At the edge of the beach, the silhouetted figure of a man stood at the rear of one of the larger boats. The way her associates were angling, it was easy to determine he was their contact.

"THAT'S THEM," Emery snapped as they drove past a group of people making their way around the barriers toward the beach. Surprised, Kerry instinctively started to slow the van. "Keep moving dammit!" Emery commanded. Kerry accelerated slowly to not attract attention. He continued driving while his commander remained focused on his side view mirror watching the trio.

"All right," Emery began as the images in the mirror diverted his attention. "Twins, at the corner slide out and make your way onto the beach. Use the darkness as your concealment as you make your way down the coastline. We won't be able to see you so stay about fifty meters from whatever boat they're taking. You'll provide cover fire for me and Kerry. We'll circle back and come at them from the other side. They should be at the waterline by then, and we'll have the high ground. We have flashlights we'll shine down on them to get their position."

"The plan is to pin them down with fire from both sides so they won't be able to mount a viable defense." He turned to look first at Kerry then at the twins. All were nodding in agreement. "I don't have the intelligence on these folks I'd normally like. I don't know what they'll have for firepower. Between their limited amount of time and their need to keep a low profile, I assume they'll be carrying handguns and limited ammunition. So, don't be heroic. We have superior firepower and more ammo. We can wait them out."

"What about the cops around here?" Ewen asked.

"Small, quiet town with a small police force that hasn't

seen action in decades," Emery responded. "Assume they'll be taken by surprise. They'll bumble around trying to figure out what to do. It will take time to reach whatever arsenal they have, organize then deploy to deal with us. I imagine we'll have a good hour before we should start to be concerned. We've got three targets. This Sheehan asshole and his associate are not known as hard types. I don't expect resistance from them. The South African, however, is a pro. She's experienced and dangerous. I need not remind you that in the last few day's she's killed a police detective, five of our men and quite possibly two more cops today."

"We've reached the corner," Kerry informed them.

The van didn't stop; instead, it slowed to an idling speed. The twins finished preparing their weapons and had them laid out. They included additional attire for the mission. They stretched surgical latex gloves over their hands and slipped dark, slick raincoats over their bodies. They added black knit ski masks that left only the eyes visible. This was all done to protect against forensic testing later if the team was in any way detained. The van also came equipped with a cleaning kit, alcohol pads, fresh clothes, and soap, if they had to wash themselves off.

Ewen and Ellen grabbed AKS-74s and canvass side bags carrying extra magazines. Unlike the more traditional models, AK-74 and 47s, the AKS had a triangular, retractable stock that made it more compact. They rolled the van's side door open and quietly slipped onto the road. Ellen slid the door closed before following her brother behind the van and then over the side into the darkness of the beach. Behind them, they could hear the van pick up speed as it rounded the corner. Unlatching the capture hook on the rifles, the steel shoulder stocks sprang from their locked positions into a rigid elongated state.

The rocks were both slick and jagged as they worked their way down to the waterline. Disciplined professionals that they were, neither spoke as they communicated by touch. Feeling the water at their feet, they began trekking back toward the trio Emery had seen. Ewen led the way; his sister followed closely. Both held their weapons in tactical poses; Ewen held his arm out in front of him and aimed in the direction they traveled; Ellen held hers against her body with the barrel pointed toward the ground ready to bring it instantly into action.

Sound normally carries at night creating echoes. Luckily, the sound of waves crashing against the rocky shore masked the sound of their feet crunching on gravel. Nearing their objective, the sound of men's voices could be heard, not shouting, but speaking loud enough to communicate over the noise of the water and the growing intensity of the wind.

Ewen reached back and tapped his sister on the shoulder signaling her to take a position behind one of the boats. Being the female in the unit, Ellen had accepted she would have to endure a certain degree of paternalism. Since she was able to go on missions, the annoyance of having to always be directed to the safest position or given the safest job of the operation was something she simply tolerated.

Without argument, she slipped away from her brother, drew her weapon up to her chest, and aimed in the direction of the men's voices as she walked over to the edge of the boat. Dropping to her knee she steadied herself as she took an aiming position.

Ewen felt around his immediate location for any sizeble object he could use for cover; there was none. Instead, he carefully lowered himself to a prone position as he placed his rifle slightly ahead of his body. The rifles were the shortened versions and had nothing to use for a shoulder rest to help tighten their control. Firing 5.56 ammunition promised less kickback.

Nash Emery directed his driver to the side of the road. The headlights went dead the last few feet before stopping. Kerry kept the engine running. This was a tactical precaution. When the battle was over and the team in a rush to make their escape, they could quickly take off and didn't have to get the vehicle started.

Emery slipped out of the passenger seat and slid to the other side. Kerry was already opening the side door of the van. Like the twins, the two men grabbed their rifles and some canvass side bags holding additional magazines. Kerry stepped inside and reached into a small cardboard box wedged between the driver and passenger seats. He backed out holding two large mag flashlights. He handed one to Emery.

Tucking their weapons up under their coats, the two men started across the street toward the barrier line. The lighting from the houses along the road was non-existent and street lamps offered little better along the coastline. Anyone driving by or looking out a window would be able to see virtually nothing. Stopping a few feet short of the white barriers, the two IRA men pulled out their weapons. Like the twins, they extended the steel shoulder stocks and locked them into position. "Shame to use such fine weapons on this mess," Emery muttered as he thought about how they would have to dump these armaments after the attack. Kerry nodded but said nothing.

Emery raised his hand. "We'll separate here and stay twenty meters apart. You take your light and shine it from the south and scan north. I'll start north and scan south. Anyone there is to be considered a target."

Kerry walked past his commander and took up his position. In like fashion, Emery walked a distance from his subordinate toward the north. When they were at the desired distance, they both walked until they were at the barriers. Lowering themselves to their knees, they rested their rifle barrels on top of the concrete barrier, pressing the magazine weld against the post base for stability. They grabbed their mag lights and rested their free hand at the base of the shoulder stock to better secure the weapon. Positioning the mag lights so they were seated over the top of the rifles, the light would shine where they intended to shoot. The lights would block their weapon's steel sighting, but it mattered little because they were shooting in the dark.

Sauwa moved cautiously as she navigated the last few feet down the rocky beach line. She was concerned with the loose, slimy rocks beneath her feet and the situation in general. She was still leery of the circumstances working with strange men at a critical moment and meeting some strange contact in the dead of night in some old boat. If it was a setup, she didn't want to make things easy for them. She also couldn't shake the nagging feeling about the van that had passed them.

It was a lengthy vessel in comparison to other boats that sat alongside it. The boatman stood at the bow like a manservant preparing to receive guests at a mansion. A small greenish light just above him outlined the perfect silhouette of a small frail looking man. As she got closer the silhouette transformed steadily into the image of a bookish-looking man, pushing the age of sixty.

"It's good to see you all. Rudy, it's been a while." The boatman was cordial, and one whose relationship with the men was seemingly more than business.

"Fergus, we appreciate this more than you can ever know." Banker's voice was distinct to her now, even over the noise of the crashing waves. Still, she had never heard the name Rudy before. To think that was Banker's real name was strange to her. Even though she knew that Banker had always been a code name, it was the name she was used to.

"No trouble lads," Fergus replied in a warm, friendly manner. "I was going out anyway. Besides, I'll enjoy the company." He turned and, even in the dark, Sauwa could tell he was looking at her.

"Well, you're a lifesaver none…" Banker was cut off.

"What the hell?" Fergus shouted as he raised his arm, pointing up.

Everyone turned to see two powerful glowing beams shining down. They were aimed in opposite directions but were moving quickly to cover the beach. Instinctively, Sauwa closed one of her eyes to protect her night vision, while at the same time, reaching for the gun hanging from her pocket. It wasn't long before the lights were blaring down on the group. Seconds later the crackling sound that was all too familiar began echoing. The men, who apparently were not accustomed to gunfire stood by confused, as Sauwa dove to get out of the light.

The ground around them was erupting as the bullets

tore into the area. Sauwa hit the ground just in time to feel a wave of bullets slam into the gravel in front of her. It sent rock fragments flying in all directions, including her face. Surprised, Banker and his partner seemed paralyzed as the bullets came closer. The shooters above were watching where their rounds hit and were guiding them closer. Eventually, Banker and his partner snapped out of their paralysis. They reached into their coats and began fumbling about.

By now, Sauwa had drawn her weapon and was trying to fire back. But the lights shining down were blinding and the gunmen were trying to sight in on her. She could feel bullets continually tearing up the ground just inches from her. She figured out quickly that the group was too close together and were being boxed in by the gunmen. Keeping close to the ground, she stayed in the darkness. The ground itself offered protection as the gunmen had to sight closer to the ground to target her and, therefore, found most of their rounds hitting into the rock piles. From the way they were shooting, she could tell they were professionals. The gunfire was not wild. Instead, there was a series of short, controlled bursts with the gunmen taking their time firing one after the other.

Banker and his partner had managed to retrieve their weapons. They were raising their hands firing erratically toward the lights. The shots were wild and, with the blinding lights, were not likely to hit anywhere near their gunmen. Still, it was enough to draw attention away from her as both lights moved onto them. Sauwa started to crawl away from her position and was suddenly met by another blast of fire. This time coming from a direction off to the side. The firing was well over her head, and she could see it was landing close to her two allies. She could see the flashes from the rifle muzzles glowing in the distance. Like the shooters above, these other two were also using controlled fire and overhead lights to help them aim.

During the time the attention shifted from Sauwa, she drew her coat off and laid it spread out next to her in the water. Using the protection of the darkness, she began crawling slowly up the hill. Her gun tightly clutched in her hand, she took pains to keep it well above the ground. She looked back to see a burst of gunfire tear into Banker's partner. She watched as the burly man clutched his chest and fell against the boat and finally dropped to the ground. Banker, seeing this, began firing even more wildly in fear and desperation. He was completely terrified and oblivious as bullets were getting closer to him. As if in some action movie, he began screaming as he exhausted the last of his shots.

Sauwa managed to get to a spot where she could now see the outline of one of the gunmen. He was situated somewhere between standing and kneeling as he tried to maintain a good firing position. Feeling confident they had neutralized the threat of the men, the glow of the mag lights turned back to where Sauwa had last been. The light caught her jacket floating in the water. A couple of shots rang out hitting the water close to her coat. In the excitement and tension of the moment the shooter, as she predicted, assumed it was her body, wounded or dead, floating in the water.

Taking advantage of the moment, she sighted in on the outlined figure. Using the faint lights of the street lamps behind him, and the light of his own mag light, she was able to see enough of her rear and front sights to line them up. Aiming toward the thickest portion of his center mass, she let loose quick rounds from her Sig. The bullets ripped into the man somewhere in his chest cavity from the way he clutched his body a few seconds later. He maintained control of his rifle but had dropped his flashlight.

EMERY WAS FOCUSED on the man below. He felt it more sport than combat by the way the fool was wildly shooting, hitting nowhere near either of the IRA men. The twins were doing their part and firing controlled bursts that had eventually caught the man's attention as he turned to the side to fire just as wildly into the darkness along the beach. The IRA man was focused on this wild shooter and the clump that used to be the other man. He hadn't noticed that Kerry had stopped shooting altogether. Another quick burst from his rifle and the wild shooter below, like his cohort, fell to the ground. He smiled with a feeling of satisfaction when he began to hear a loud deep groan resonating off to his side. He turned to see his subordinate doubled over clutching his chest.

"Shit!" Emery cried, as he looked at Kerry. He wanted to say something, but realized, that someone was shooting back. Immediately, he veered his mag light and rifle in the direction where the South African had been spotted. A cold chill crept over him as his light caught nothing but boats, water and the gravel of the beach. She was nowhere to be found. It started to dawn on him that he was no longer in control and a stone cold, professional killer was stalking him.

The gunfire from the top to the beach had stopped, leaving only the flanking fire off in the distance. As the only other mag light was now sweeping sporadically over the ground below, even the flanking shooters had stopped, no longer having a marker to sight off. When the gunfire ceased, Sauwa had to move more carefully. The sound of the waves and wind still masked her movements, but in the absence of shooting, eventually the alien noise would be noticed. The light moved about, staying along the waterline. She took advantage as she raised her body and began climbing with her free hand and knees.

"I can't see her!" A gruff Irish voice of a man shouted. She presumed he was shouting to his allies on the beach. Sauwa continued climbing until she was able to catch the outline of the other gunman. Lowering onto her side, she aimed her weapon. Again, the illumination of the street lamps gave her just enough light to see the tips of her sights and the body of her assailant. She was still concerned about the other gunman — whether he was dead, injured beyond function or a danger to her. If she took the shot on the other man, she would be giving away her own position if he were still armed and ready to fire.

The glow of the moving mag light was gradually rising up the beach as the gunman realized she was no longer down there.

She was losing time. He would eventually find her. Even if he didn't, the explosive exchange of gunfire had no doubt woken several of the town's people. Soon the police would be here in force and her chances of escape would be lost. This was possibly the prime strategy of her assailants all along.

The light was turning in her direction. As close as she was, and the way her body was positioned, he would have her the second she was in his line of fire. She gripped her weapon and shifted her legs and body to get a steadier position. The man's silhouette was now turned in her direction. The light was coming up fast, and she needed to act. Aiming the weapon, her sights were aligned with the gunman's body. Taking a breath, her Sig touched off three quick shots. The bullets pounded into the barrier he was supported against.

EMERY NARROWLY MISSED BEING CAUGHT by the bullets as they smashed into the concrete pole he knelt against. The surprise took him off guard as he lost his grip on both his rifle and his mag light, they fell to the ground. Fragments of the post had flown into his eyes blinding him. His hands were busy brushing at the fragments in his eyes. In the confusion, he had, for a brief moment, forgotten his adversary. His mind became awash with fear as he realized the danger he was in. His initial thought, in his injured state, was to call the twins. They were his only hope for protection if the South African was close and moving to make her final strike. He didn't.

He fought to regain his eyesight while feeling around for his weapon. He was still batting his eyes when he found his rifle and started to grip it. He had gained a kneeling position when he looked over to see the blurred image of a young woman emerging. Kerry was doubled over, and even with obscured vision, Emery could see he was in the throes of death. Grabbing for his rifle, he attempted to take up his firing position, confident he could still kill her and complete his mission.

Sauwa, herself had knelt down and was still protected somewhat by the darkness of the beach. She had seized on the moment of the gunman's weakness to race up the rest of the way and close the distance. Now, only a few feet from him, she aimed her Sig as she steadied her herself and prepared to fire. The gunman was not phased in the slightest as he tried to ready his weapon. With his silhouette firmly in her sights, she aimed directly at his chest cavity and waited.

He lifted his head after being hunched over his rifle. It was the moment she needed. As he attempted to raise his rifle in her direction, two rounds of 9mm gunfire destroyed the brief period of silence.

Initially, the bullets felt like a painful succession of heavy bee stings as the hot lead pierced Emery's body. He could feel the metallic objects punch into his chest and stomach, crash through the bone and cut through his organs. They kept coming as the South African continued to fire. He couldn't even count as each round brought another sensation of throbbing pain. Emery thought he was firing back, he could still feel the rifle in his hands and his fingers on the grip. But, there was no return fire. He hadn't realized he did not have his finger on the trigger.

Sauwa fired her remaining shots, not sure in the darkness how many had actually hit him. Finally, the upper receiver was ejected all the way back, signifying she had run out of ammunition. The gunman had dropped his rifle and commenced a pattern of heavy breathing that could be heard from her location. She emerged from her position and walked out onto the road, approaching the man quickly. Throwing the first gun off into the darkness she produced the second from her waistband as she came up to him.

"Make a finish of it, bitch." Emery's voice was deep with a tone that denoted both vengeful bitterness and tired defeatism as he saw the assassin. He knew his time was over and he was going to go out like a man, a soldier.

Sauwa wanted to walk away. She wanted to end her career as an assassin right then. He was wounded, and she could have simply walked away. But, it wasn't how the game worked. He would come after her, or try again to kill her as she tried to escape. There was still the rest of the kill team out on the beach somewhere. Lifting the Sig, she fired a round straight into his eye socket. Emery fell over onto his side motionless. Sauwa grabbed his rifle and lifted the strap of the side bag over his head.

She started back to where the other gunman laid. He too was motionless, and the moaning and coughing he had been doing a short time before had completely ceased. She wanted to walk past him and let it go. Yet, the professional in her told her she had to finish it. Pumping two more shots with the Sig into the man's head, she kicked the other man's discarded rifle onto the beach and continued walking. She told herself he could still be a threat; it still didn't make her feel any less than a stone, cold killer.

Remembering the other members of the hit team roaming about, Sauwa moved to duck back into the shadows of the beach. She had been out in the light too long and by now had given away her position. Tucking the Sig back into her belt, she took up the rifle in a tactical grip as she moved back down the hill in a zig-zag pattern with the hope of distorting any visual marker the other gunmen might be using to keep tabs on her location. As professional as this team was, it was an easy deduction that they had seen her kill their comrades and had begun moving toward her position.

With that thought, she moved back into the darkness of the beach. Once out of sight, she began doubling back along the coastline until she was parallel to the location of the gunman she had retrieved the rifle from. Then, she moved down the hill until she was along the water line. Sauwa waited a short while, listening for any sounds that might give away the location of her adversaries. When she didn't hear anything, she started moving toward the boat and her compatriots. Momentarily out of harm's way, she took the opportunity to change magazines from the side bag. Like a soldier in combat, she tucked the shoulder stock into the pocket of her shoulder and aimed the barrel out in front as she started to move. Like the weapon's previous owner, she realized the futility of trying to sight in the darkness. Still, she matched her eye up with the general direction she wanted to aim the weapon.

After passing one of the other boats, she caught sight of the green light on Fergus's boat. Though excited, she maintained her tactical discipline as she continued a steady approach. Coming closer, she could also make out the outline of Fergus himself. He was out of the boat on the rocks, appearing to be tending to Banker and the other man. As she neared, she could hear the faint sound of loose gravel being crushed by feet rapidly approaching.

She stopped and held her position as the sound became louder and more defined. A pair of figures soon emerged into the area partially illuminated by the boat's green light. Sauwa could only make out parts of what were human outlines as she focused her rifle in their direction.

The mysterious silence and disappearance of the mag light illumination had confused the twins. Not understanding what had happened, they began moving up the hill toward the road. Witnessing the situation atop the hill, the twins quickened their pace to aid their comrades. They arrived too late to help.

Someone, a woman, armed with a rifle, was moving off the road. They watched, as she slipped into the darkness, heading in the direction of the boat and people they had been pinning down. With little time to assess the situation, and recognizing they were on their own, the twins retreated back down the hill and began moving toward the boat in hopes of catching the woman and killing her.

Guided by a green light from the targeted boat, they came upon a scene illuminated by that light. A small man was kneeling before two bodies sprawled out on the ground.

"Where's the woman?" Ewen shouted as he and his sister aimed at the man. The frail-looking man looked about confused as he struggled to collect the words needed to answer.

"Answer the fucking question!" Ellen demanded as she moved closer toward the old man.

Suddenly the night exploded with the crackling of gunfire. They saw the rapid white flashes from a rifle muzzle aimed in their direction. Soon they were besieged by a hail of bullets whistling all around them. "Shit!" The twins screamed in unison as they found themselves caught entirely off guard. In the confusion, Ellen dove for the water as her brother dove for the limited safety of the ground. In the heat of the battle, both in panic had dropped their weapons.

Sauwa kept up the rapid-fire until her magazine was exhausted. She pressed the small latch that released her spent magazine. She was reaching into her bag for a spare as she moved to where Fergus was lying curled up in a ball. "Hurry, we have to get Banker and the other guy aboard," she snapped.

"They're both dead!" the old man cried as she pulled him upright. "I checked. They're both torn to shreds, neither is breathing."

In the darkness, Sauwa could hear the two assailants, one was thrashing about in the water, and the other was crawling about on the ground. Since neither was firing back, she could only assume they had dropped their weapons and were trying to locate them. "Then get on the boat! We have to get out of here!"

Fergus began climbing over the side while Sauwa stayed behind him ready for the next attack. To keep her assailants disoriented, she continued to fire sporadically in the direction of their noise. She could hear Fergus hacking away at his docking rope trying to free the boat from its restraint. She kept up her sporadic bursts of fire that served well to keep the aggressors diving for cover.

At this point, Ewen had only one thought on his mind, rescue his sister and escape. Between the pitch darkness and the South African's shooting in his direction, he had given up on trying to win this battle. "Ellen!" He finally shouted. "Ellen!"

"Ewen, I'm here!" Ellen screamed back, as she thrashed about in the water. Ewen raced toward the sound of his sister's splashing. It was only short distance, but it felt much farther. Grabbing hold of a human form he was well acquainted with, Ewen took hold of his sister as they both wobbled across the field of loose, uneven gravel back up the coastline.

Confident her attackers had fled, Sauwa backed her way over the bow of the boat. Fergus had started the engine and was trying to navigate his way past the neighboring boats as he headed out to sea. Aiming her rifle over the side, she watched until the boat was well out in the water.

The old man asked if he could turn on his floodlights. With a sigh of relief, Sauwa agreed. Soon the boat was encircled with the illumination of white lights. Lowering the rifle back into the boat, she fell back onto a pile of ropes. Her adrenaline high had started to dissipate, leaving her physically drained.

EWEN AND ELLEN had little time to mourn as they stood over the bodies of their fallen comrades. Ellen was like a statue as she mourned the bullet-riddled body of Nash Emery. Her only comfort was the hands of her brother, holding firmly to her shoulders. The hole where Emery's eye had once been sent a cold chill down both their spines. It was not the work of a soldier but of a cold-blooded assassin. Emery, a fighter of a cause, was a soldier in the service of oppressed Catholics and, most of all, the father who practically raised them. He had not deserved such an end.

"We have to settle this Ewen," Ellen's voice was cold.

"We will," Ewen responded in a tone meant more to comfort his sister than to reinforce his words. He tugged at her shoulders, reminding her they had to escape. For Ellen, the idea of leaving Nash alone on a deserted street seemed unforgivable. But she, like her brother, knew how the business worked. You left comrades and loved ones where they were and mourned their deaths in secret. It was their world.

Quietly, the two walked back toward the van. Neither said a word, but both agreed with an unspoken understanding. This was not over. Sauwa Catcher was going to die for this.

27

Detective Sergeant Ryan Youngest looked out over the virtual war zone on the rocky beach. The grizzly display of bullet-riddled bodies sprawled everywhere reminded him of something out of a war movie. He looked around, getting more of the picture, as the forensic teams set about placing the tall standup lamps to better light the area.

"Jesus!!" Jeffery Talamadge exclaimed bitterly as he walked about observing the teams working. Coors Ravenhoof and Detective Glenahaughan stood by watching silently. Until the forensic crews did their walkthrough, there was not much they could do. The citizens of the village were forming up around the hastily created blockade guarded by a few of the local police. The town's police chief, a short, pudgy man who looked like he hadn't done exercise since his patrol days, moved about putting on a show and pretending he was in charge of the whole investigation.

"He's got to do something to prevent looking foolish.

His men responded to this mess badly in the first place." Ravenhoof whispered to Youngest who nodded in agreement.

"We're not even sure if this shooting is related to our case," Youngest replied. "We're only here because it was a massive shooting, and an informant told our people that Sheehan was possibly driving somewhere north tonight. Otherwise, we're wasting our time on this."

"What did the locals see?" Glenahaughan asked walking up.

"The folks that live along the road thought it was kids shooting off firecrackers," Youngest replied. "They didn't even think to call the police until someone looked out the window and saw bodies on the street. Then it took the local police nearly half an hour to get here because they've not seen a murder in my lifetime. The last gunfight this town's seen happened when Michael Collins was around."

"I'm looking for either Detective Sergeant Youngest or Detective Glenahaughan!" A man wearing a mask and covered by a baggy, plastic suit shouted as he emerged from the beach line.

"Over here!" both men shouted as they simultaneously waved to the cartoonish figure. The man trotted over carrying a blackened object in his hand.

"I was asked to see if the corpses could be identified, and if one of the bodies belonged to a Rudy Sheehan?" the white-coated figure explained.

Both detectives nodded. The suited figure handed them a plastic evidence bag. "The ones down by the water were carrying these wallets: one belonged to a Rudy Sheehan and the other belonged to Colin Christie. Both were from Dublin."

Talamadge joined the gathering of investigators just in time to hear the announcement. "She had to have been here."

"If so," Ravenhoof walked over to barriers separating the road from the beach, "we have to assume since all the bodies are male, she obviously didn't die here."

"Which leaves one of two possibilities." Youngest began looking about. "We have four dead in an obvious gunfight, but only one means of travel. We have to assume that our other set of bodies had accomplices who managed to escape. They either abducted our Ms. Catcher, or the gunfight ended in a stalemate with the survivors going their separate ways. If that is the case, we have to ask how Ms. Catcher would have escaped."

"They were here meeting a boat." Ravenhoof turned and started back to his colleagues. Our friends down there were here to meet a boat and apparently got ambushed by these ones on the road. It appears there's a gap between boats down their right where Mr. Sheehan and his friend are lying. We can assume that Ms. Catcher probably slipped away and did so on the water."

"So, we're looking for two sets of suspects," Glenahaughan muttered. "Her, and whoever was with these other two fellows." He pointed to the bodies laid out on the road.

"I'm betting these two additions to the story will turn out to be IRA," Youngest surmised as he started over to them, with his three colleagues assisting.

"Judging by the look of this scene, these boys were higher caliber operators than those from the warehouse shootings," Ravenhoof observed as he began scrutinizing the area. "They attacked from above, keeping the high ground. The big police flashlights I'm looking at helped give them good visibility to what was going on down below as well as blinding anyone having to look up at them."

The seasoned operator spoke from years of experience. "The way they were dispersed gave them means to control more ground below. My guess is if you extend your crime scene perimeter, you'll find a lot more bullet casings in one direction or the other where their comrades were delivering flanking fire to box these fellas in."

"So, then the next question is what?" Talamadge interjected with frustration. "She's taken to the bloody high seas?"

"That would be my guess," Youngest said calmly. "And, if that's the case, she and our remaining IRA hitters have the better part of a four-hour head start."

"To where?" Talamadge scratched his head. "Whatever boat she's taken isn't big enough to get her across any ocean and certainly no further than south of the country."

"No," Ravenhoof spoke up. "But, if the intention all along was to have her meet up on the water with someone else…"

The group was silenced with that thought. "All the cargo vessels and ocean-going yachts would be moving out along the Irish Sea…"

Youngest cut in, "With all the shipping traffic coming and going between Liverpool, Swansea and Cardiff alone, she'd be meeting a ship out on the open waters."

"She's gone!" Glanahaughan muttered angrily. "One of Ireland's most vicious killers, and she slipped right through our fingers, after a three-day spree that's left how many dead? Our own policemen as well." He swore profusely feeling defeated.

"We can try to contact the coastal patrols. But it would take a significant amount of time and we don't even know what to have them look for. In any case, it's a safe bet she's out of Ireland's jurisdiction." He turned to Ravenhoof and Talamadge. "What's next for you?"

Both men shook their heads. Ravenhoof finally spoke up. "We could wait until the man ferrying her returns. I would imagine he'll at least be coming back. However, as you say, by the time they give us any information, the ship in question will be out in international waters and not likely to cooperate knowing they're housing a fugitive they deliberately helped sneak out of the country. No, I'll see this investigation through and glean what information I can from it. That way, I can report something back to my people that hopefully will help us pick up her trail again and quickly."

"My government can't let this go either," Talamadge said. "As long as she's in the UK, she's a priority of MI-5 and we will take her down. If she's gone abroad, rest assured, British intelligence will consider her a threat and pick up where we left off. Who knows, someone may decide to take this matter up with The Hague and the international courts."

Ravenhoof took a deep breath before releasing a long deep sigh. "In any case, this is far from over."

THE WATER WAS FREEZING SO EARLY in the morning. Neither Ewen nor Ellen relished the sensation of ice cold liquid splashing over their bodies as they soaped up a thick lather trying to catch every nook and orifice that might even remotely carry traces of their evening's affairs. The sun was slowly rising delivering a mystifying pinkish red aura across the water and skyline. Soon their naked bodies would be exposed to anyone passing by. Exiting from the water, they were met by the equally piercing chill of the early morning ocean breeze.

Shivering, they practically dove for the two plastic bags sitting a few feet away. Ripping the parcels open, they enjoyed the first sensation of warmth, as they wrapped towels over their bodies and proceeded to dry off. Afterwards, they dressed in the extra sets of clothing they had brought along for the mission. The whole time neither one spoke. There was nothing to be said. They had lost Nash, their mentor and protector, the family they had never had. And, it had happened right in front of them.

Dried and dressed in warmer attire, they took one last look around before placing the van in neutral, releasing the emergency brake and pushing the vehicle and all its contents off a nearby cliff. The van crashed into the water with a powerful splash. They had left all the doors open to allow it to flood quickly. They watched as it rapidly sank into the murky depths of the Irish coast. They continued to watch after the van had completely disappeared from sight. It was not so much for professional reasons, but it was a token way they could finally grieve for Nash Emery.

They waited silently at the edge of the cliff until the sun began to overtake the darkness. Turning, they started across the fields to a waiting station wagon and a nervous looking middle-aged woman. As they walked, they had the same thought. "This isn't over Ewen," Ellen gritted her teeth. "Nash didn't deserve to go out like that — being killed by some psychopath — and we let it happen."

"No sister, this isn't over in the slightest," Ewen replied as he placed a reassuring hand on her shoulder. "Nash is never going to be with the angels until we make this right. We have only one cause now and that's killing Sauwa Catcher."

The twins made their way to the car. Ellen slipped into the back while her brother took the passenger seat up front. The woman said nothing as she got behind the wheel and drove the car onto the main road. Keeping a safe steady pace, she looked around once to see if any other cars were approaching as they sped toward the border.

SAUWA HAD TRIED NOT to fall asleep while in the boat, but the exertions of the day had finally caught up with her. She awoke to the old boatman shaking her awake. "Miss, it's time; we're here."

Realizing she had completely crashed, she rose to a sitting position. "How long was I out?" she asked as she felt her faculties slowly returning.

"Around three hours or such," Fergus replied as he walked back to his post at the helm.

She looked up and saw a ghostly looking frame, noticeable by a scant circle of lights. "How do you know it's the right ship?" Butterflies began to emerge in her stomach. She was about to step into a world of uncertainty.

Fergus clicked his light switch flickering a pattern that was obviously some sort of code. In the distance, she saw a tiny light, no more than a flashlight, flicker back in reciprocation. "I know, Miss, because our mutual friend gave me the general coordinates and timeframe of the ship's location. He also gave me the codes I was to use to make contact."

The boat neared the large cargo vessel. As it did, a succession of lights began to run down the side of the larger ship. With masterful skill, Fergus wheeled his boat up to the lights until they could make out the outline of a ladder well. "Here's where you get off, Miss."

Sauwa was hesitant, as her nerves began to twist knots in her stomach. "What will happen to you?" She looked back at Fergus. "I mean, after all that went on back in your town, the police are sure to be waiting for you."

In the darkness, she couldn't make out the expression on the old man's face. "Don't worry about me. I'm an old man who everyone knows goes out in the late hours. As far as the world knows, some desperate people caught me when I was leaving. The shootout should be proof enough of that. One of them, trying to escape took me at gunpoint and forced me out to the water where they directed me to some mysterious ship. That's all I know. It's an easy sell. And nobody but you knows of my connection to Rudy and Colin."

Colin, that was the name of the other man, she thought. She had fought alongside a man she had known only for a few brief hours before he died, and she had not even known his name until this moment. The boat bumped up against the hull of the ship. The sound of chains clanked as it nestled against the ladder well. "It's time," Fergus said.

"Thank you," Sauwa said to the old man. "I wish I could..."

"You owe me nothing and you don't have time for pleasantries," Fergus stated warmly. "After they start investigating, the police won't take long to figure you're out at sea, and they'll be sending their patrols looking. You can thank us all best by not taking extra time."

He was right. Throwing on her bergen, she balanced herself as she stepped off the boat onto the narrow scaffold of the ladder well. She was barely climbing when she heard the sound of Fergus's boat drive away. As he had pointed out, time was of the essence. He hadn't even taken the time to ensure she got aboard safely. With nowhere else to go, she ascended the metallic stairs, balancing against the buoyancy of the heavy ocean waters.

Finally reaching the top, she was met by a set of powerful hands that heaved her the rest of the way over the topside. She hit the slippery metal floor with a thump and barely kept from dropping to her knees. "Welcome aboard," a deep voice with a heavy East European accent said in a sinister way. "A man has paid me a considerable amount of money to help with your travels out of this beautiful land."

It was hard to see the man's face, but she saw the outline of a giant with a large round frame and quite possibly excessive facial hair. "Thank you," Sauwa replied, lamenting that she had not kept any of her weapons.

"My name in Yorgi. I'm captain of this ship and your host while you're aboard." It was hard to tell if he was being sarcastic or genuine by the way he spoke. In either case, it didn't matter, she was at his mercy. "Come," he commanded. "I take you to your lodgings."

She hesitated until Yorgi pressed the issue with a powerful slap to her bottom; she followed obediently.

Seconds later they were through a door and heading down another ladder well that took them deep into the bowels of the ship. Walking through a narrow hallway, he led her to a door. She found herself standing in a room equipped with a small bed and a closet.

"You are only female aboard," Yorgi said. "So, don't expect much accommodations. If you need shower or potty, the facilities are two doors further down. Men mostly shower in morning and early evening to catch work shifts. So, you'd be well served to shower mid-morning or late evening."

Sauwa turned to face the captain. He looked like someone out of an old pirate movie. A large, muscled frame suggested years of hard work in a rough demanding business. His beard was full and unkempt and hygiene was not a priority. He wore a blue P-coat over a thick, grey wool sweater and a pair of dark brown workmen's pants. In any other world, she would have considered him a threat. Here and now, he was the only friend she had.

"How do I know I can trust you?" she inquired. The question, she knew, was futile but in a way necessary to gather more knowledge of him.

"Because I have been paid," he replied with a shrug. "A man with my side business doesn't live very long if he gets a reputation for betraying his clients. Besides, when it was known I was transporting Sauwa Catcher, a professional killer, I figured betrayal would only guarantee my death."

It wasn't the best answer. Still, it seemed sincere. She relaxed a little. With nothing more to be said, Yorgi turned and started out the door.

"Where are we going?" Sauwa asked, nervously.

Yorgi didn't turn as he continued through the door.

"Sarajevo. It's a good place for a wanted fugitive to get lost. Also, a person of your skill and reputation is sure to find work quickly." He exited the room shutting the door behind him leaving Sauwa alone to collect her thoughts and ponder an uncertain future.

SO, WHAT DID YOU THINK?

THANKS FOR READING! I hope you enjoyed the book.

Would you please take a minute to leave a review on Amazon?

Honest reviews help other readers make informed decisions about which books might appeal to them. They also help me to better understand my audience, what I'm doing right, and where I might improve the reader experience.

I greatly appreciate your feedback and your time.

—J.E. Higgins

THE ORGANIZATIONS

CCB — Civil Cooperation Bureau

Concilium — Former headquarters of South Africa's National Intelligence Service

DONS — Department of National Security

IRA — Irish Republican Army

Irish Garda — Irish national police

MK/Umkhonto we Sizwe (*Spear of the Nation*)—Military wing of the ANC

RUC — Royal Ulster Constabulary; South Africa's National Intelligence Service (NIS); predecessor to the Department of National Security

The Dark Chamber — A special, deep cover infiltration unit of the CCB

UDA — Ulster Defense Association

UVF — Ulster Volunteer Force

ZANU — Zimbabwe African National Union

THE PLAYERS

Sauwa Catcher — Former CCB operative now fugitive mercenary

THE SOUTH AFRICANS

Mr. Gahima — ANC Liaison to NIS

David O'knomo — ANC head of unit investigating war crimes

Coors Ravenhoof — Member of the Department of National Security; Member of O'knomo's team

Jamie Nawati — ANC Intelligence; Member of O'knomo's team

Dr. Eugene Walderhyn — Analyst and Researcher; Member of O'knomo's team

DUBLIN UNDERWORLD

Rudy Sheehan *(Alias: Banker)* — Sauwa Catcher's contact in Dublin

Mr. Larky — Forger

Victor — Walhalla (money handler)

IRISH GARDA

Marston Donovan — Intelligence Officer; Informant for the IRA; Sauwa's Target

Ryan Youngest — Detective Sergeant

Ian Rose — Ryan Youngest's Commander

Hilter Dagden — Detective; Works with Ryan Youngest; Investigates Marston Donovan's murder

Glenahaughan — Criminal Investigator

Harry Curly — Detective, Crime Special Surveillance Unit

Ian Galligan — Detective, Crime Special Surveillance Unit

MI-5

Jeffrey Talamage — MI 5 Counter Intelligence Officer

TERRORISTS

Ellen Calloway — Part of IRA action service unit

Ewen Calloway — Part of IRA action service unit

Nash Emery — IRA action service unit

Seamus Nally — Ranking IRA Officer

Cork Regan — IRA enforcer

Rowan & Shanna — UVF support workers

Simon — UVF leader (recruits Sauwa Catcher)

Devon Williams — CCB commander; Sauwa Catcher's former boss

ACKNOWLEDGMENTS

To Rod, Gloria, Shannon, Bob, and Louis Rakovich as well as all the many others who contributed to the making of this book, I would like to extend my sincere thanks.

ABOUT THE AUTHOR

J.E. Higgins is a former soldier who spent twelve years in the U.S. military, first as infantryman in the Marine Corps and then in the military police with the Army. He holds a B.A. in Government and a Masters in Intelligence; intelligence operations.

The Dublin Hit is his debut novel.

You can reach J. E. Higgins at his website: www.thehigginsreport.com where he publishes monthly papers on international political trends.

Made in United States
North Haven, CT
20 June 2022